BUT NOT FOREGATHERED

A CLINT WOLF NOVEL
(BOOK 24)

BY

BJ BOURG

WWW.BJBOURG.COM

TITLES BY BJ BOURG

LONDON CARTER MYSTERY SERIES

James 516
Proving Grounds
Silent Trigger
Bullet Drop
Elevation
Blood Rise

CLINT WOLF MYSTERY SERIES

But Not Forgotten
But Not Forgiven
But Not Forsaken
But Not Forever
But Not For Naught
But Not Forbidden
But Not Forlorn
But Not Formidable
But Not For Love
But Not Forborne
But Not Forewarned
But Not Foreboding
But Not Forespoken
But Not For Blood
But Not Foreknown
But Not Fortuitous
But Not For Fear
But Not Foreseen
But Not For Lust
But Not Forspent
But Not Forsworn
But Not Foregone
But Not For Vengeance
But Not Foregathered

BUT NOT FOREGATHERED
A Clint Wolf Novel by BJ Bourg

This book is a work of fiction.
All names, characters, locations, and incidents are products of the
author's imagination, or have been used fictitiously.
Any resemblance to actual persons living or dead, locales, or events
is entirely coincidental.

Cover design by Christine Savoie of Bayou Cover Designs

PUBLISHED IN THE UNITED STATES OF AMERICA

CHAPTER 1

Mechant Loup, Louisiana
Ten hours before landfall

My wife was stubborn. While it was one of the things I loved about her, it would also be the predominant cause of me turning gray before my fortieth birthday. I had glanced at myself in the mirror while getting dressed for work this morning, and I seemed to be holding onto the dark brown the Lord had given me, but I knew those days were limited, especially after a day like today.

As I stood on the solid concrete porch of our raised police department, I looked to the south. So far, everything was relatively calm, except for an uptick in wind speeds. The sun was even shining. Were it not for our trusty meteorologist, we would never know that a monster of a hurricane was heading straight for town. It was the kind that could potentially knock us off the map, and there was nothing we could do about it except hunker down and pray for the best.

The door opened behind me. I glanced over my shoulder to see my wife standing there, her mouth turned down into a frown. These days, she wore a large uniform shirt and she kept it untucked to accommodate her belly. I shook my head. Even when we were fighting, she was still the most beautiful woman in the world, and it was hard to be mad at her.

"Clint, I know you're upset about me being here," she said softly, "but it's my job. I'm the chief of police. I can't evacuate during a crisis. It would be different if I weren't the chief, but what kind of leader would I be if I left?"

She was right, of course, but I didn't care about her job. I only cared about her safety and the safety of the baby that was growing inside of her. She was about a week shy of six months pregnant, and I didn't believe the place for her was right in the middle of a monster hurricane.

Meteorologists had dubbed Hurricane Ursula the *Storm of the Century*, and I had vowed to name our baby Storm if Susan didn't evacuate with her mom, my mom and dad, our daughter, Grace, and our two German shepherds, Achilles and Coco. In response, Susan had only placed a warm hand on my face and told me I could name the baby whatever I liked, but that she was staying put.

I turned to fully face Susan, resting my back against the concrete railing. "I'm just worried about you and the baby," I said. "What if something happens to y'all?"

"We're in a hurricane-proof building," she said. "We'll be fine."

"It's not the hurricane-force winds I'm worried about," I said for the umpteenth time. "It's the possibility of tornados."

She pounded a fist on the side of the building. "These concrete walls are sixteen inches thick. There's no safer place for me to be."

Again, she was right and I didn't want to dwell on the point for long, but I needed one small victory.

"Will you at least promise to stay inside?" I asked, raising an eyebrow. "No matter how bad it gets out here, will you promise to stay within the confines of these concrete walls?"

"I promise to stay inside." She smiled and moved closer, kissing me with her soft lips. "Now, you need to promise not to be mad."

I sighed, turning back toward the south.

"I'm not mad. I'm just worried." I pointed up and down Washington Avenue, where people were bustling about. There were even a dozen or so tourists ambling up and down the street, apparently waiting to see if a hurricane was everything it was cracked up to be. "There's a chance the entire town could be flattened, but there's still a ton of people out here."

"I checked with the mayor a few minutes ago," she said, "and no one's gone into the shelter yet."

"Well, I just hope everyone has a safe place to ride this thing out." I shook my head slowly. We couldn't force people to leave their homes, but we had done the best job possible to let the townsfolk know that they would be completely on their own once the storm hit. I'd spoken personally with some of them, and I wasn't sure they fully understood what that meant.

One man asked me if the fire department would respond in the event of a house fire.

"Once the storm hits, no one's coming until it passes," I'd told him. "You and your family will be completely on your own until it's safe for our first responders to get back on the road and begin attempting rescues and assessing the damage. The roads might not even be passable. Trees, electric poles, and other debris might be blocking the streets and highways. Some houses will be completely destroyed. We'll be out of power for weeks, maybe longer. You'll have to boil your water before drinking it, so if you have an electric stove, you're out of luck. If you don't have enough food to feed your family for at least a week, you'll go hungry."

His eyes had grown wider as I'd talked to him, but then he waved me off.

"It's never gotten that bad," he had said. "We're staying."

That had been yesterday, and I'd had a dozen similar conversations since then. Some of the people had heeded my warning and promptly packed up their families and headed north, while others had doggedly announced they were staying put. Kind of like my wife.

I smiled and turned to follow Susan inside. She was like a wild horse that couldn't be broken, and—although it caused me grief at times—I loved her for it.

I nodded to Melvin Saltzman as I entered the dispatcher's station. Melvin was Susan's patrol lieutenant, and the most seasoned patrol officer on the force. He had also been in Mechant Loup longer than anyone else in the department.

"Got everything you need?" I asked him.

He nodded.

We had gathered enough food and supplies for our entire police department to remain self-sufficient for at least a month following the storm, and our officers were going to continue making patrols through town until the weather dictated otherwise.

"I think Lindsey's got a call for you," he said, indicating our dispatcher.

Lindsey Savoie had been with the police department longer than I had, and she was our lifeline. We had offered to let her leave town for the storm, but, like my wife, she had insisted on staying to help out.

"Yes, ma'am," she was saying, nodding her head compassionately. "I understand. We'll get on it right away."

I moved closer as she dropped the handset to the cradle and asked, "What's going on?"

"Three boys are missing," she said, the concern evident in her voice as she read from her notes. "Cory Verdin, Allen Foret, and Ruben Foret are their names. Ruben and Allen are brothers. Ruben's fifteen and Allen is sixteen. Cory's also sixteen. Their parents haven't seen them since yesterday, and their cell phones go straight to voicemail. They went to the ball park and then were supposed to go camping on the east side of town. They were supposed to be home first thing this morning, but they never showed up."

I glanced at the clock on the wall. It was twelve-thirty. Although Hurricane Ursula wasn't supposed to make landfall for another ten hours, we had already begun seeing some gusts of wind that neared tropical storm force, and they would only increase in intensity as the day drew on. The last report I'd seen had warned that the weather could begin to dissolve within the hour, and those boys did not want to be caught in the woods during the storm that was coming.

"What's the address?" I asked.

"Mrs. Valerie Verdin called it in," she said. "They live on the corner of Market Street and Back Street. The Foret boys live next door."

"Want me to come along?" Melvin asked.

I hesitated, thinking it through quickly. Ideally, before we started searching the woods, we would want to know for sure if they had actually gone camping, but that would require some leg work and we didn't have time to wait. If the parents knew the location of the campground, I could send Melvin to give it a quick search. He was the best man tracker I knew, so if the boys were there, he would find them.

"No," I finally said. "I'll take Amy along and go meet with the parents. Who's patrolling town right now?"

"Shade and Regan," he said. "Baylor and Takecia are resting up for the night shift."

Shade Rankin was Susan's newest recruit, and he had graduated from the police academy a little over three months ago. Along with Regan Steed, who had been with the police department for two years now, Shade worked one of the day shifts, while Baylor Rice and Takecia Gayle each worked a night shift. On a normal day, there would only be one officer on duty at a time, but during times like this, everyone came together and worked around the clock.

"Okay, I'll call you if I can find out where they were camping," I said. "And you can take Regan or Shade with you and give it a quick search to see if they were even there. I'll try to find out if there were any problems at home that might've prompted the boys to run away."

I hurried toward the wing of the building where my office was located, and I could see Amy Cooke strolling down the hallway. She was coming from her office and she was carrying a wedding planner.

"Are you busy?" I asked.

"Nope, just bored." She shot a thumb over her shoulder. "Bay's taking a nap, so he's no fun. Me, I was about to take a walk to the bakery to see if they're still open. We need some sweets to ride out the storm."

I told her about the missing boys. She was the only other detective we had in town, and she was as overworked as I was, but we usually collaborated on the more serious cases. Even though I had many more years of experience as a detective, she brought a different perspective to every situation, and she was a tremendous asset.

"Care to come along and interview the parents?" I asked.

"I wouldn't miss it." She did an about face. "Let me pick up this book. If I lose it, I won't even remember what day we're getting married."

I did the math in my head. Today was the fifth of July and they were getting married at the bayou side park on the thirteenth of August. If the storm did even a fraction of the damage as was being predicted, there was no way the town would be cleaned up enough to have their wedding. I wasn't about to be the one to tell her that, so I only smiled when she returned from picking up her wedding book and followed me outside to my Tahoe.

CHAPTER 2

When Amy and I reached the corner of Market and Back, we saw a woman with a black shirt and jeans standing on the front porch of a Victorian-style home. Her arms were folded across her breasts and she was glancing nervously toward the Market Street Bridge. I was driving a black unmarked Tahoe, so she didn't realize who we were until I parked on the street in front of her house and we stepped out.

Due to the impending storm, Amy and I wore drab green 5.11 tactical pants with tan Polo shirts, rather than dress slacks and button-up shirts. Valerie Verdin took one look at our outfits, the badges clipped to our belts, and the guns on our hips, and rushed off the porch.

"Thank God y'all came!" she said, brushing back her wavy, dirty blonde hair. "Ray said the police don't consider someone missing until twenty-four hours have passed. He thinks it's all a big joke anyway."

"I've got a daughter," I said in a knowing voice, "and twenty-four hours is a long time when your child is missing."

"Tell me about it." She wrapped her arms around herself again and rubbed opposite shoulders. "Cory was supposed to be home at nine, and I already can't take it anymore. I could never wait twenty-four hours. Can y'all go look for him? I would go, but I'm not familiar with the woods. Besides, I hate snakes and spiders and Cory's always talking about all the snakes he sees when he's out there."

"Do you know where he goes camping?" I asked.

She shook her head. "It's somewhere on the other side of the bayou. That's all I know. I think Ray knows where it's at."

I had scribbled down some names in my notebook after getting the information from Lindsey, and I consulted it now. "So, Ray is Allen and Ruben's dad, right?"

She nodded her head.

"Has this ever happened before?" I asked.

"That they've gone camping?"

"No, that they were late coming back?"

"Um, well, it did happen a couple of times," she admitted. "Once, they didn't come back until late the next night because they said the fish were biting and they didn't want to stop."

I nodded, feeling a bit of relief.

"But Cory would never do that again," she quickly continued. "I grounded him for a week and I never let him go camping again until he promised to never be late. He's never been late since then. And then this storm is coming. I'm just…I've got a bad feeling about this."

"Lindsey said their cell phones are going straight to voicemail."

"Yeah, but that always happens."

"Have you tried to track Cory's phone?"

"I did, but it says he's out of range or the phone is turned off, which always happens, too." She puffed out her cheeks and blew out a lungful of air. "I hope I'm not overreacting again."

"Again?"

"I've done it before," she admitted. "That boy's gonna give me high blood pressure before I turn forty."

I had never formally met Valerie Verdin before, but I recognized her from seeing her around town. I thought I knew what her son looked like, but I asked if she had a recent picture of him anyway.

"I do." She hurried up the steps and across the wooden porch. "Y'all can come inside."

I glanced at Amy and she shrugged, so I led the way as we followed Valerie to the door that she'd left open. I took a cautious step into her house and waited just inside the breezeway. I never liked invading the private space of another, so I stood there until she called out to us.

"Y'all can come in," she said from somewhere deeper in the house. "I'm in the living room."

We followed the sound of her voice until we reached a large room with high ceilings. The house was at least a hundred years old, but the interior had gotten one hell of a facelift. The floors appeared to be original, but it had been refinished and was almost as shiny as my badge had been when I'd first taken it out of the box. Valerie was standing in front of a mahogany mantel fussing over a picture frame. When she finally wrestled the picture free, she turned and handed it to me.

It was a picture of her standing next to a boy with bushy brown hair and eyebrows. He wore a yellow Polo shirt with a white undershirt, and he was holding up some sort of plaque.

"This was two months ago," she explained. "He made the honor roll at school. It was the first time since his dad passed away four years ago."

I immediately apologized, and frowned as I studied the boy's face. It was rough to lose a parent at the vulnerable age of twelve, and although he was smiling in the picture, I could see the sadness in his eyes. I didn't ask how his dad had died. Instead, I asked if he was involved in sports. I could only imagine how hard it was for a sixteen-year-old boy to participate in sports without the support of his father, but it seemed he was doing it, because Lindsey had mentioned him and his friends going to the ball park.

"Yeah, he plays football for his school and then he plays baseball during the summer months," she explained. "He doesn't really like baseball, but his friends are all doing it and it keeps him busy throughout the break, so I encourage him to do it."

"Do you mind?" I asked, pulling out my cell phone and indicating that I wanted to take a picture of her son.

"You can have the picture," she said. "I've got more of them. I've even got digital copies."

I thanked her, took a clear picture of her son, and then texted it to Melvin, along with a message asking him to disseminate it to the rest of our officers. He replied that he and Regan were waiting on the east side of town for me to send them the location of the camp.

While I was communicating with Melvin, Amy took over the interview.

"How have you and Cory gotten along lately?" she asked. "And look, while some of these questions might seem strange, I'm just trying to get a handle on how things were in his life. Sometimes, a kid might have a bad day—something that would seem trivial to us— and then decide to run away from home. If his friends are similarly disgruntled, they might decide to go along with him. Or, there could be some event that the boys really wanted to attend but were told no, so they run away to attend that function. There's just a lot to consider, and I want to get you thinking about all of the different possibilities."

Valerie nodded her understanding. "I get it, I really do, but Cory and I get along great. When his dad died, he became the little man of the house. It's like he grew up overnight. He became real protective of me and of the property. At night, he would make the rounds of the house and make sure all of the doors and windows were locked, just like his dad used to do. If there was a knock at the door, he would tell me to wait while he checked it out."

"Have there been any changes at home that might've threatened that balance?" Amy asked. "Like, a boyfriend?"

Valerie hesitated and I knew Amy was on to something.

"It's okay," Amy said. "We're here to help. You can tell us anything. And remember, just because something has changed, it doesn't mean it has anything to do with Cory being late. They could've gotten lost or delayed because the fish were biting again."

"I sure hope that's all it is." Valerie let out a nervous laugh. "Um, I did start seeing someone recently, but Cory likes him. In fact, Cory kind of set us up."

"Really?" Amy asked. "Well, it certainly helps the situation when your son likes the man you're seeing. So, there's been no tension between your boyfriend and your son?"

"No, like I said, Cory loves him. He's been working for him for two years now. He cuts Elton's grass and does other work around his house and shop for him." She frowned a little. "As soon as Cory found out Elton was single, he started trying to set us up. It was Cory's idea to invite him over that first time. He seemed eager to have a father figure in his life. I guess I was the one who was a little hesitant. I mean, I'm still hesitant. If it would be up to Cory, we'd already be married and moving in, but this is all new to me. I like to take things slowly, you know?"

"I understand perfectly," Amy said. "Does the fact that you want to take things slow upset Cory?"

"No, he doesn't really know." She waved a hand around the living room. "Elton comes over once or twice a week for dinner and Cory sees us interacting like normal. I don't know if I would call us boyfriend and girlfriend, but there's definitely a spark between us. I'm just nervous. I still love my husband, you know? He died when Cory was still little, and things were so great at the time. I remember those good times and I feel like it would be such a betrayal to start seeing someone else."

I knew the guilt she felt all too well, but I didn't interject.

"Where does Elton live?" Amy asked. "Is it possible Cory's with him?"

"No, that's the first place I checked." She shot a thumb in the direction of the Foret home. "Besides, he's with Allen and Ruben, so they wouldn't be at Elton's house."

Amy nodded and turned to me.

"We're gonna interview Mr. and Mrs. Foret in a second and find out where the campsite is located," I said. "We've got officers ready to start searching immediately."

"Thank you, and please hurry," she said. "I don't know what I'd do if they were stuck out in that storm. The forecasters are saying we could have twenty-foot sea surges and that the damage could be catastrophic."

I nodded. I'd seen the same reports, and I didn't want them stuck out in that weather either.

CHAPTER 3

"Are you kidding me?" Ray Foret asked when he answered the knock at the door and saw Amy and me standing on his concrete porch. He knew immediately why we were there. "She called the cops? I can't believe this!"

"She's just worried," said his wife, Wendy, who stood beside him. She was tall, close to five-nine, and about the same height as her husband. "To be honest, I'm worried, too."

"They'll show up!" Ray said in obvious disgust. "They're boys. They have no sense of time when they're in the woods. Hell, when I was a kid, I would leave on Friday and not come back until Monday morning just in time for school. It gave my mom fits—just like it's giving you fits—but my dad didn't care. As long as I made good grades and got to school on time, he didn't give a shit how long I stayed in the woods."

"Mr. Foret, do you know where their campsite is located?" I asked. "Mrs. Verdin is concerned, so we're gonna send an officer out there to check on them. Just to make sure they're okay and they're aware that a storm's coming."

"They already know about the storm," he said. "They're looking forward to it."

"Still, where's the campsite?" Although Ray wasn't worried, I was going to get the location and check out the site for Valerie's sake. Cory was all she had left in this world, and I was going to make sure he was okay.

Ray sighed. "Um, once you get to the other side of the bayou, you cross the highway and head toward where they have the spring festival every year. There's a canal that runs east to west that crosses under Cypress Highway. You know it?"

I nodded. "It's before you get to the Waxtuygi Nature Park, right?"

"Yeah, that's it," he said. "Anyway, you follow that canal for about a mile into the woods. The trees are pretty thick all along the canal until you reach this large oak tree. It looks like someone planted a whole grove of oaks in that area at some point—probably over a hundred years ago—because they're all spaced evenly and lined up in a grid. Anyway, they have a tree house in that first oak tree. It's where I used to camp as a kid. In fact, I built the first tree house there, but it got blown down during a storm about twenty years ago. When Allen was ten, I went back there with him and rebuilt it. It needs some more work, but I haven't had time to take care of it yet."

I nodded and asked for a photo of his boys. As though waiting for something productive to do, Wendy hurried inside and returned with a photo of two redheaded boys. Their faces were covered in freckles and they could've passed for twins.

"Which one's Ruben and which one's Allen?" I asked.

Wendy pointed a slender finger toward the boy on the right. There was a cowlick sticking up in the front of his hair, and his ears were bigger than those of the other boy.

"That's Ruben," she said. "He's our youngest."

I took a screenshot of the picture and sent it to Melvin, along with a message describing where he could find the campsite.

Ray stepped forward. "What's that for?"

I didn't look up until I had finished sending the message.

"It's to send to our officers in the field," I explained when I was done. "They're on the east side of town as we speak, just waiting to hit the woods to find your boys."

"I really don't think any of this is necessary," he said. "I think Valerie is overreacting because she's a woman. If her husband was still alive, he would tell her this is nothing to worry about, and we wouldn't be standing here bothering y'all."

"It's no bother," I said calmly.

"It's a bother to me," he said in a loud voice. "There're other things I could be doing right now."

I stepped closer to him and, in a low voice asked, "Would it make you feel better if we only searched for Valerie's son and didn't give a shit about your boys? Would that be less of a bother for you?"

He saw the way I was looking at him and took a half step backward. He swallowed and glanced at his wife, who was nodding her disapproval.

"No, it's okay," he finally said. "If you want, I can take you to the campsite."

"You can come along," I offered, "but Melvin will beat us to it. Meanwhile, can you think of any reason why your sons might be out late?"

"It could be anything," Ray said. "Once they go in the woods, they don't know when to come out. And I'm fine with that."

"Have y'all had any disagreements lately?" I pressed. "Any reason why they would want to run away or anything?"

"What are you saying?"

"I'm asking a question," I continued patiently. "I need to get a sense of the mood around here prior to them leaving—just in case."

"Just in case of what?" he asked.

"I've worked a lot of missing person cases," I explained. "Some people—especially teenagers—usually go missing because they want to be missing. They don't want to be found. Is it possible your boys and Cory set out on their own for some reason?"

Before Ray could answer, Wendy interjected.

"You did yell at them for not picking up their baseball bats and gloves yesterday morning," she said. "They weren't happy about that."

"That's because they act like slobs," Ray said. "They just leave their shit dragging around and expecting us to pick them up. My dad would've never put up with that shit, and I sure as hell won't. They're lucky I didn't take the belt to them."

I groaned inwardly. If I was this man's kid and had to listen to this shit every day, I'd probably run away, too. However, I needed to keep him agreeable, because I needed information from him.

"Look, is it a normal thing for them to leave a mess?" I asked. "After all, they're boys, and boys aren't the neatest creatures out there."

He laughed at that. "Yeah, there's nothing neat about Allen and Ruben. They're boys through and through. But yeah, I have to stay on them constantly about the mess. Yesterday was nothing new, and they don't take it personal. They know I'm only doing what's best for them."

Wendy frowned and shook her head. I glanced in her direction.

"What do you think?" I asked.

"I think he's too rough on them and I don't think they like it," she said defiantly. "If he's not careful, he'll piss them off so bad, they'll leave and never come back home. I overheard Ruben saying when he turns eighteen, he's moving as far as he can from this place."

"Do you think that's what happened here?" I asked.

Ray's face was burning red, but he only glared at Wendy. I figured he would've given his wife a tongue-lashing had we not been standing there. Instead, he took a breath and exhaled forcefully and addressed Amy and me.

"Look, I don't understand what's happening here," he pleaded. "The boys are fine. They're just playing in the woods. That's all. I don't know why you're asking all these questions. I mean, they're not even missing. They're just late."

"I hope that's all this is," I said with a nod. "If they're at the campsite, then this will have all been for naught. But if they're not at the campsite, we'll have a head start on searching for them. Now, do they have any friends or family members who live out of town? If they would've run away, where would they go?"

Wendy was thoughtful, while Ray turned in frustration and stormed into the house.

"They have some cousins in Ohio," she said, "but they rarely ever speak to them."

I jotted down the information and then reviewed the notes I'd taken from Lindsey.

"Mrs. Verdin told our dispatcher that the boys went to the ball park yesterday," I began. "What time was that?"

"Oh, it was later in the afternoon. I think they left on their bikes a little before four, and the practice started at four-thirty." She rubbed her face with her hands and glanced past me and Amy. "Did the other officers get to the campsite yet? Did they find them?"

"No, ma'am, they'll call when they do. Now, you said the boys were on their bikes," I continued. "Did they ride their bikes to the campsite, too?"

"Yeah, that's how they travel. They once rode their bikes all the way to Attakapas High." She shook her head. "I was so mad at them. It was during the summer and they wanted to practice kicking field goals on the football field, so they jumped on their bikes and left. I thought they were just riding around town, but when I put supper on the table and hollered for them to come in, they were nowhere around. I called their cell phones and that's when they told me they were heading back home, but they were still far away. Ray had to go get them in his truck. He was some mad!"

"Was Cory with them?" I asked.

"Oh, yeah, they do everything together."

I nodded thoughtfully. It seemed like the boys liked to be adventurous. From what we'd learned so far, if they weren't at the campsite, they were probably just cruising on their bikes, living the dream and enjoying the summertime. Hell, it was also possible they had ditched baseball practice to start their camping trip early. That was another angle I'd have to pursue, so I asked for the name of their baseball coach.

"Stewart Finane," Wendy said.

I scowled, remembering my prior dealings with Stewart. I would've never guessed him to be a coach of anything, except maybe chess. "The principal of Attakapas High?" I asked. "Is this the same Stewart Finane you're talking about?"

She nodded. "He's the coach for their summer league. He's pretty good, too, because they're undefeated."

I glanced at Amy, who shrugged and said, "You never can tell about a man."

I only shook my head and studied the sky. It was overcast now and the wind was starting to pick up, but there were no obvious signs that a monster hurricane was barreling down on us. It was quite possible the boys were oblivious to the dangers that lurked just beyond the horizon.

"I know Ray said the boys already know about the storm," I began slowly, "but do they know how bad it's supposed to get?"

Wendy shook her head. "When they left, it was still forecasted to hit Texas. It was during the night that the news said the track had changed and it was coming here. I tried calling them to warn them, but their phones went to voicemail like they always do when they're camping."

I asked a few more questions and jotted down her answers. In closing up the interview, I promised Wendy that we'd keep in touch, and then Amy and I headed for my Tahoe.

CHAPTER 4

Mechant Loup East

Melvin wiped the sweat from his eyes as he and Regan trudged along the canal east of Cypress Highway. The weeds were tall and he was having trouble locating any bicycle tracks in the packed earth beneath their feet. It hadn't rained in a couple of weeks, and the heat had dried most of the ground in this area to the point of cracking. Thankfully, the clouds were beginning to roll in and the wind was picking up, so things were cooling off.

"It's on days like this that I really miss Tellico Plains," Regan said. "It gets hot there, don't get me wrong, but I never felt like I was in hell. This place is downright miserable at times. And the mosquitoes are relentless. Do they ever take a vacation? I swear I was fighting them all winter long."

Melvin laughed as he glanced over his shoulder at the shorter woman. Her long brown hair was drenched and her large blue eyes were glassy from the beads of sweat that poured into them. She dabbed at them with a hand and trudged on.

Regan had first landed in Mechant Loup two years ago by way of Tellico Plains, Tennessee, and Melvin had been impressed with her from the very start. She had worked as a patrol cop with the Tellico Plains Police Department for ten years prior to relocating here because of her husband's job, and those years had served her well. She had spoken often of traversing rugged mountain terrain in search of missing people, and she had described some of the areas as downright impassable.

"At least the ground here is flat," Melvin commented as they rounded a bend in the canal. "We can cover a lot more area than in the mountains, I'm sure."

"That's the truth," she said, "but we didn't have giant lizards lurking around just waiting to take a bite out of us. Do you know that I responded to a call the other day about an alligator in a ditch in someone's front yard? When I got there, the lady pointed to the ditch and told me to get rid of the alligator. There was about eight inches of water in that ditch. I didn't see an alligator, and I asked her what in the hell she was talking about—only, I didn't use the word *hell*. She threw a stick in the water and that ditch exploded with action. I didn't realize they could hide in such a small spot. They give me the creeps!"

Melvin laughed some more and asked her what she would do if they encountered Godzator. Everyone around here had heard the stories about Godzator—including Regan—but few people had actually had the pleasure of seeing the monster.

"If I ever run into him, I'll be the last person to do so," she said with a crooked smile. "And I hope I'm carrying my shotgun when it happens, because I'd hate for it to be just me and my pistol against that armored beast. I heard Clint shot it a few times with his Glock, but he wasn't able to put it down."

Melvin smiled thoughtfully, remembering back to the early days when he had first met Clint. He remembered the time Clint had gone missing himself, and how he had been the one to find Clint alive in the swamps. It had been a glorious feeling, and he hoped this search would have a similar outcome.

"Those were the good old days," he finally said, stopping when he reached the giant oak tree that stood on the edge of the canal.

Regan pulled up beside him. "What days were good and old?"

"Back when Clint first came here," he said absently, his brow furrowing. The ground under the oak tree was mostly bare and dusty, with broken acorns littering the area. Closer to the base of the tree, he could see the remnants of an old campfire and some waste that had been left behind by irresponsible campers, all of which confirmed that he had located the campsite. However, there was one thing that was missing—evidence of recent activity.

He approached the campfire and knelt next to it. He stabbed his fingers directly into the ash. It was cold. He scanned the area carefully with his eyes, but there were no signs of bicycle tires approaching from any direction.

"From the looks of it, this place hasn't been disturbed in a while," Regan said from behind him. "Those boys haven't been here recently, right?"

"No, they haven't." Melvin straightened and walked past the tree toward the oak grove. He waved for Regan to follow him. "Let's check the rest of this grove in case they approached from the south. They might've wanted a change of scenery—a new challenge."

As he led the way deeper into the grove, neither he nor Regan spoke much, except to point out a thing or two along the way. Mostly, they found old animal tracks in the dried mud, but no recent tracks. As hard as they searched, they couldn't find any signs that any humans had been here since the last rain. Sure, the ground was dry and solid so there would be no impressions in the mud, but they were searching for other sign as well. A crushed leaf, a snapped twig, a rub mark in the dirt—all of these were signs of someone's passing.

Melvin pointed out a number of sign that indicated the presence of animals. Coyote scat, a piece of fur stuck to the bark of a tree, rabbit pellets, and partially eaten leaves were all indicators that there was life out there, but none of it had been human.

Melvin sighed heavily as they made their way back toward the canal. He didn't know why the boys had lied about camping out here, but they had picked the wrong time to be getting into trouble.

Not only was it cooler in the shade of the trees, but the wind was growing increasingly stronger and Melvin was no longer sweating. He glanced at Regan just as the remnants of the old campfire came into sight.

"It feels better now, doesn't it?"

"Yeah," she said with a nod. "The wind's keeping the mosquitoes away, so that's a nice touch, too."

He stopped near the campfire, sat on a stump that had been used as a bench, and pulled out his cell phone. As he called Clint, he wondered how much progress Claire and Delilah had made on their trip out of town. For the storm, he had wanted them to hunker down at the police department as a family, but Claire had overruled him. She had insisted it would be safer to take Delilah northwest to Arkansas rather than staying in town, and Melvin didn't want to force them to stay. If he was wrong and they were injured or killed, he would never forgive himself.

However, he didn't like the idea of his wife and seven-year-old daughter driving alone on the roads during an evacuation. He knew all too well the dangers that lurked on the highways and byways during a state of emergency, and he was worried sick about them.

CHAPTER 5

Clint's Tahoe

I parked on the shoulder of Back Street and searched for Stewart Finane's cell phone number. I had spoken to the principal a few times over the years, and he had proven to be helpful when the need arose. As the phone rang, I tried to imagine him standing out in the sun at baseball practice barking orders at his team. Try as I might, I couldn't do it.

"Hey, there, Detective Wolf," Stewart greeted, sounding out of breath. "What can I do for you?"

"I hope I'm not catching you at a bad time," I began, "but I have some questions about baseball practice yesterday."

"Nah, it's okay," he said. "A couple of the teachers and I are out here boarding up the windows at the school. Apparently, the storm has shifted its course and is now heading right for us. I don't know how they could've gotten it so wrong."

"I hear you," I said politely, wanting to get right to the point. "Look, do you know Allen Foret, Ruben Foret, and Cory Verdin?"

"I sure do. They all attend Attakapas High and they're on my baseball team. Why? Is something wrong?"

"I don't think so," I said. "Mrs. Verdin reported them missing when they didn't return home this morning from camping out. She said they were heading for the ballpark in town when she last saw them. They told her they had baseball practice. I was just wondering if you saw them yesterday."

"Yeah, they were there." Stewart paused. "Let's see, if I remember right, they got there right after I did, so that would've been around four o'clock. Practice is at four-thirty every day, and I usually get there thirty minutes early."

"How'd they get there?"

"Like they usually do—on their bikes."

"Were all three boys together?"

"Yep," he said. "They're inseparable. Even at school. Where you see one, you see the other two. They take all the same classes, they go to lunch together, they've been seen heading to the bathroom together, and they even get in trouble together. In fact, I had to suspend them last year for fighting. If one of them fights, they all jump in."

"Who'd they fight with?" I asked.

"Four of the senior football players," Stewart explained. "Ruben had walked out on the field before Allen and Cory could get there, and the seniors started messing with him. Well, when Allen and Cory saw what was going on, they jumped right on those big boys and started fighting."

"How'd they fare in the fight?" I asked.

"Oh, they lost," Stewart said flatly. "They all got beat up pretty bad, but I still had to suspend them because they started the fight. I also suspended the seniors, but none of the parents agreed to press charges, so we handled it in-school."

"Was there any bad blood after the fight?"

"Surprisingly, no. Although they were getting beat up, they never quit fighting until the coaches jumped in and broke them up. That earned them the respect of the entire football team, and even the coaches." He grunted. "Hell, even I admired them after I watched the tape. Those boys are definitely gritty."

I was glad to hear they were fighters. If Melvin didn't find them and they were stuck out in the approaching weather, they would need to be tough.

"Do you know what time they left practice?" I asked.

"Yeah, they actually cut out early," he said. "They said they were heading to the woods for a camp out and they wanted to get there before dark, so they left around seven. Practice ended around eight."

"Did you see what direction they headed when they left the ballpark?"

"Um, they went west on Coconut."

I was thoughtful. It would've been quicker for them to head east on Coconut and then turn up a cross street to get to Market Street, but there could've been any number of reasons for them to head west. They probably went to the convenience store to grab some snacks and drinks for the camp out. It's what I would've done.

"What about gear?" I asked. "What kind of gear did they have with them?"

"They each had backpacks," he said. "They looked like camping backpacks."

"What about their baseball equipment?"

"I saw Cory put his glove inside a zipper compartment and he shoved his bat into a cooler pouch on the side of the backpack," he said. "I think they all did the same thing."

Not only did they have their camping gear, but they were also toting around their baseball equipment. They wouldn't have wanted to go far lugging around all of that stuff. I started to question why they hadn't brought the gear home before crossing the bayou, since they had to roll right past their houses, but I dismissed the thought. If they wanted to make it to the campsite before dark, they wouldn't want to waste even the minute it would take to unload their gear.

"You know, I told them to keep an eye on the weather," Stewart continued, "but Allen said his dad told him the storm wasn't coming. I thought the same thing, but boy, was I wrong."

I turned and gave Amy a nod. I was feeling better that the boys had made it to practice and left early to go camping. I was sure I would hear back from Melvin to say that he had located the boys at the campsite and they had just lost track of time. And then we could all go back to preparing for a long and battering day ahead.

As if on cue, my cell phone began buzzing in my ear. I glanced at the screen and saw that it was Melvin.

"Mr. Finane, I have to go," I said, "but thanks for the information. You've been a big help."

"Clint, they're not here now," Melvin said when I answered his call, "and they never were here—at least not in recent time."

I wanted to echo Stewart's words about being wrong, but instead said, "Oh, shit!"

"Yeah, we even walked through the rest of the oak grove, but there's no sign of them or their bikes. You need to find out if there's another camping spot that they used. If they're out here, we need to find them before dark, because the outer bands of the storm will start reaching us at any time."

He was right. I ended the call and whipped my Tahoe around. We were still within spitting distance of Valerie Verdin's house and were knocking on Ray Foret's door within seconds. Ray answered again and his face dropped just a little when he saw us standing there.

"Do you know of any other camping spots the boys might've

used?" I asked. "They weren't at the place you described."

"What?" He looked from me to Amy and then back to me. "What do you mean they weren't there? They have to be there. It's the only place they know they're allowed to be. My dad was friends with the old man who owned the property, and now I'm friends with his grandsons, and they let them camp there."

"Well, they're not there." I shook my head. "Melvin searched the entire oak grove and didn't find any signs of the boys or their bikes or their gear. He said no one has been at that campsite in recent time."

"That's impossible." Ray's own head was shaking, but in disbelief. "They were there last night. That's where they camped. Allen told me that's where they were going after baseball practice."

"Well, they never made it," I said. "They did go to baseball practice though, and they told Stewart Finane that they had to leave early to go camping, so it looks like that was the plan."

"If that's what they said, then that's exactly what they did." Ray nodded his head confidently. "Your guy messed up. My boys are back there and I'm gonna go find them myself."

"I promise you they're not there," I said patiently. "Look, can you check to see if your boys dropped off their baseball gear when they rode past your house? It doesn't make sense that they would bring it on the camping trip, especially since they'd have to ride past the house to get to the east side. It's possible they were in a hurry and didn't want to take the time to do it, but can you check to be sure?"

Ray nodded and disappeared inside the house. I could hear some movement from inside the garage, and Amy grunted from beside me.

"It sounds like he's destroying things, not searching for them," she said. "That man's got anger issues. I wouldn't be surprised to find out he hit his boys."

I furrowed my brow. "You think they're running away from an abusive father?"

"Everything's on the table at this point, am I right?" she asked.

I nodded and looked toward the garage door when it creaked open. Ray came out huffing.

"No, they didn't drop it off, and that's unusual." The reality of the situation was starting to settle like an anchor to the ocean floor. "Something smells wrong about this—"

"What's going on?" asked Wendy, who had appeared in the doorway and stared from Ray to us. "Did y'all find the boys?"

At that same moment, I heard Valerie's voice as she approached from her house. Ray's noisy banging from the garage was loud enough to wake up everyone in the cemetery nearby, so it was no wonder Valerie and Wendy had heard the commotion.

"Is Cory okay?" Valerie asked. "Did y'all find him?"

I waited for her to reach us. Once she and Wendy had joined us in the front yard, I repeated what I'd said to Ray, and how we had just learned that the boys hadn't dropped off their sports gear.

"No!" Valerie said, throwing her hands to her face. "This can't be happening! I can't lose my boy!"

Wendy rushed down the steps and wrapped Valerie in her arms. "It'll be fine," she said. "They'll be fine. They just changed their minds about where they wanted to go camping. They probably went to a different spot. You know how they are, always wanting to discover new places to explore."

My mind was racing as I stood there watching the two women comfort each other. The wind was picking up rapidly, so there was no way we would be able to get helicopters up in the air. And we could forget about getting dogs out here or assembling a search team. Even if we knew where to start looking, the rain would be falling soon and would wipe away whatever scent or tracks the boys might've left behind.

I felt Amy's eyes on me.

"What are we supposed to do now?" she asked in a low voice, not wanting the parents to hear. "The storm's getting closer and we're running out of time."

I'd been wondering the same thing, and I was starting to devise a plan. I didn't know if it was the right plan, but at the moment, there wasn't much else we could do.

CHAPTER 6

While we had a handful of officers at our disposal, we had nowhere to send them at the moment. I turned back to Ray, hoping to extract more information from the man.

"Are you sure you can't think of any other possible camping spots?" I pressed. "Maybe someplace you've taken them before, or someplace you've told them about, or someplace they've heard about from someone else?"

"There's just the one place." Ray's face was twisted into a deep scowl. "I can't believe they're not there. That's where they said they were going. If they're not there, I have no idea where they could be."

"Okay, then," I said, turning to the women. "Valerie, I need you to call the parents of every friend that Cory could possibly have. Find out if they know where their kids are, and find out when's the last time their kids spoke with Cory. Wendy, I need you to do the same thing for each of your sons."

"What about me?" Ray asked when I turned to leave with Amy. "What should I do?"

I glanced at his pickup truck. I knew I would need to keep him occupied so he would stay out of trouble and not bother us while we were trying to work. If he stayed around here, he would drive Wendy crazy and he might do something stupid.

"Why don't you get in your truck and start driving around town?" I suggested. "We'll have officers doing the same, but an extra pair of eyes won't hurt. If you find them and they're okay, don't go ballistic and start yelling at them. If they're in trouble and need help, dial 9-1-1 right away. If you find their bikes or anything that belongs to them, don't touch it."

"Wait a minute—are you saying someone might've taken our boys?" He scoffed. "There's no way they were kidnapped. Maybe one of them—if they were alone—but not all three of them."

"We don't know what happened," I explained, "so if you find anything of theirs and they're not around it, it'll be considered evidence. If you were to touch these items, you could destroy our chances of figuring out where they are and what happened to them."

As Wendy and Valerie watched the exchange, they both began to cry. I turned to them.

"Listen, I need y'all to stay positive," I said. "It's more likely than not that they sought out new adventures and got lost, but because of the storm, we need to cover all of our bases in a hurry. While y'all contact their friends, I need y'all to give Detective Cooke access to their computers."

"But why?" Wendy asked. "What will she look for?"

"I'll look for any little thing that might give us a hint as to where they went," Amy explained. "If one of them searched the internet for buried treasures, we'll have an idea that they might be searching for gold. If they typed in the name of a town, that might mean they're trying to go there. Everything's a clue. I'll also be searching to see if they had trouble with anyone on social media, or if they met any girls. It wouldn't be the first time a boy has gone on a road trip and taken his buddies along to meet a girl. We might find a social media post about a hurricane party that's taking place. It's possible they ditched the camping trip for such a party and got too drunk to come home this morning. Everything's possible and no idea is off limits."

"Wait a minute!" Valerie snapped her fingers. "Cory did meet a girl from out of town!

Amy and I exchanged glances.

"Do you have her name and number?" Amy asked.

"Um, I think her name's Stacy, but that's all I know." She was thoughtful and then shook her head. "No, there's more. She lives in Northern Chateau somewhere. Um, he met her at a football game."

Amy was jotting the information down in her notepad.

Meanwhile, Ray was already backing his truck out of the driveway and speeding off. I was hoping if he found anything, it would be his boys and Cory, and that they would be okay. I didn't want him finding their bikes or their back packs, because I was sure he would touch them. But what were the chances of him finding anything?

I considered this. If someone had kidnapped the boys, it would be hard to dispose of their property. Three bikes and three backpacks would be easy to spot, so if a kidnapper wanted to get rid of their stuff, it would have to be done in a remote location—someplace far away from the public eye. And why would someone want to kidnap three boys? That just seemed like too much trouble and too much of a risk. If Stewart was right, these boys could put up quite a fight collectively, so they wouldn't go down easy.

No, I thought, it was more likely that they had gone off and gotten lost in the swamps somewhere. Since there were no bike paths throughout the swamps around here, the boys would've been forced to park their bikes on solid ground someplace and set out on foot. Depending on where they entered the swamps, it might be possible for someone to find their bikes and gear and phone it in, but first they would need to know what they were looking for.

Amy was asking Wendy and Valerie if they could access their cell phone accounts and provide live updates of the boys' phone activity, and both women readily agreed to do so.

"Hey," I said, stopping them as they set off to follow Amy's instructions, "do y'all have pictures of the boys' bikes and backpacks?"

"I took a picture of them on their first day of baseball practice," Valerie explained with a nod. "They were just leaving for practice and I made them line up and smile for the picture. It was a few weeks ago, but it's the same bikes they have now."

"I need that picture," I said.

"Sure, it's on my phone." Valerie bent her head and moved her thumbs rapidly across the glass screen. She looked up once to ask for my cell number, and then nodded. A few seconds later, she said, "You should have it by now."

I did, and I went into action. I immediately forwarded the picture to the group text message that Susan had started a while back between all of our officers, and then I asked them to forward it to everyone they knew in town. I wasn't on social media, so I asked them to also share it to whatever local social media pages they were a part of or knew about.

When I was done, I looked up to see Melvin and Regan pulling up in front of the house, both of them in their respective police cruisers. Amy had already entered the Foret residence, where I knew she would begin scouring the cell phones and social media accounts of Allen and Ruben.

CHAPTER 7

After speaking briefly with Regan and making sure she was up to the task, I waved Valerie Verdin over and introduced her to Regan.

"Mrs. Verdin, can you give Officer Steed access to all of Cory's social media accounts and his cell phone records?" I asked. "If there's anything there that'll help us find your son, she'll uncover it."

Valerie nodded, her face a mix of fear and relief, and hurriedly led Regan to her house.

"The dad doesn't believe us," Melvin said when Valerie and Regan were gone. "He showed up on Cypress Highway just as we were leaving and he set out toward the campsite."

I shook my head. "I suggested he start driving around town to help look for the boys. The more eyes we have out there the better, but if he plans on second-guessing everything we tell him, he'll just get in the way."

"I guess he has to see for himself." Melvin shrugged and then asked about my plans going forward.

"I'm gonna try and retrace their footsteps, beginning with the ballpark."

"I'll just start driving around then," he said. "I'll drive along bayous and canals and check every camping spot I can think of."

I thanked him and walked to my Tahoe. I called Susan to give her an update as I headed for the ball park. I began by checking the dugouts, tennis court, and outbuildings, hoping they might've returned to the park to hang out, but I had no such luck. On my walk back to Coconut Lane, I paused for a moment to pay my respects to the statue of Lieutenant Jack Jackson, a Mechant Loup police officer who had died in the line of duty.

Once I was back on Coconut, I paused near my Tahoe and surveyed the houses heading west from the ballpark, which is the direction Stewart Finane had seen the boys heading. There was an elderly couple sitting on a gliding rocker at the brick house almost directly across from the park, so I headed there first. I smiled and gave them a nod as I introduced myself. I couldn't help but notice that their shutters remained open and their potted plants were still on the concrete porch.

"Are y'all ready for the storm?" I asked.

"We're not worried about that storm," the man said with a grunt. "They don't know where it's heading. First, they said Texas, and then they said Lake Charles, and now they've moved it all the way to here?" He shook his head in disgust. "They don't know a damned thing anymore since our favorite meteorologist retired."

"Well, it might be better to play it safe, just in case they're right," I offered gently.

"How old are you?" the man asked.

"I turned thirty-eight last week."

"You're still a baby. You wouldn't remember this." He shook his head. "Anyway, there was a Cat Four storm in the Gulf about thirty years ago, but it wasn't supposed to hit us. Well, it supposedly made a turn and the weather man come on the TV in the middle of the night screaming that we were all gonna die. I come out here and boarded up every window on this house—and I've got a lot of them! I had the wife running a drill and the kids holding up boards while I was cutting them to size. I finished up by screwing the door closed from the inside and hiding the family in the attic with a chainsaw. I even had my flatboat waiting in the front yard, tied to a long rope that I could reach from the roof. Turns out, that Cat Four dropped to a One and we barely got a pisser of a rain storm. Since then, I don't pay attention to nothing they say."

His mind was set and there was no changing it, so I moved on to the problem at hand.

"Do y'all sit out here every day?" I asked.

"Yeah, most every day," the man said.

"Would y'all have been out here yesterday when the kids were practicing baseball across the street?"

"Oh, yeah," the wife said with a smile. "I was watching them play. Herb was reading the newspaper like he usually does. I like watching them hit the ball to see how far it goes. Sometimes, it even goes over the fence. There's some strong boys out there in that field."

"Baseball's a game of cowards," Herb said. "What do they do? They hit an unarmed ball with a stick and then they run away like bums. They call it America's game or some such nonsense. Americans don't run. We stand and fight. Take boxing. Now, that's an American sport. Two people standing in the middle of the ring and slugging it out until somebody drops. There's no tapping or running or quitting. You fight until somebody dies. After watching that, why would I want to watch kids hit a ball and then run for their lives?"

The woman shook her head and waved off her husband. "Don't mind him. If you sit here long enough, he'll tell you his opinion about everything from potato chips to the price of a Big Mac."

"Well, it's ridiculous," Herb continued. "When they first opened the McDonald's in Chateau, you could get a Big Mac for sixty-five cents. The other day, they tried to charge me five bucks for the same sandwich. It hasn't changed in fifty years except to get smaller. It's ridiculous."

I couldn't argue with the man, and even if I could, I wouldn't. I didn't have time to talk about a Big Mac.

"Ma'am, were you out here between seven and eight o'clock last night?" I asked.

"Oh, yeah, we were out here until it got dark." She pushed her glasses higher on her nose. "When the mosquitoes got too bad, we went inside."

"Did you notice three boys leave the ballpark early?" I dug for my phone. "They would've left around seven, before everyone else left."

Her brow furrowed as she thought about it. "Let me see…"

I found the picture of Cory first and showed it to her. Her expression didn't change. Next, I showed her the picture of the Foret boys.

"Ah, I remember those redheads!" She nodded. "You can't miss them. Yeah, I saw them get here with another boy, but they came from the back of the street. When they left, they went that way"—she pointed westward toward Main Street—"and they seemed to be in a hurry, like they were excited about something. You know, they were standing up while they rode their bikes to make them go faster."

"Did you notice any cars in the area when they left?" I asked. "More specifically, did any cars leave right after they did and travel in the same direction?"

"No, I didn't notice any." Her expression suddenly turned quizzical. "Is something wrong? Did they steal something?"

"No, they're not in trouble," I said quickly. "It's just that they didn't come home this morning, so we're trying to find them before the storm hits. Their parents are worried about them."

"Oh, no! Do you think someone kidnapped them?" She was clutching at the front of her blouse now. "When I was a little girl, a boy from our neighborhood was kidnapped. They never did find him."

"Ain't nobody kidnapped them boys," Herb said impatiently. "They wouldn't be able to catch them. All them boys do is practice running away. They're good at that, don't you know it? You watch them run in circles every night."

"Square," the woman said.

"What?" Herb glanced sideways at his wife.

"They don't run in a circle," she said. "They run in squares."

I thanked them and walked off, leaving them to argue about the shape of a baseball field. As I was moving toward the next house, I saw Ray Foret's truck rumbling down the street. He stopped in front of the ballpark and stared intently toward the baseball field.

I shook my head. Something in my gut told me that we would have trouble with this man.

CHAPTER 8

Ray Foret saw me standing on the opposite side of Coconut Lane, so he whipped his truck around and pulled up beside me. Sliding down his passenger side window, he leaned forward.

"They weren't at the campsite," he said breathlessly. "They never even went there."

I wanted to tell him I had already told him that, but I didn't. The man was in pain, and I wasn't about to add to his misery.

"Well, they were definitely at practice," I said. "I've been able to confirm it with some of the neighbors here. They remember seeing two redheaded boys and another one leaving on bicycles. They also confirmed the boys were heading west on Coconut when they left the ballpark."

Ray looked toward Main Street. "Where in the hell were y'all going?"

He was mumbling and directing his question to his sons, so I didn't answer. Instead, I reminded him to call me if he found anything.

"We need to work together on this," I said. "I'll keep you up-to-date about everything I find, and I'll need you to do the same."

"Right." He nodded and sped off, heading west on Coconut.

I proceeded to the next house, where a man and a young boy were busy closing brown shutters and locking them in place. I questioned them, but neither of them knew anything about the missing boys, and neither of them had been outside on the previous night.

I knocked on a few doors, but those who answered didn't know anything. The ones who weren't home were probably long gone, heading north or west to avoid the storm, so I headed back to my Tahoe. I wasn't sure if the boys had gone north or south along Main Street, but I headed north first, intent on checking every business along the street for surveillance footage.

As luck would have it, nearly every business was closed and boarded up, except for Cig's Gas Station. I parked in their lot and decided to call Regan and Amy before going inside.

"Anything?" I asked Regan when she answered.

"Nothing much," she said. "The last time Cory used his cell phone was yesterday around five, and when we try to trace it, it shows that he's out of service or the phone is turned off. His last known location was at the ballpark."

"What about his social media accounts?"

"He's not very active on social media. I did find that girl Stacy from Northern Chateau. They connected on social media and she sent him her cell number over a private message."

"Did you call her?" I asked.

"Yeah, but she hasn't spoken to him in about a week," she said. "When I asked if Cory ever made plans to visit her, she said that he had talked about riding his bike to Northern Chateau, but then changed his mind when he realized how far it was. He told her if he snuck out in the middle of the night, he would have to be back by the time his mom woke up for work, and there was no way he could ride his bike to Northern Chateau and back in five hours."

A powerful gust of wind suddenly blew through the parking lot, rocking my Tahoe roughly and causing the metal sign above the gas station to rattle loudly.

"What about search history?"

"Well, it looks like he's fascinated by alligators," she said. "He looked up wrestling alligators, owning them, and whether or not it was illegal to keep one as a pet."

"When was that?" I asked.

"Within the last month." She grunted. "He also looked up one-way trips to Mars, something about video game cheats, the toughest breed of dog, and how to make a girl want you."

"That's quite an array of topics," I said with a laugh. I asked her to let me know if she found anything helpful, and then called Amy.

"Hey, old man, give me a second," Amy said in a low voice when she answered. I heard some movement in the background, and then she came back on the phone. "I wanted to get away from Wendy so we could talk freely."

"Did you find something?"

"Yeah, I found some stuff," she said, "but not much of it is useful."

"Shit!"

"You can say that again. First off, they haven't used their phones since yesterday afternoon. Wendy has one of those apps that track their phones, but the last location shows the ballpark. She says that's normal, because they're always letting their phones die."

"Hold up," I said, rubbing my chin. "Both boys' phones just so happen to have died at the same time while they were at the ballpark?"

"Yeah, that's what it looks like."

"The last location of Cory's cell phone was also at the ballpark," I said. "Does that seem odd to you?"

"Are you suggesting that their phones didn't die, but that they all turned them off at the same time?" The curiosity seemed to be mounting in her voice.

"I don't know that for sure, but it seems odd that all of their batteries would die at the same time, don't you think?"

"Yeah, it does seem odd," she admitted, "especially since it happened before the camping trip. Had it been during the night of their trip, then that would make more sense, because they would've all been out in the woods for about the same amount of time without power. But I guess it's also possible that they hung out together all day and neither of them charged their phones."

"Ask Wendy while you've got her there," I said. "Find out if they were together all day."

Amy was gone for a brief moment, and then came back to the phone.

"Nope, they weren't together all day," she said. "And get this: Wendy also said she never got an automated message from the app saying they needed to charge their phones. She says she gets those messages about once every two days telling her that one or both of her boys' cell phones are losing power, but she didn't get a message like that yesterday."

What did that mean? I settled into my seat as the SUV rocked gently from the rising wind, and considered this information. Had the boys intentionally gone off-grid upon arriving at the park? Or had they simply turned off their phones to conserve the batteries because they knew they would be out camping all night? I figured the latter was more feasible, and asked Amy what she thought.

"I guess it's possible," she said, "but if we don't find them soon, we'll never know, because this storm is coming hard."

I glanced at my radio. I'd been too busy to listen to it. "Have you heard the latest reports?"

"Wendy's got the TV blaring over here. It's nonstop coverage. They're talking about a twenty-foot tidal surge, total inundation along the coast, and winds that could give an EF-5 tornado a run for its money."

My mind immediately went to Susan, who had decided to stay here and ride out the storm with her officers, as well as the three boys who were out there somewhere, no doubt completely unaware of the hell that was heading our way.

"Is there a chance it might turn?" I asked, knowing that the cone of uncertainty was narrowing by the minute.

"Nope, it's coming right for us."

I cursed under my breath and opened the door to my Tahoe. I cursed again when it was almost jerked out of my hand by another strong gust of wind. I hurried across the parking lot, wondering where on earth the boys might be. If we couldn't find them before the storm arrived, I was hoping that they were at least on high ground.

If they had ridden their bikes to Central or Northern Chateau, they would be in a lot safer position than if they were stuck in the swamps around town. Hopefully, the surveillance system from Cig's would show them crossing the bridge and heading north. If it did, it would buy us some time to find them. If it didn't, we would be forced to keep searching for them right up until the storm hit. Otherwise it could spell the end for all three boys.

CHAPTER 9

The clerk at Cig's was some new kid I'd never seen before. Truth be told, I hadn't been inside the store in quite some time. It was the place I used to purchase my alcohol when I was going through a rough patch in my life, so I tried to avoid it. Not because I thought I would revert back to my old self, but because it reminded me of things that were better left in the past.

"Hey, how are you?" I asked the kid.

"We're closing in fifteen minutes," he said. "I've got to lock up and drop the garage doors before the weather gets too bad."

"I'll only need a second," I said, pointing to my badge. "I need access to the surveillance equipment. We've got three young boys who went missing last night, and we're trying to find them before the storm gets here. I need to see if they crossed the bridge."

The kid behind the counter hesitated. "Um, I'm not familiar with the system…"

"I've got it," I said. "In fact, I'll show you how to use it while I'm at it."

He nodded and led me to the office where the surveillance system was located. I quickly accessed the files, explaining everything as I went, and pulled up footage from the camera facing Main Street. After making sure the time and date were correct, I began playing the footage from the previous evening, starting from seven o'clock. I had increased the speed to eight and watched carefully for any bikes that might pass.

"What are we looking for?" the kid asked.

I pointed to the stretch of highway that was visible in the camera. "We're looking for three boys to ride by on bicycles. They're fifteen and sixteen years of age, one's got brown hair, and the other two have red hair."

"The Foret boys?" the kid asked, cocking his head to the side.

"Yeah, do you know them?" I was tempted to look at him, but I didn't take my eyes off of the monitor.

"I go to school with them," he explained. "They're missing, huh?"

"Yeah, would you know anything about that?"

"I'd check with Cory Verdin, because they're always together." The boy nodded admirably. "I heard about a fight they got into at school once and they got suspended. They were pretty much legends after that. Everyone in school was talking about them and Cory. They say Cory's the toughest out of the three of them, but Ruben and Allen are okay."

I wanted to delve deeper into the idea that three boys could become legends at school just for being suspended, but I didn't have time at the moment.

"Do you know of any other trouble they've gotten into at school?" I asked.

"Like what?" he asked.

"Have they been involved in other fights? Or have they ever played any pranks at school that might've gotten them in trouble?"

"Not that I know of."

"What about enemies? Are there any kids out there who don't like them?"

"I don't think so. Ever since the fight, they've pretty much been liked by everybody. It was some bully football players who beat them up, but even though they lost the fight, they showed that you could stand up to even the biggest bully and come out a winner."

"What about any of the parents of students from school?" I offered. "Have you ever heard parents complaining about them, or maybe other students saying their parents didn't like the Foret boys and their parents, or Cory and his mom?"

"No, sir, everyone likes Cory's mom. She's hot."

I nodded idly and frowned as the time in the video drew on and there was still no sign of the missing boys. I would've expected them to reach the bridge within minutes of leaving the ballpark.

"Have they ever come into the store?" I asked as the video footage continued to play. According to the time stamp, it had just rolled past nine o'clock at night, and I still hadn't seen any signs of the three boys.

"Not while I was working," the kid said.

I nodded, my mind moving ahead to something else now. I figured if the boys had left town, they would've done so immediately after leaving baseball practice. They wouldn't have waited, so it was a waste of time to continue playing past nine-thirty. I slid the cursor back along the timeline until I reached six o'clock and played it forward from there, just in case Stewart Finane had been mistaken about the time they left. When the footage reached seven o'clock, there was still no sign of the boys.

I sighed and maneuvered back to the home screen. I stood from the chair I'd been sitting in and thanked the kid.

"You're welcome," he said. "I've always wanted to be a cop."

"Well then, keep your nose clean and always do the right thing— even when no one's looking."

He frowned, as though he didn't understand what I was saying.

"Look, it's easy to do the right thing when people are watching you, but it's when no one's looking that it really matters." I pointed at him. "Not only should you do the right thing because it *is* the right thing, but if you ever apply to become a cop, they'll polygraph you and ask you all about your dirty little sins."

The boy gulped. "Really?"

"No, they'll just ask you about any crimes you might've committed," I said with a smile. "They want to make sure they're hiring a good person."

"What if someone might've done something wrong when they were younger?" he asked cautiously. "Like, what if they made a mistake and they're sorry for it now?"

"Just be honest about it and chalk it up to youthful indiscretion," I said on my way toward the door. "We all do dumb things when we're young."

"Youthful indiscretion." The kid smiled broadly. "I'll have to use that one on my mom."

I shook my head and stepped out into the whipping wind. It was still early in the day, so it wasn't raining yet, but the wind speeds were increasing almost by the minute, and the clouds were growing meaner and darker along with them.

"God help those boys if we don't find them in time," I said to myself. I was deeply disturbed that I hadn't seen them riding their bikes out of town, because that could only mean they were somewhere in town or in the swamps. If they were hiding out at a friend's house—or perhaps a girl's house—that might not be so bad, except for when their parents got a hold of them.

However, if they were out in the swamps, they would be in grave danger from all directions. Not only could the rising water and flying debris get them, but they could also be crushed by wind thrown trees. I'd been caught in the swamps during a storm before, and it had been a minefield of falling trees. I didn't know which way to go to avoid them. When I went one way, I'd come upon a tree falling from the opposite direction. It was less than ideal. I had made it out alive and unhurt, but I'd heard of others who hadn't been so lucky.

I was backing out of the parking lot when Melvin's voice came over our private police channel—the one that nosy townsfolk couldn't access with their scanners.

"Headquarters, be advised I've located three bicycles on the west side of town near the water tower," he said. "Please advise Clint."

"I'm en route," I said quickly over the radio. I glanced at my cell phone, which I'd forgotten on the dash, and saw that Melvin had tried calling me three times. He'd also texted me, but I didn't bother reading the messages now. I already knew what they would say. Besides, I needed to spend the next minute trying to figure out what their bikes would be doing next to the water tower.

CHAPTER 10

The wind whistled against my Tahoe on the drive to the water tower, and I wasn't even driving fast. When I arrived, I saw Melvin's F-250 parked near a large corrugated metal building at the end of Jezebel Drive. The building was old and rusted in spots. I'd never been inside the place, but I knew it was where the town's maintenance department kept tools and equipment to service the water tower.

I stepped from my Tahoe and approached Melvin's truck. He was still sitting inside and didn't open the door until I was right beside it. I could see that he was on his cell phone, so I didn't interrupt him.

"Hey, I was checking on Claire and Delilah," he explained. "They're still in Louisiana, but they're close to the Texarkana line."

I nodded and turned my attention to the space between the metal building and the six-foot cyclone fence that surrounded the water tower. Tucked into this narrow alleyway were three bicycles. They had been pushed up against the building and dumped on their sides in the tall grass.

"How in the hell did you spot them?" I asked. Even though I knew they were there, it was almost impossible to see them.

"I drove by here twice before I saw them." He pointed to the cross street opposite our location. "I was driving there when I looked this way and saw something round sticking up out of the grass. It was one of the tires."

"Did you check it out yet?"

"I called your phone a couple of times and then checked the building to make sure it was secure," he explained. "Once that was done, I came back to my truck and waited. I figured you'd want to photograph the bikes as they were found."

"And the building?"

"It's all locked up and there's no sign of forced entry, so they definitely didn't go inside."

I surveyed the area, looking from right to left, in front of me and behind me. "If they're not in the building, then where are they?"

Melvin raised his eyebrows and glanced upward. I followed his gaze to the top of the water tower.

"No way," I said. "There's no way they went up there."

"Then where else could they be?"

I pulled out my cell phone and called Amy. "Hey, are y'all done?"

"Yeah, Regan and I are heading back to the office so I can jump in my Charger and get on the road. Ray's back. He's freaking out a little. He told Wendy he checked everywhere and couldn't find their bikes, so he's convinced they're no longer in town. He's blaming Cory for luring his boys off to some place. I had to talk him down a few times, but I'm sure he'll explode at some point. The man's out of control."

"Well, then he can't know that Melvin found the bikes at the water tower."

"Hold up—y'all found their bikes?" Amy had obviously not heard Melvin's earlier radio traffic.

"Yeah, Melvin and I are here now," I said. "Did y'all find any information on their computers about water towers or terrorist attacks or poisoning water supplies—anything like that?"

"No, nothing like that," she said. "I saw enough breasts and soft porn to lose my breakfast, but there was nothing terror related—just your run of the mill, teenage boy stuff."

I glanced at Melvin. "Do you really think they're up there?"

"It's worth a look." He squinted against the wind and stared toward the top of the dome. "If they got the hatch open, they could be inside. Do I think they're trying to poison the water supply? No, but it's quite possible they climbed up there for shits and giggles and then got into trouble. Maybe they can't get the door open again, or maybe one of them got hurt inside. Either way, we have to check it out."

"You're not going up there!" I could hear the excitement in Amy's voice over the phone. "Are you seriously gonna climb the water tower?"

"I climbed one when I was a teenager, and I was drunk and wearing cowboy boots," I said with a sigh, "so this should be a piece of cake."

"But those things have to be 100 feet tall," she protested. "If you fall, you'll surely die."

"Try 165," I corrected. "And it's windy, so yeah, it's definitely risky."

"Right, so if you fell 165 feet you'd be even deader. Plus, you'd have more time to think about all the sins you've committed on your way down." She paused for a second and then said, "That's why I have to do it. You've got a daughter and another baby on the way. It's probably a boy. He'll need his dad to be around when he's playing sports and beginning to date girls and stuff. Save yourself, old man, and leave the water tower climbing to me. I've got this."

"We'll pull straws," I said with a laugh. "Just hurry and get your ass over here. We need to recover the bikes and process the area before it starts raining. And I'd like to be gone before Ray finds out what's happening. We don't need him showing up and starting problems."

While waiting for Amy to arrive, I pulled out my camera and photographed the area. After I'd gotten some overview shots, I moved in closer for some intermediates and close-ups. The ground was dry and there were no discernible tracks in the area, but I waved for Melvin to come over and have a look.

"It looks like they left here walking," he finally said, pointing beyond the metal building. "My guess is they set off in an easterly direction behind the equipment barn, but that's just a guess. The wind's been blowing for hours and it's whipped the weeds in all directions, so it'd be impossible to track them with any accuracy."

I scowled. "Do you think the sheriff would send one of his K-9 deputies out in this mess?"

"Gretchen would do it." Melvin nodded positively. "She's not scared of shit, but I think it would be a waste. The trail's almost a day old, and once they hit any of the surrounding streets, it's anybody's guess where they went."

Gretchen Verdin and her German shepherd, Geronimo, made up the best K-9 team anywhere in the state, and probably the country, but I knew he was right. She would track the boys to the street, and that's where it would end.

I shook my head. There was no way they would've abandoned their bikes to travel the streets on foot. They had either gotten into a vehicle from here, or climbed that water tower, or set off into the vast swamplands to the west. I didn't like any of those choices, but we were about to either confirm or eliminate one of them, because Amy was just arriving and it was time to pull straws.

CHAPTER 11

Mechant Loup was a small town, and it didn't take long for information to travel from one end to the other. Apparently, someone in the neighborhood of the water tower had seen all of us congregating in the area—Takecia, Shade, Regan, and Baylor had all decided to join Melvin, Amy and me—and word had quickly made its way to the ear of Ray Foret, and he arrived moments after I'd drawn the short straw.

"You did it wrong," Amy said, waving her long blade of grass at Melvin. "It should've been six short straws and a long one, because we would all volunteer for the assignment."

Shade was the youngest and most athletic among all of us and he would've made the shortest work of that tall climb, but I was glad I'd pulled the short straw. The wind gusts were rocking our vehicles and some would even push us off-balance, so it was going to be a harrowing climb. I was just walking to my Tahoe to retrieve a harness and safety lanyard when Ray's truck turned the corner on what seemed like two wheels and raced toward us on Jezebel.

"I've got him," Melvin called, stepping into the road and waving for Ray to stop his truck. Takecia and Shade joined him in blocking off the road, and Ray immediately slowed his vehicle when he saw them standing there. They made him pull to a stop about twenty yards away.

"Where're my boys?" he demanded when he leapt from his truck. "I wanna see my boys!"

"We don't have them yet," I heard Melvin say in a patient voice. "We're about to check—"

"Bullshit! I got a call that y'all found my boys!"

As I stepped into my harness, I watched what was happening.

"We only found what we believe to be their bicycles," Melvin said. "They're identical to the ones in their picture. Right now, Detective Wolf is about to climb the water tower to see if that's where they went."

Ray looked in my direction and our eyes locked. I saw him take a deep breath and exhale it forcefully. He grabbed his face with his hands and walked in a circle. "Oh, my God, are you sure y'all didn't find them dead? Are you telling me the truth? Someone told me y'all found their bodies."

"I wouldn't lie to you," Melvin said. "We only found the bikes. We think they might be up in the water tower, so Detective Wolf is heading up there now. If you can remain calm, I'll let you stand over by our vehicles, but you've got to promise to stay put. We don't have time for interference. You have to let us do our jobs."

Ray nodded his head and Melvin led him to where his truck was parked.

I finished strapping into my harness and grabbed my safety lanyard. By the time I made it to the gate, Melvin had already cut one of the links to the chain and swung it open.

"Be careful," Melvin said. "The wind's blowing pretty hard down here, and it's much worse up there."

I nodded and made my way to the base of the ladder. I took a breath and glanced up. The last time I'd done this, I was young, dumb, and drunk, and I didn't have a harness or safety lanyard, so I figured this would be much easier. However, when I saw how far it was to the top, I swallowed. I didn't remember it being that high.

"I'll do it if you're having second thoughts," Amy chided from beside me. "I know you're getting kind of old for these things."

That was all the motivation I needed. Without another moment of hesitation, I grabbed onto the round, metal rungs and began climbing. Once I'd gotten about twenty feet off the ground, I began using my safety lanyard. I'd reach as high as I could, snap the carabiner onto a rung above me, climb a few steps, and then repeat the process. I never looked down and I never stopped moving until I reached the top.

When I stepped over the guard rail and dropped to the catwalk that circled the giant water tank, I felt my legs wobble. My arms were fatigued and I was breathing hard. I took a look over the edge and felt dizzy. Right then, a powerful gust of wind blew in from my right side and nearly knocked me over. I clutched onto the railing and held on for dear life. Once the winds died down, I clipped my carabiner to one of the vertical bars of the railing and took a few breaths.

It had been a long time since I'd been this high in the sky, so I was a bit awestruck for a moment. The water tank was blocking my view to the south, so I turned and looked to the north. I felt like I could see straight into Mississippi from my perch.

When my breathing had normalized, I unclipped from the railing and turned to the final ladder—the one that extended upward and then curved over the top of the tank. It was a little unnerving, because it looked like I would be hanging onto the side of this giant dome like a lizard clutching onto a windshield, just waiting to be blown off by the next gust of wind.

Saying a silent prayer and reaching high to clip my carabiner onto one of the metal rungs, I took three careful steps upward. I repeated the process about a dozen times—stopping often to grip the ladder with both hands as the powerful wind threatened to snatch me from my position—before I rounded the top of the water tank.

When I looked up and to the south, I gasped. Dark, ominous clouds stretched from left to right as far as my eyes could see, completely covering the southern horizon. Intermittently, I saw brilliant flashes of lightning erupting far inside the clouds, and even from that distance, I could hear the deep rumbling of thunder.

"Holy shit, are we in for it," I said, shaking my head as I thought about the missing boys. I couldn't see the square hatch that led into the belly of the water tank, but I was hoping I'd find the lock cut and the boys inside. Maybe they'd gotten drunk and fallen asleep inside the tank, or the door had locked behind them. Whatever the case, I needed them to be inside and doing well.

Gripping the nearest rung as hard as I could with my left hand, I removed the carabiner with my right hand and was stretching out for the last rung with my right hand when it happened.

My right foot had raised just an inch or two from the rung I'd been standing on when the next gust of wind decided to take a swipe at the top of the water tank. The force of this one was greater than any I'd felt thus far, and it was enough to shove my body to the left and knock me off balance.

I twisted violently and was spun away from the ladder. In a desperate attempt to save myself, I fought to hold on with my left hand, but the force of my body being twisted caused my wrist to bend awkwardly and it broke my grip on the rung. I gritted my teeth and fell.

CHAPTER 12

From somewhere below me, I heard a collective gasp as the world opened up beneath me and I fell. In that brief moment, I could hear Amy's words from earlier very clearly in my mind: *you'd have more time to think about all the sins you've committed on your way down.*

Even before her words came through my mind clearly, I was abruptly jerked to a rough stop. My heart stuck in my throat, I wriggled around to see what had happened. The ground spun beneath me and something curious caught my eye, but it was gone in a flash. I continued spinning and banged into the ladder.

I quickly grabbed onto the rungs and righted myself. Although the wind was blowing hard and it was cool up here, I could feel beads of sweat dripping down my face. I looked at the rung directly in front of me and realized that I'd somehow managed to clip my carabiner to it as I fell. It had been purely instinctive, because I had no independent recollection of doing it.

I puffed in a breath of fresh air and attacked the ladder once again. I was a little banged up from clattering against the iron and my wrist was sore, but I was ready to be done with this mission. I wanted to feel the solid ground beneath my feet, and I wanted it now.

Clipping ahead only one rung at a time, I made my way to the top of the water tank and glanced at the hatch.

"Shit!"

I took a breath and sagged on the ladder. The hatch was locked with a large round padlock that was thought to be bolt-cutter proof. Cursing some more, I descended the top ladder and was grateful to feel the solid catwalk beneath my boots. I turned and looked down at the ground. A small crowd of onlookers had gathered near our vehicles, and they were standing there with Ray.

I shook my head. Did they not know a storm was coming? Had they seen what I had seen on the horizon, they would've all jumped in their vehicles and raced in the opposite direction. I pulled out my radio and addressed Melvin.

"The hatch is locked," I said, looking directly beneath me to where he stood with Amy and the rest of our crew. "They didn't come up here."

"Damn it, Clint, you gave us a scare," he said. "What the hell happened?"

"A gust of wind caught me by surprise," I admitted. "It's rough up here. I can actually feel the entire tower swaying."

"Well, hurry up and get down. I don't like you being up there."

"Just a second." I stood tall and leaned out over the railing. I was clipped into one of the vertical bars just in case, but I still gripped the top of the railing with both hands. I scanned the ground carefully, searching for what I had seen while dangling upside down. I tried to recreate the fall and subsequent point of view I might've had, and then found it.

I glanced at Ray and the crowd of people who had gathered down below. I didn't want to draw any attention to the area, because Ray was the type of person who would have to run over and see for himself, so I leaned casually on the railing and called Melvin on my radio again, using our private channel.

"Hey, Mel, while I was hanging upside down speaking to God," I said in a low voice, "I saw some tire tracks on the back side of the metal building. Don't go now, but there are a few piles of busted up concrete and shells at the center of the yard, and then there's a pile of dirt closer to the building. It's overgrown with grass, but it looks like a car drove right up against the back of the building and smashed a track through the edge of the dirt pile."

"Oh, really?" he asked, keeping his eyes on me.

"Yeah, it looks fresh, because the grass in that one area is still pushed down." I noted the tall grass whipping in the wind all around the tire track. "It would've been impossible to see from the ground."

"How do you want to handle it?"

I told him what I had in mind, and then began my long descent. Once I was gratefully on solid ground again, I pulled out of the harness and walked to my Tahoe. I waved for Ray to join me. While I explained to him what was going on, I caught movement from the corner of my eye and knew that Melvin and Amy were heading for the back of the building to check out the tire track.

"What're we supposed to do now?" Ray asked in frustration. "If their bikes were here, then they were here. So, where are they now?"

"We don't know for sure, but we're thinking they either headed into the swamps to the west of here or got picked up by someone in a car." I closed the back gate on my Tahoe. "Do you know of anyone who might've picked them up by car?"

"No." He shook his head. "That doesn't make any sense. They were supposed to be camping on the opposite side of town. They were looking forward to it. They *loved* to go camping."

"We didn't find their gear with their bikes, so they definitely took it with them," I explained. "That could mean they decided to go camping out here instead of on the east side, but I'll need some kind of confirmation before sending a search party out there to look for them."

"I'm not afraid of this weather," he said with a snarl. "I'll go look for them by myself if I have to!"

"It's not just about the weather," I said. "If we send five or ten people in the wrong direction, then we won't have enough people to search in the right place. We'll be on our own out here until this storm passes, so we need to utilize our resources as efficiently as possible. Our number one goal is finding your boys before that storm hits. If we don't, they could be in real trouble."

He thought about it and then nodded.

"I need you to cooperate with me in every way possible," I said pointedly. "Can I have your word that you'll do that?"

"Yeah, I give you my word."

"Okay." I pointed toward the top of the water tower. "Your boys weren't up there, but it wasn't a complete waste of time. From that vantage point, I saw some tire tracks that we would've never seen from the ground—"

"Where are they?" he asked hurriedly, staring wildly about. "Where do they lead?"

"You need to calm down and remember your promise," I said. "I need you to stay right here with me while those tracks are being looked into. I also need you to think really hard about who might've picked them up by car."

"I can't think of anyone."

I sighed. Why would someone park a car behind this metal building and pick up three boys who had just abandoned their bicycles along the opposite side of this same building? I couldn't think of a single good reason for meeting like this, but I could think of a few bad ones.

"Have your sons ever experimented with drugs?"

"Hell, no!"

"How can you be so sure?" I asked. "There's no way you can know everything your sons are doing all the time."

"Oh, I know."

He sounded extremely sure of himself. Either he didn't want to believe they could get one over on him, or he really did know.

"And how do you know?"

"It's none of your business how I raise my boys," he said defiantly. "If I tell you they're not on drugs, then that should be enough for you."

"It's not," I said. "Your boys are missing and their lives could be in danger. I already told you not to waste my time. I don't want to have to keep saying it over and over. For the sake of your boys, I need to know everything. My number one goal is finding them. I can't do that without your help."

He folded his meaty arms across his chest. "I drug test them every weekend."

I tried not to look surprised, but I was. "Did something necessitate these drug tests?"

"When Allen was in middle school, I found a little wrapper with marijuana inside his school bag." He cleared his throat. "Um, ever since then, I started buying those home drug test kits and I make them pee in a cup once a week. Sometimes, I change it up to keep them on their toes, you know? I might pop in on them on a Wednesday morning before school and make them do it, or a Monday afternoon right when they get back from practice."

I tried to keep a flat affect, but on the inside, I was starting to wonder more and more if the boys had actually run away from home. What if they had packed more than their camping gear inside those bags? If their toothbrushes and some clothes were missing, that might be a sign that they had run away. If they had a piggy bank that was now empty, that might also be a sign that they had willingly run off.

"Look, I need you to go home and search your boys' rooms," I said, still trying to rectify the one doubt I had. While the Foret boys might deem their house a prison, Cory seemed to be happy with his mom and his living arrangements. Of course, that was according to his mom, so she might be overlooking some things.

"I already searched their rooms," Ray said. "There's nothing there."

"But what about those things that aren't there?"

"What do you mean?"

"Were their toothbrushes there? Were any clothes missing? What about their money jar—was it empty?" I could tell by the blank expression on his face that he had been searching their rooms with a different idea in mind. I shot a thumb toward his truck. "Go back and see if any of those things are missing, and let me know as soon as you find out. I'll let you know what we turn up here."

As he nodded and hurried off, I pulled out my cell phone and had the same conversation with Valerie Verdin. She scoffed at the idea. "There's no way Cory ran away from home," she said, a sense of dread bleeding into her voice. "If he left in a car, he was forcibly taken."

"We don't know that," I said softly. "Try to stay positive. Just go through his things with an eye toward what might be missing. I'll let you know if we find anything more out here."

"What's that?" she asked. "I can barely hear you over the wind."

I cupped a hand over my phone and repeated what I'd said. When she acknowledged that she'd heard me, I walked over to where Takecia, Shade, and Regan were talking to the people from the neighborhood who had gathered to watch.

CHAPTER 13

Takecia told me they had questioned the neighbors, but no one had seen anything of substance.

"One lady did hear a car drive up late at night, but she doesn't know where it went or what time it came by," she said. "Amy told us the boys left the park earlier in the evening, so I doubt the car had anything to do with the bicycles."

I thanked her and started to walk away when she grabbed my arm. "I'm glad you didn't die," she said in her thick Jamaican accent, "because it would've upset my friend, and I would have been forced to kill you."

I laughed. Takecia and Susan were more than best friends. Back in the day, when Susan was a mixed martial arts fighter, Takecia was her training partner. When two people share sweat and blood in combat, there forms a special bond between them, and the friendship between Susan and Takecia was special.

I made my way around the metal shed and found Melvin and Amy squatting near the pile of mud I had seen from my perch above Mechant Loup. I looked up at the water tank and shook my head. Moments earlier, I had been hanging from my harness up there, thinking it was all over.

"Clint, you have to see this," Melvin said. "I found a partial shoe impression in the mud. It looks like it could be from an athletic sneaker."

I got closer and stopped when I was standing over them. The shoe impression was very faint and it was positioned at the edge of the mud pile. I calculated the distance between the tire track and the shoe impression. They were about three feet apart. The shoe impression had to be related to the tire track, but were they related to our missing boys?

"Is this it?" I asked.

"Yep," Amy said, strands of her blonde hair whipping in the wind. "We did a thorough check of the area and that's all we found. I've got some good photographs, but there's no way we'll have time to cast it before the rains come."

Typically, we would cover the track with a bucket or set up a tent to preserve the evidence from the rain, but either a bucket or tent would be instantly blown away in this weather.

"If the boys did get into this vehicle last night, they could be anywhere by now," Melvin said. "But I can't say for sure if they did. It's impossible to start a track from the bicycles. The ground is hard. The grass is blowing everywhere. I just can't say for sure where those boys went."

I cursed under my breath and squinted as I studied our surroundings. There were no cameras on the metal building, or on any of the apartments across the street, or on the trailer behind the building. Toward the front of the street and beyond the trailer, there was an apartment complex for the elderly, but most of them were gone. I'd seen buses coming in and out of there all morning long to pick them up and evacuate them to higher ground. Also, I already knew there were no cameras on any of the buildings, so we would be getting no help from there.

"What're you thinking?" Amy asked, raising her voice to be heard over the wind. It was really howling now. The power lines were whipping in the wind. Loose metal clanked loudly from somewhere on the large shed. Even we humans were being pushed around and had to keep adjusting our footing to maintain our balance. Scattered rain was starting to fall, and that prompted the onlookers to scatter.

"We need to put the bicycles in the back of my Tahoe and get them printed," I said. "And then we need to have a tough conversation with the Forets and Mrs. Verdin."

Amy nodded and we all trudged to the opposite side of the shed, where we donned latex gloves and each grabbed a bicycle. Shade opened the back gate to my Tahoe, and we put two of the bikes in there. Thanks to the gear I kept in the cargo area, my SUV was getting a little cramped, so Melvin threw the third bike in the back of Takecia's marked Tahoe.

Now that Shade had graduated from the police academy, he was driving Takecia's old Dodge Charger, and she had been issued a new

Tahoe. Susan had convinced Mayor Pauline Cane to upgrade all of the patrol vehicles to Tahoe four-by-fours because of the muddy terrain we often encountered, but she wanted to phase the older vehicles out over time.

"Hey, Clint," Melvin said, waving me over to where he stood on the edge of the road with Shade. "Do you mind if we hit the fields back here and see if we can find anything?"

"I can't ask y'all to do that," I said. "The storm's almost on top of us and there's no evidence that they even went off in that direction. It could be putting y'all at risk for nothing."

"You risked your ass to climb that water tower," Shade said, "so this is the least we can do. I'm with Melvin if you're okay with it."

I licked my lips. "I would never ask y'all to do it, but I'm also in no position to say no. Y'all work for Susan, not me, though."

"Should we ask the chief if it's okay?" Shade asked.

Melvin flashed a devilish grin and slapped Shade on the shoulder. "There're a few things you need to learn about police work, young man."

"What's that?"

"Sometimes," Melvin said, "it's better to ask for forgiveness than for permission."

Shade nodded his head knowingly and both men hurried to their cruisers. They each grabbed a raincoat and a rifle and then headed off into the fields of tall grass that stretched for miles to the east. I watched them go and wondered if I would regret not doing more to stop them. Part of me thought they were risking their lives for nothing, but part of me wasn't sure.

CHAPTER 14

Once Amy and I had driven to the police department and stored the bicycles in our evidence room, I gave Susan a brief update on the case and told her where Melvin and Shade had gone.

"You let them go out in this weather?" she asked, her mouth wide. "Clint, that storm's breathing down our asses. If they're not back before it hits, they'll be the ones in trouble."

"I know, Sue," I said with a sigh, "but you would've done the same thing if you weren't carrying Baretta in your stomach."

For a brief moment, the serious expression on her face vanished and she laughed. "I already told you, we're not naming our kid after some TV detective from the seventies!"

I kissed her quickly and left to find Amy. She was in the break room tearing through a bag of chips. She tossed me one and then followed me to my Tahoe.

The heavier clouds were starting to roll in now, and they cast the town in a dark and ominous shadow. I caught Amy looking to the sky as I drove to Valerie Verdin's house, and there was a look of concern on her face.

"Do you think we'll lose everything?" she asked.

"I don't know," I said, "but if it's as bad as they say, then I believe some of us will."

I could never quite understand how Mother Nature selected her victims. I'd seen firsthand—and on more than one occasion—the aftermaths of tornados that had flattened entire neighborhoods, and invariably, there would always be one or two homes that had been left completely unscathed. While witnesses would say that the tornado skipped over those particular homes and resumed cloud-to-ground contact on the opposite side, no one could ever explain why that particular house was spared. If this storm was as bad as the weather service was predicting, I had to wonder if anyone would be so lucky as to come away untouched.

I parked in Valerie Verdin's driveway and we knocked on her door before going to the Foret home. While both families were equally worried, Ray and Wendy Foret had each other but Valerie was all alone, so I wanted to meet with her first.

As soon as she opened up, the wind gushed into her house and sent the door slamming into the inner wall. She waved for us to enter and I quickly shut it behind us. I could already feel the walls of the house trembling against the onslaught, and the storm hadn't even made landfall yet.

"Did you find anything?" she asked breathlessly.

"No, ma'am," I said with a frown. "It was definitely their bikes, but it turned out to be a dead end."

She gasped and took a seat on a recliner in the living room.

"Did you check to see if any of Cory's things are missing?" I asked.

"Other than his camping gear, nothing's gone," she said. "I checked his savings like you said, and his toothbrush, and everything, but he didn't take anything with him."

"He didn't take a toothbrush to go camping?" Amy asked, scrunching up her face.

"He did take one, but it's a camp toothbrush," Valerie explained. "He only takes his good one when we go on vacation. So, what does all of this mean? Where's my son?"

"I'm sorry to say this, but we don't know." I shifted my feet, feeling the weight of her eyes on me. "We don't even know where to begin looking at this point. The shed's locked up tight, so it doesn't look like anyone went inside. We checked the water tower, and that's locked up, too. Lieutenant Saltzman and Officer Rankin are searching the fields west of where we found their bikes, but there's no indication they headed off in that direction."

"This can't be happening." Valerie was no longer staring at me. Her gaze had fallen to the floor and she just stared.

"Did you call his friends?" I asked.

"Yeah, but none of them knew anything. Most of them haven't talked to him since the last day of school." She shook her head slowly. "He's not one to play on his phone a lot. He prefers spending his time outdoors or next door at the Forets."

Windows suddenly rattled as another strong gust of wind battered the house.

"Ma'am, do you have some place to stay during the storm?" Amy asked. "Your house is really taking a beating, and the storm's not even here yet."

"I…I guess I could stay with Elton." She rubbed her hands down her legs, smoothing out the skirt she was wearing. "He wanted to come over and even offered for me to go there, but I didn't want him seeing me like this. I guess it'll be better than being alone."

Amy stepped forward and put a hand on Valerie's shoulder. "If you'd feel more comfortable, you can stay at the police department with us. I'll let you have my office. It's tucked into the corner, out of the way, and you'll have lots of privacy."

"It's okay," Valerie said. "I'll stay with Elton. He said his house is pretty new and was built to post-Katrina codes, so it can withstand a bad hurricane."

"Would you like a ride to his place?" Amy asked.

"No, I'll call him to come pick me up." Valerie shifted her eyes to me. "Will y'all keep looking for my son?"

"We'll keep driving around until the storm makes landfall."

"But what about the swamps?" She rose to her feet. "Will y'all check the woods and the swamps?"

"I'm sorry, ma'am, but we don't even know where to begin searching," I explained. "We won't be able to get a plane or helicopter in the air until this weather passes, so our response is limited. Even if we did know where to look in the swamps, we wouldn't be able to deploy search parties under these conditions. I'm so sorry. I really am, but I promise that I'll continue driving around town myself until it's absolutely too dangerous to stay out there."

Valerie dropped back to the recliner and stared off again. After a brief moment of silence, she slowly nodded her head. I could almost see the realization sweep over her.

"I know you're doing all you can and you have to think about the safety of everyone, not just my son. I wouldn't want anyone getting hurt trying to find Cory." She brushed a tear from her eye. "Will my cell phone still work in this weather?"

"Not likely." I scowled. "Cell service is usually the second to go, right after the power."

"Then how will I know if y'all find my son?" She was looking up with sorrowful eyes that broke my heart.

"Give me a minute," I said, and hurried outside to my Tahoe. I was surprised by how dark it had gotten just in the minutes since we'd first arrived here. It was almost five o'clock in the afternoon, but it looked closer to eight. When I returned to Valerie's living room, I handed her my satellite phone.

"What's this?" she asked.

"We'll be working off of our SAT phones when the lines go down," I explained. "This is mine and I want you to hang on to it during the storm. If we get any word at all about Cory, somebody will call this phone. It's fully charged, so it'll be good for a few days."

Valerie leapt from her chair and wrapped her arms around me. I could feel her warm tears dripping down my neck.

"Thank you so much!" she said. "This means a lot."

I patted her back awkwardly. "It's okay, ma'am. Really, it's no big deal."

When she let go of me, she clutched the phone in both hands. "Okay, I'll stay at Elton's house. I'll call him and ask him to pick me up just as soon as I pack. He lives at the corner of Seventh and Green Grove. I...I guess you don't need the number there, since I have this phone."

I nodded. "I'll call you on the SAT phone if I need anything."

"But what if Cory comes home during the storm or tries to call me?" Valerie asked as an afterthought. "If I leave, he won't know where to find me."

I was thoughtful. If Cory had, indeed, left in a car, he could be anywhere—even another state—so he might have phone service wherever he was going, and he might try to call home at some point."

"Leave a note on the refrigerator telling him you've gone to Elton's house," I said, pulling a business card from my wallet and writing down the number to the SAT phone. "Also, change the message on your voicemail. Say that you're staying with Elton and give him this number to call. Even if your cell phone dies or the lines go down, he'll get the message if he calls you."

She thanked me again and hurried to her kitchen to write the note. Amy and I followed, and Amy asked if she wanted us to wait until Elton arrived to pick her up.

"No, I'll be okay," she called over her shoulder as she wrote the note. "Just please find my boy!"

CHAPTER 15

Six hours before landfall

Melvin lowered his head against the bullets of rain that pelted his rain suit. The department had purchased the very best rain gear that money could buy, but a few drops of water found their way under his suit and dripped down his neck. He shivered as the water slid like icy fingers down his back.

"Hey, Mel," Shade hollered from the opposite side of the ditch to his right. "The temperature dropped all of a sudden. Doesn't that mean tornado?"

"Yeah," Melvin shouted back, trying to be heard over the storm that raged around them. He turned his head toward the sky, squinting against the driving rain, but all he saw was a ceiling of blackness.

The field in which they walked was surrounded on three sides by ditches. They had begun by making their way westward along the ditch that bordered the field to the north, searching for shoe impressions in the soft mud, and were now making their way southward along the ditch that bordered the field to the west. So far, they had found no evidence that the boys had crossed either of the ditches, and he was beginning to think the rain would make their search a lost cause.

His plan had been to scout the edges of the entire field where the mud in the ditches were soft, and if they could find no evidence of the boys' passage, they could safely rule out the possibility that they had ventured out into the swamps beyond the pastures. So far, they hadn't found anything, but the rain was now falling in sheets and would wash away any tracks that might have been made by the boys.

Still, they pushed on. The original plan was that once they reached the gate at the far end of the field—the one they could no longer see thanks to the rain—they would head east along the last ditch, climb into the warmth of their vehicles, and get the hell out of there before things deteriorated even worse. That is, unless they found tracks showing the boys had entered the swamps. They had both agreed to keep going if they found evidence that the boys were out there. Together, they believed they could survive anything Mother Nature threw at them, but those boys would be helpless once Hurricane Ursula battered down their front door.

They pushed on for another ten or fifteen minutes, both of them straining to see the mud at the bottom of the ditches, when the gate finally came into view. Knowing the boys wouldn't have crossed the ditch in this area with the gate so close by, Melvin waved for Shade to advance at a quicker pace.

Once they reached the road that crossed over the ditch, Melvin and Shade stopped to inspect the gate that blocked the road from vehicular traffic. Melvin chuckled when he saw a sign that read, *You are no longer trespassing, you are a target!* He checked the chain and verified that it was locked. He had planned on searching the metal surface for rub marks in the rust, but the rain was making that nearly impossible.

Shade was scanning the ground on the opposite side of the gate when Melvin noticed a red glow from his left. He turned and realized it was coming from the post to which the gate was attached. He hollered at Shade.

"Look," he said when Shade glanced up from his search, "there's a game camera!"

Shade took one step forward then was over the gate in an effortless leap. He joined Melvin, who was inspecting the camera.

"It's not locked," he told Shade. "We can check it to see if the boys came through here, but if I open it, I'll break the water seal and it might get damaged."

"I've got this," Shade said, mounting the lowest bar on the gate and hovering over the camera to use his body as a shield from the rain.

Melvin nodded his thanks and squatted under the human umbrella that Shade had made for him. He was pleased to see that the camera was a Browning Recon Force Edge, because they allowed instant playback, and the quality of the footage was excellent. The sensors also worked off of heat and motion, so there wouldn't be many false alerts and empty footage.

After reaching inside his rain suit to wipe his hands dry, he released the latch and swung the small door open. After pressing the *Mode* button, he selected *Playback*, hit *Enter*, and then began searching through the files, working backward from the video of him and Shade approaching the camera.

There were only two files from the current day, and both of them were videos of crows picking at the ground. Throughout the previous night, there was footage of a coyote, two raccoons, and an opossum. There were only four files from the previous day, and all of them were videos of birds landing in the area to peck at the ground.

"No sign of the boys," Melvin said as he closed the door and latched it down. Shade dropped from the bottom post and he straightened. He glanced at the ditch that bordered the field to the south and shook his head. It was already full of running water, and they could no longer see the bottom. Melvin shrugged. "I don't think they would've jumped that ditch anyway. Let's get out of here."

Shade nodded and fell in beside him as they headed toward their vehicles which were about four hundred yards away.

They had traveled about twenty yards when Melvin felt a difference in the way the raindrops were hitting his rain suit. They were no longer pelting it. They were actually slamming into it and they felt much heavier. He turned to look at Shade, who had also noticed and was searching the sky.

Melvin held out a hand and confirmed his fears. Marble-sized hail was falling into his palm at a rapid clip. He turned to search the fields to the south and his mouth dropped open. The rain was coming in sheets and the clouds were black from the horizon to the sky, so it was hard to see a funnel. However, with the intermittent backdrop of lightning flashing from out of the south, there was no mistaking the mud and debris that were being kicked up from the ground in the distance. The most troubling thing was that the destruction was moving toward them at a blinding pace.

"Let's get the hell out of here!" Melvin shouted, grabbing Shade by the arm and urging him to run.

Shade heeded Melvin's warning, but Melvin recognized right away that Shade was holding back. The younger man was as fast as anyone Melvin had ever witnessed, yet he was keeping pace with Melvin.

"Get out of here!" Melvin shouted, looking toward the south to check the progress of the tornado. It was rapidly gaining on them and seemed to be making a beeline for their exact location. While that was a good thing because there were no houses in the area, it was also a bad thing because there were two people in the field. The base of the tornado had to be over one hundred yards wide, so there was no way they could dodge it. Even if they stopped, they were in trouble. The only thing that could possibly save them was for the tornado to change course. If it didn't, they were screwed.

Shade didn't react to Melvin's shouts. He just kept running beside his lieutenant while glancing periodically to his right, measuring the progress of the tornado.

Melvin could see that they were never going to make it to their vehicles. At least, he couldn't make it. Shade still had a chance.

"Shade," Melvin bellowed, "I'm giving you a direct order—get your ass out of here now and call for help!"

Melvin bristled when Shade ignored him and continued keeping pace with him, but he was moved by the younger man's commitment to his fellow officer.

Knowing he would do the same thing if he could outrun Shade, Melvin realized he couldn't be mad at the younger officer.

Melvin's legs were burning and his lungs were screaming. He had sprinted almost two hundred yards over uneven ground, running at max capacity, but it felt like his legs were on a treadmill. Whether they stopped or continued at this point, it would be useless. It was too late. The devil's finger of destruction was upon them and was about to swallow them whole.

Thinking quickly, Melvin hollered a warning and then dove right into Shade, lifting him from the ground and tackling him. As they flew through the air, Melvin felt a blast of wind the likes of which he had never felt before, and ground debris blasted them like fully automatic gunfire.

CHAPTER 16

The home of Ray and Wendy Foret

After leaving Valerie Verdin's residence, Amy and I walked across her yard to meet with Ray and Wendy Foret. They let us in immediately.

"Did you find anything?" Ray asked, his face a contorted mess of anger and worry.

"We found a tire track and one shoe impression in the mud behind the metal shed. It could mean something, or it could not." I indicated him with a nod of my head. "What about you? Did you find anything over here?"

Ray sighed. "There's nothing missing except for their camping gear. I'm telling you, they went camping. There's no way they left in a car with somebody. They wouldn't have done that—especially without telling me about it."

I realized that Ray would remain in denial, so I chose to change the subject. "We've got two officers searching the field west of the water tower. If the boys headed out in that direction, they should find some evidence of their passage through there."

"And if they don't?" Wendy asked.

I hesitated, knowing the next bit of information wouldn't go over well.

"If they don't," Ray interjected, "then they're not gonna look for them until after the storm passes. Right, detective?"

I frowned. "We don't have the manpower to search every field, lake, or swamplands, and we have no clue where to begin looking. At this point, it would be a suicide mission for no good reason and with no real chances of success. Now, if we did know where to look, I'd be the first one out there trying to find them. Hell, even when the storm passes, we'll be shooting in the dark, but once the winds die down, we can get some planes and helicopters in the air to help broaden our reach."

"This is bullshit!" Ray said, stabbing a finger in my direction. "What if this were your daughter? I bet you'd be out there right now trying to find her. Instead, you're in here making excuses! That's shameful!"

My daughter had been taken once, but under very different circumstances. She hadn't wandered off and gotten lost or failed to let us know where she had gone. No, she had been taken in a violent attack on our home, and people had died during the abduction. While I could've said a lot of things in response to Ray's outburst, I knew the man was hurting.

"I'm real sorry," I said again. "If you can tell me where to look, I'll be glad to head out there right now and search. Just tell me where to go. You know your sons better than I do, so tell me where to search."

Ray opened his mouth, but then clamped it shut as he stared at me. I could tell he was starting to realize that what I was saying was true. Sure, he wanted to do something, he wanted to take some sort of action to find his boys, but so did we all. The only problem was that we had no direction in which to go. Until and unless we could find a piece of evidence to point us in a direction, we were stuck.

"Did you talk to his friends?" I asked. "Do they know anything?"

"We've called every one of them," Wendy said, "and no one knows where they are. Most of them haven't even spoken with our boys since school let out, so they don't know what they're up to. They usually just hang out with Cory. They're always together and they're always somewhere in town."

I looked back at Ray. "Have they ever mentioned the west side of town for any reason?"

"No, I don't know what they would be doing back there." He shook his head. "It's got to be that somebody kidnapped them and ditched their bikes. They planted the bikes there so we would think that's where they are, but they're somewhere else. I just know it."

"You think someone could've kidnapped all three boys without at least one of them getting away?" I asked. "Or without there being a report of a disturbance or some evidence left behind that a fight and abduction occurred?"

"I don't know what to think," he said in frustration. "That's your job."

"But you know your sons," I countered, thinking I had already gotten my answer from Stewart Finane. "Would they fight if someone tried to abduct them?"

"Absolutely." He nodded his head. "They would go down fighting."

"If that's true," I said, "then I doubt they were abducted. It would take more than one man to overpower three strong teenage boys and abduct them in broad daylight in the middle of town. Even if there were three abductors to the three boys, there would still be yelling and fighting and enough of a disturbance to alert someone in the neighborhood. Have you ever seen videos of multiple cops trying to get one handcuffed man in the back of a police car? Now imagine someone trying to get Cory, Ruben, and Allen into the back of a car all at the same time."

He sighed heavily, as though hating to admit it. "I guess you're right, but that would mean they willingly got in the car."

I was running over the possibilities in my mind. We hadn't gotten a report of any crashes in town since yesterday, but what if they had left town in this mysterious vehicle? I remembered one particular case where a teenager had snuck out of her room at night and gotten into a car with a friend. She'd ended up driving the vehicle, crashed, and died in the crash. The next thing the parents knew, an officer was knocking on their door to make the death notification. They argued with the officer and led him to their daughter's room, only to find the window unlocked and her missing.

"We'll stay in touch," I said to Ray and Wendy, not wanting them to know what I had in mind. Amy and I then left and hurried through the rain to my Tahoe.

It was storming something fierce now, and I knew the eye of the storm had to be getting close to shore. As bad as things seemed now, I knew we hadn't seen anything compared to what was coming.

I called the Chateau Parish Sheriff's Office as we headed back to the police department. A dispatcher answered and I asked if they had received any reports of an automobile crash between yesterday and today, but she said they hadn't. I then asked if there had been any complaints involving Ruben Foret, Allen Foret, or Cory Verdin. After a brief pause, while she sat there humming to herself, she finally said that those names didn't appear anywhere in her system—not today, and not ever. I thanked her and then called the state police.

After speaking with the desk sergeant and learning that there hadn't been any fatal crashes in our area over the past week, I then contacted the hospital. I sat parked under the building as I waited for the head nurse to take my call. When she did, I gave her the names of the three boys and asked if any of them had come into the ER since yesterday.

"Nope," she said. "We've been quiet. Thankfully, it looks like a lot of people have decided to get out of town for the storm."

I ended the call and shook my head.

"Where can they be?" Amy asked. She wasn't expecting an answer, so I didn't provide one. Instead, I got out of my Tahoe and took the back entrance into the building, because we could do so without getting wet.

Susan was in the dispatcher's station with Lindsey and they were fielding calls like crazy. There were a number of lines lit up, so Amy and I jumped into action and each grabbed a phone to help out. Most of the calls I took were from people who were starting to regret their decision to stay in town. We had opened up the middle school as a shelter, and I told them they could head there if they could do so safely.

"Things are starting to heat up outside," I warned one man, "so it would probably be best for y'all to hunker down and ride this thing out where you're at."

"What happens if a tornado comes?" one woman asked, her voice laced with panic as the wind howled in the background outside her home.

"Get your family into a room at the very center of your house, one with no windows, and cover yourselves with blankets and mattresses," I advised. "In fact, it would probably be a good idea to sleep in that spot throughout the night. If a tornado does come, you'll have little warning, and you might not have the chance to get to safety before it hits."

That did nothing to comfort the woman, but my goal hadn't been to make her feel better. I wanted her to take the storm seriously and take steps to protect herself and her family.

I had just ended that call and pressed the button on another line when I suddenly heard a voice screaming on the other end.

"Tornado!" the voice of a woman screamed. "There's a tornado heading straight for town, and it's the biggest thing I've ever seen! We're all gonna die!"

"Calm down," I shouted. "I need you to focus. Where are you?"

"I'm at the end of Orange Way," the woman shouted through sobs. "Oh, my God, I need help! Please come help us!"

"Where are you right now?" I asked.

"Me and Blue are in the bathtub," she wailed. "Please, you've got to hurry!"

I knew instantly that the woman was Phoebe Watts. She lived at the end of Orange Way with her son, Blue.

"Stay right where you are, Phoebe," I said. "This is Clint Wolf. I'm heading that way now. But first, I need you to tell me where the tornado was when you last saw it, and in what direction was it traveling?"

"I saw it coming from behind Lacy Court," she said, her voice still trembling. "Trees were flying in the air."

"It was heading toward Orange from Lacy?" I asked, quickly viewing the map of town in my mind's eye.

"Yeah."

I dropped the phone and picked up the base station mic.

"Melvin, Shade, get the hell out of there!" I shouted. "There's a tornado heading straight for y'all!"

I then dropped the mic and ran for the door, not offering an explanation or waiting for anyone.

CHAPTER 17

When I pushed open the door to the police department, it pushed back and sent me reeling, the wind slamming the door with such force that I thought the glass would shatter. Refusing to be deterred, I hit the door again, this time expecting the resistance, and squirted through the opening. I heard Susan yelling from somewhere behind me demanding to know what I was doing and what was going on. I didn't have time to answer.

There was rumbling all around me. The day had turned to night in a flash. I could hear whistling and howling coming from the west side of town, and it was in this direction that I raced. I mumbled desperately to myself as I sped up Washington Avenue a lot faster than I would have on a normal day. Thankfully, the streets were empty and the sidewalks abandoned.

I peered toward the sky as I approached Main Street, but I could barely see through the sheets of rain. I said a silent prayer that the tornado was nowhere near Melvin and Shade, but if what Phoebe had said was accurate, then it was heading right for them.

I snatched up my mic and called out again on the radio, asking for their status and telling them to get the hell out of that field. From the popping in my ears, I knew I was already too late. The tornado was upon us, and I had no clue if I was driving right into it or if it had already passed.

I sped across Main Street and continued on Washington Avenue, heading straight for Jezebel Drive. My automatic headlights had come on and they were on the high beams. In the distance, I saw something flying across the air. It was big and round and it looked to be flailing about as it was tossed around like a sheet of toilet paper in the wind.

"Holy shit!" I said aloud, unable to avert my eyes. "That's a cow!"

I swallowed and my ears popped just as I was reaching Jezebel, but I didn't even have time to consider what it meant, because a wave of leaves, dirt, and twigs slammed into my Tahoe with such force that it cracked the windshield. I felt the front end of my SUV leave the ground slightly, and then my tires screeched as it was suddenly dropped and I was heading left instead of straight on. I quickly hit the brakes and watched in awe as the outer wall of the tornado whisked right past me, heading due north, tearing through the back side of town.

In an instant, it was gone and I was able to see in front of me. I quickly backed out of the driveway I had been twisted into, and then raced toward the water tower. My guts were turned inside out as I scanned the fields where I'd last seen Shade and Melvin. While the structures along Jezebel had been spared, I couldn't say the same for the cow pasture and woodlands that stretched to the west.

For a width of about one hundred yards, and only God knew how long, everything on the ground level had been peeled away and tossed about like Godzilla swiping pieces from a chess board. As the tornado continued northbound, it left behind a mess of snapped tree branches, broken barn wood, fence posts with streaks of barbed-wire dangling from them, and metal roofing scattered everywhere.

I got on my police radio and switched to the Chateau Parish Sheriff's Office channel and let them know that a tornado was heading their way. I then parked my truck next to Melvin's truck and Shade's car, and jumped out on shaky legs. All of the windows on both vehicles had been shattered, and there was a large tree branch protruding from Melvin's back window.

I stumbled into the open field toward which I'd last seen them heading, calling out their names as I ran. If the tornado could toss a 1600-pound cow through the air, my friends didn't stand a chance.

"Melvin!" I hollered, dodging a large wooden board still affixed to a corner post. "Shade! Where in the hell are y'all?"

I surveyed the sky to the north, where the tornado looked to be losing strength and releasing its hold on the floating debris, praying that I wouldn't see them falling to the earth.

After a moment, I continued forward, staring in amazed fear at the trail of destruction that had been left behind by the tornado. The entire field was a tangled mess of twisted barbed-wire, farming equipment, and tree limbs. While this might have appeared better than the debris fields from other tornados I'd encountered, which had consisted of furniture, mattresses, and other personal belongings, it was worse to me. *Much* worse. Two members of our law enforcement family were somewhere in that field, and there was nothing standing—not even a single fence post.

There was no way either of them could've survived such an ordeal. Even if the tornado hadn't snatched them into the air, the flying debris would've been enough to kill them instantly. And the barbed-wire...I shook my head and shivered as I thought about the possibilities of them getting ripped to shreds by that unforgiving wire.

Screeching tires could be heard over the howling of the wind, and I glanced over my shoulder to see two vehicles drive up. Takecia had Baylor with her in her Tahoe, while Amy and Susan were in Susan's Tahoe. I wanted to protest my pregnant wife's presence out here in the chaos, but I was too numb to do so.

Instead of waiting for them to join me, I began hurrying through the debris, trying to pick out anything that looked human from the mess of limbs, posts and wires. While the sky had lightened up a little now that the tornado had dissipated, the wind was still battering us. I hadn't thrown my rain suit on when I'd left the police department, so I had gotten drenched from head to foot when I'd first stepped out of my truck. Hell, I'd even felt water seep into my boots. Thankfully, there had been a break in the rain, but I knew it was only temporary. Soon, another band would come swirling around and, with it, there might be more tornados. I knew we had to find Melvin and Shade and get the hell out of here before things got worse, because it surely would.

I suddenly found myself surrounded by the others. They were joining me in searching and yelling for Melvin and Shade. Even Susan—our unborn baby leading the way—was scouring the field in search of our friends.

I had been working my way toward the southern side of the field when I thought I heard something. It was faint and hard to hear because of the wind swirling in my ears, but it definitely sounded like a human grunt.

"Melvin!" I shouted. "Shade! Where the hell are y'all?"

I heard the noise again, and it was clearly a grunt. It was followed by a cough. I ran in the direction of the noise, hollering for the others to join me, but I saw nothing but a tangled mess of leaves and branches in the area where the sounds had originated. And that's when I saw it—a hand pushing out from under the rubble.

"Here!" I hollered over my shoulder. "They're here! They made it to the ditch!"

As soon as I reached the large branch that had dropped across the ditch, I grabbed an end of it and began tugging. It was too heavy for me to move. I grunted and pulled with all of my might, spurred on by the possibility that Melvin and Shade were being crushed beneath the weight of the tree.

Baylor ran up first and grabbed a different branch and began pulling in unison with me. I heard more coughing, some cursing, and a lot of grunting beneath us as Melvin and Shade worked to help free themselves from their tomb.

Amy reached our spot next and we all managed to drag the tree a dozen feet to the west, creating a hole big enough for Melvin and Shade to crawl out of. My jaw burned with emotion and relief as I saw two very wet and muddied men slipping and sliding as they fought to climb out of the ditch. Susan was closest and she planted a boot in the mud and offered each of them a hand. They took it and were able to finally climb onto higher ground.

I laughed in relief as I stared at them. Their entire faces were covered in mud. Their rain suits were tattered and ripped in different places. Melvin blinked and mud rained down his face.

"I didn't think that shit would really work," he said, his breath coming in gasps.

"I thought we were dead," Shade agreed. "I can't believe we survived. I mean, holy shit that was close!"

Before any of us could respond, I heard Melvin let out a string of obscenities. I turned to follow his gaze and saw a van from a local Fox affiliate parked near the field, and a cameraman was filming in our direction. I turned back to my friend and realized that wasn't why he was cursing. He was cursing because of that giant tree limb protruding from his truck window.

CHAPTER 18

"Detective Wolf, may I have a word with you?" asked the reporter when we all approached Melvin and Shade's damaged vehicles.

Other than being a little banged up and bruised, both Melvin and Shade were in good spirits. They were actually giddy with excitement that they had lived through a tornado, and that was a healthy approach to the job. I had known of officers over the years whom had gotten depressed after living through harrowing experiences. They had been unable to focus on the positives and, rather, had become consumed with the negative aspects of the incident—namely, that they could've died. Some of them had become so obsessed with that reality, that they had actually taken their own lives.

I had already known Melvin to be the type of officer who possessed a sense of humor and who was mentally prepared to do this job, and I was relieved to see that Shade was of a similar mindset. I had seen him in action during one life-and-death situation, and he had survived the incident both physically and mentally, and he had grown stronger because of it. This appeared to be another incident that would add strength to his character, rather than destroy him mentally.

I turned away from the others and approached the reporter, who wore a rain coat and baseball cap. Even though she was outfitted for the storm, there was no mistaking the long blonde ponytail that whipped in the wind beneath her cap, and I knew it was Laura Cavanaugh. The cameraman was still filming, so I smiled and told her I wouldn't be doing any on-camera interviews.

"Jack," she said to her cameraman, "film the officers who survived the tornado and get some good shots of the damage to their vehicles."

Jack nodded and turned to follow Melvin and Shade around as they inspected their vehicles. Melvin realized they were being followed, so he began to loudly curse the tornado and the tree that had destroyed his truck. I stifled a chuckle and asked Laura what it was that I could do for her. She and I had worked together before and, although I didn't trust many reporters, she was a standup person. If she told me she would stay quiet about something, I trusted her to do so.

"I was interviewing some of the neighbors just now," she said, shooting a slender thumb toward some onlookers who had gathered after the tornado had passed, "and one of them said you're working a missing person case. Is it true that three boys are missing in the swamps while this storm is coming?"

I glanced toward the small crowd that had gathered and recognized some of them from earlier. Realizing Laura could actually be of help to the investigation, I pulled out my cell phone and showed her the pictures we'd obtained from Valerie and the Forets.

"These boys are missing, but we don't know if they're out in the swamps." I indicated Melvin and Shade. "They were searching the fields in hopes of finding some evidence that the boys went in that direction when the tornado blew through here."

"How'd they survive?"

I pointed toward the south. "They took cover in a ditch over there and rode it out."

"Huh." Her mouth was partially open and her expression curious. "That really works?"

"I guess so." I tapped the screen on my phone, which she was still holding. "Can you get these pictures out and ask anyone with information to call the police department? There's a chance they left in a vehicle last night, so they could've gotten anywhere from here to Amarillo by morning."

"Is there any indication they're heading west?" she asked. "Or are you just a George Strait fan?"

"The latter," I explained. "The truth is, we have no clue where to begin looking, and the family has no idea where they could've gone. They were supposed to be camping on the east side of town, but we checked out the campsite. It hasn't been used in weeks."

Laura had given me back my phone and was jotting down some

notes. "Can you send me those pictures?" she asked. "You still have my cell number, right?"

I nodded and scrolled to her number in my contacts to send the pictures.

"Is it true you almost died climbing the water tower?" Laura suddenly asked, throwing me off-guard.

"No," I said quickly, feeling my face flush.

"Then explain this." She turned her own cell phone in my direction and I stared in shock as I saw myself on video being blown off the ladder and then dangling from the safety lanyard. I hadn't remembered reaching over with my right hand to snap the hook onto one of the rungs, but now I knew I clearly did it. It must've been purely instinctive, because I didn't remember having a conscious thought to do it. Also, now that I'd watched the video, I realized exactly how close I'd come to missing the rung.

"Where'd you get that?" I asked.

She shot a thumb toward the crowd. "One of your lovely citizens gave it to me. I know you won't like this, but it'll be on television before your clothes dry, along with the footage of Melvin and that cute guy surviving the tornado."

I groaned inwardly. "Is there anything I can do to change your mind?"

"Nothing at all," she said with a coy smile. "My bosses sent us down here hoping we would get some good hurricane footage. The storm hasn't even made landfall yet, and I've already got a potential viral video on my hands."

I smiled wryly, but was cursing under my breath.

"Please don't let the story about the missing boys get lost in the storm coverage," I finally said. "We're out of options here. We don't know where to begin looking, and their families are devastated. We'll definitely need the public's help to find them."

"I'll take care of it," she said. "The neighbor I talked to said you and your officers are out here risking your lives to find those boys, so their story will be tied to the storm. I'll make it a race against time to find them."

I thanked her and was turning to walk away when she stopped me.

"Do you know where I can find the parents?" she asked. "I'd like to do an interview with them."

"I'll go ahead and give them your cell number," I said after thinking about it for a few seconds. "If they want to do an interview, they'll contact you. I think it'll help us find them, but it's not my call to make."

"If they're willing to talk," she said, pointing toward the sky, "they'd better call fast, because I have a feeling this town will be out of power and cell service soon."

She was right and I knew it, so I immediately called Ray Foret and asked him if he wanted to do an interview.

"Do you think it'll help us find my boys?" he asked in a rare moment of calm and rational thinking.

"It couldn't hurt," I admitted. "Our officers didn't find any sign of your boys in the field west of the water tower, and if they did hit the swamps, that's most likely where they would've entered. They even found a trail camera on a gate post, and no one has approached the gate in days."

"Okay, we'll do it," he said. I was about to end the call when he stopped me. "Detective, was there really a tornado in that area?"

"Yeah, there was," I admitted.

"Is it true that those two officers died out there while looking for my boys?"

"No," I said. "Where'd you hear that?"

"A friend of a friend lives in the area and he said y'all were looking for their bodies," he explained. "I'm real sorry about what I said earlier. I don't want y'all getting hurt looking for my boys. If y'all have to wait until the storm passes, I understand and I respect that. In fact, that's what I want. I don't want anyone dying to try and find my boys—especially since they left on their own."

"What makes you say they left on their own?" I asked, wondering if he had discovered something.

"It makes sense what you said earlier," he admitted. "Wendy and I were talking, and it makes sense that they parked their bikes and got in the car with someone else. They've done it before."

"When?" I asked, feeling my blood boil that he hadn't mentioned it earlier. "And why didn't you tell me this sooner?"

"I was afraid you wouldn't take their disappearance seriously," he said meekly. "Two years ago, when Allen was in middle school, too, he and Ruben left on their bikes like they always did, but then hid the bikes in the trees across from the school and got picked up by their older cousin. They went down to the beach to hang out for the day, thinking they'd get back before school ended, but they didn't realize the principal would call and report them missing."

"Have you spoken to this cousin?" I asked, growing a little excited.

"Yeah," he said. "He hasn't seen them in months."

"Damn," I said, letting out a sigh. After a moment, I asked if Cory had gone with his boys to the beach.

"No," he said. "Cory refused to skip school. He said his mom would be disappointed in him."

I ended the call and then called my SAT phone. Valerie answered right away.

"Hey, detective," she said, huffing. "I'm packing my bags. Elton's on his way to pick me up. Did you find out anything?"

"No, ma'am, and I'm sorry," I began, and then told her how Melvin and Shade had searched the field west of town. I was going to leave out the part about the tornado, but she had already heard from Wendy that two officers were dead. I corrected the rumor, and explained that there had been no signs of Cory or the Foret boys in the field. "I'm calling to find out if you want to talk to a reporter. Her name's Laura Cavanaugh and she—"

"Oh, I know her!" Valerie said excitedly. "I mean, I don't *know* her, but I watch her every evening. Do you think I should talk to her?"

"It wouldn't hurt," I said, "and it might even help. If the boys left town, we'll need to get the word out. They might not even know we're looking for them."

Valerie was quiet for a long moment. I couldn't hear her moving in the background anymore, so I knew she was taking this question seriously.

"Okay, I'll talk to her," she finally said. "But tell her to meet me at Elton's house. I just saw the latest radar track, and they said it's gonna make landfall soon. I don't want to be here or on the road when it does."

When I ended the call, I walked over to Laura and gave her the information. She thanked me and then met with her cameraman to begin organizing a live shot.

I walked over to where Melvin and Shade were offloading the equipment from their vehicles and stowing them into the back of Susan's Tahoe. Takecia, Baylor, and Amy had already left—Amy riding with Baylor—to check on Mechant Loup North to make sure the tornado hadn't damaged any homes there.

Susan's Tahoe was filling up fast, so I opened my Tahoe and helped them finish cleaning out their vehicles.

"Leave the cruisers here," Susan said. "We'll send a wrecker for them after the storm passes. Shade, you can have your old truck back and Melvin—"

"He can use my Tahoe," I offered. "It's got a cracked windshield, but it's fine. I'll drive by the house and pick up my truck."

"I was gonna give him my Tahoe," Susan said with a shrug, "but that sounds good."

I closed the rear gate to my Tahoe when they were done, and then sidled next to my wife. I shook my head.

"Not a word," she said, trying not to smirk. "Not one damned word."

"I was gonna ask about Gracie," I lied. "Have you heard from them? I've been too busy to call."

"Yeah, they're fine," she said. "I spoke with them before we came out here."

"I wish—" I felt her eyes on me and sighed, realizing it was no use to complain anymore. It was too late anyway. She was already here and so was the storm. While the eye wall hadn't made landfall yet, we were getting hit with the outer rain bands and were already experiencing hurricane force winds.

Susan turned to face me and looked me directly in the eyes. "After that stunt you pulled up on the water tower," she said, "I'd better not here another mention about me evacuating."

I stared around in shock, wondering how Susan had found out about that, but then my eyes landed on Laura. She was watching us and laughing.

CHAPTER 19

The Verdin residence

Valerie Verdin dragged the last of her suitcases to the door. She stopped and leaned against it to catch her breath. While she was still in decent shape at thirty-eight, she hadn't been to the gym in a few months, and running around the house packing three bags had worn her out.

"Damn, I need to go back to spin class," she breathed, hurrying back to her bathroom to make sure she hadn't forgotten anything. She hadn't, so they stopped to check Cory's room. She grabbed her chest and squeezed back the tears as she fell back against the door frame. There was a heavy lump in her throat that threatened to gag her. Cory was her life. He was her everything. Without him, well, there would be no reason to—

A knock sounded at the door and tore her from her thoughts. She took a deep breath and exhaled it forcefully.

"Everything's gonna be okay," she said out loud. "Cory's fine. He just went for a ride with some friends. They'll be back after the storm."

Straightening from the wall, she hurried to the front door and opened it. Elton stood there frowning, his face glistening from the rain. It was dark outside now, and she wasn't sure if it was from the storm or if it was actually nighttime already. The whole day had been one scary blur of events after another, and she'd barely had time to slow down enough to breathe.

"I'm so sorry," Elton said, and stepped inside to hold her.

In his arms she felt safe, but it also made her remember how much Cory liked him, and she broke down. She didn't know how long they stood there—her crying and him rubbing her back saying it would be okay—but she finally remembered that Reporter Laura Cavanaugh would be meeting her at Elton's house.

"Oh, we need to go," she said, pulling away and rubbing her face. "A reporter's supposed to meet me at your house. I hope you don't mind. They want to do a story on Cory and his friends being missing, and I told her I wouldn't be here, that I'd be staying with you."

"No, no, it's fine," Elton said, reaching for her bags. "Make sure everything's locked up. I'll put these in my truck."

As Valerie made one last pass through her house, she heard the wind and rain pick up outside. She couldn't remember the last time she'd heard the rain pounding against her roof with such force, and she was positive it would eventually cave in and water would flood the entire house.

"Damn, it's coming down hard," Elton said when he came in for the last bag. He hadn't been wearing a raincoat when he'd first walked up, and storm water was dripping from his hair and clothes, leaving a puddle on her wooden floor.

"Let me get a towel for you and for the floor," she said quickly, hurrying away to the bathroom.

"Don't worry about me," Elton called. "I'm just gonna get wet all over again."

When Valerie returned with the towel, Elton was gone and so was the last bag. She smiled to herself. She could get used to having a man like him around. Since her first husband had died, she had been left shouldering the burden alone. She cut the grass, she cleaned the gutters, she tended the garden, and she even threw the football with Cory. And today, she had expected to load her own luggage into Elton's truck, but he hadn't even hesitated. He did it so naturally that she knew it was a part of him.

"Do you have a rain suit or an umbrella?" he asked when he returned. He was careful to step on the towel and not let any water drip on her floor.

"I have an umbrella," she said, and reached behind the door to produce it.

Taking the towel she had brought for him and draping it over her shoulders, he led her onto the porch and opened the umbrella. Holding it over her with one hand, he reached back and pulled her door shut. He tested the knob to make sure it was locked, and then led her to his truck.

"Oh," she muttered as they reached for the doorknob to his truck at the same time and their hands brushed. She had been opening doors for herself her entire life, and hadn't expected this. "Thank you."

He only smiled and watched her climb into the truck, the water pounding him with the force of one of those giant waterfalls she had seen in the Smoky Mountains. Abrams Falls, was it? She had seen a couple of them, but this one had been thunderous, and this rain was reminding her of it.

Once she was inside, Elton closed the door and walked around to the driver's side. Although she was anxious and scared to death over her son, she couldn't help but laugh when he got in and water poured off of him.

"Oh, my God, I can't remember when it's ever rained that much before," she said.

"Neither can I," he said. "This is the worst it's ever been."

At least there was warm air blowing from the vents, and it embraced her with warm arms. They were pulling out of her driveway when she saw the news van approach her street. It turned down Market Street to follow them. She figured it was Laura Cavanaugh and that she was headed to Elton's house, but then the news van pulled into the Foret driveway.

"Oh, no," she said.

"What is it?" Elton asked.

"The reporter's going to Ray and Wendy's house," she said, watching in the rearview mirror. "I can't believe she's gonna interview Ray."

"Why? What's wrong with him?"

Valerie sighed. "Nothing really, I guess. He's just out of control. He's so mad that I'm afraid he's gonna hurt somebody. When the boys are found, I...I worry that he'll blame everything on Cory and try to hurt him. Cory's told me how he treats his boys. They hate him and they're scared to death of him."

Elton reached out and put a comforting hand on Valerie's shoulder. "Hey, it's okay," he said soothingly. "I won't let him put a hand on Cory—not him, or anyone."

Without realizing it, Valerie leaned closer to Elton. She felt safe in his arms. She was still scared to death over Cory being missing, but she sure felt safe now.

CHAPTER 20

Four hours before landfall

After Susan had brought me to the house to pick up my truck and change into dry clothes, we had driven back to the police department to hunker down. We were getting bombarded with hurricane force winds almost nonstop now, and the rain was falling sideways. We secured all of our vehicles under the raised hurricane-proof building, where they would be safe from flying debris and would be available for us to use once the storm had passed.

Susan and I had gathered with Amy, Baylor, Takecia, Regan, and Lindsey in the radio room to watch the latest radar forecast on the TV mounted to the wall. Laura's story came on again, and they replayed the video of me almost falling off of the water tower, as well as footage of my pregnant wife helping to pull Melvin and Shade from the ditch.

"That's my wife," I said proudly. "She can make babies and save lives all at the same time."

"And that's my husband," she deadpanned. "He just turned thirty-eight and he still thinks he can fly."

I moved closer to her and put an arm over her shoulder. "I'm worried about you, but I'm glad you're here," I said softly, trying not to be heard over the television. "I hate it when we're apart for more than a day."

She smiled and squeezed my hand.

Although the forecasters were preaching doom and gloom for the coming hours, we had a backup generator and supplies to last for weeks, so I knew we would be fine. However, we were all worried about the townspeople who had stayed behind and not heeded the evacuation order. Susan had spoken with Mayor Cane, who was hunkering down at the town hall building with the rest of the town council members, and she reported that the middle school was now filled with evacuees. Due to the active investigation into the missing boys, a few members of the National Guard and two sheriff's deputies had been stationed there to maintain order, and it enabled all of our officers to assist with the search.

Now, though, all we could do was wait and pray. While it was dangerous out there, we all would've risked everything to search for those boys if we had credible information regarding their whereabouts, but—as tempting as it was—it would've been foolish to go blindly into the storm just to feel like we were doing something.

As I scanned the faces in the room—the only ones absent were Melvin and Shade, because they had left to clean up from their face-to-face encounter with the tornado and were resting—I could tell that every mind was on the three missing boys. We were all praying they had, indeed, gotten into a car and run away to the north, where it would be much safer than staying in town. If they had remained behind and were to perish in this storm, I would have a difficult time delivering the news to their parents. It was never easy to give that sort of news, and the older I got, the harder it became.

My brain continued to work as I absently watched the various news reports from the southern portions of the state. Some of the other news organizations had picked up on Laura's story, and the pictures of Allen, Ruben, and Cory were everywhere. They advertised upcoming interviews with the distraught parents, while also promising around-the-clock coverage of the storm and its aftermath.

As I sat there, the information I'd recently received from Ray Foret was beginning to disturb me. Although Ray had been in contact with the cousin who had taken the boys to the beach—and that cousin had denied seeing the boys for some time—I couldn't help but wonder if they had gotten in a car with someone else and headed in the same direction.

Since the hurricane was coming, I hadn't considered it as an option, but what if they had planned on surfing the waves during the hurricane? What if they wanted to pretend to be storm chasers? What if the impending storm had awakened some sense of adventure within them, and they thought it would be cool to experience it firsthand? The thought had only just occurred to me, so I quickly went to my office, where it was quiet, and called Ray.

Wendy answered her husband's phone.

"Ray's talking to the reporter right now," she said in a haggard voice. "Did you find them?"

"No, ma'am, I'm sorry." I wanted to smack myself on the head. Of course, every call from me would have them thinking I had news about their boys, rather than me needing information. "I was calling to follow-up with Ray on something. Do you remember the time your boys skipped school and headed to the beach with their cousin?"

"Do I ever," she said with a snort. "I thought Ray was gonna murder them."

"Do you think it's possible that's where they're headed?" I asked. "And if so, is there a particular place they would go?"

"What do you mean?"

"Does anyone own a camp down there along the beach? Maybe a friend of yours or someone else you might know?"

"I mean, we do have a friend who owns a hunting camp down there," she said slowly, "but it's not on the beach and we haven't been there in ages. It's about half way from here to the beach. In fact, I think it's abandoned now. No one goes there anymore."

"Have the boys ever been there?"

"Yeah, we took them there a few times when they were younger."

"What about the owners?" I asked. "Where are they now?"

"They moved to Florida two or three years ago. They tried to sell it, but no one wanted it. The flood insurance is too high nowadays, so it just sat there."

I settled back in my chair. "Does either of the boys know anyone who drives?"

"A couple of their friends drive, but I've already been in touch with all of them," she said. "And I even spoke to their parents. None of them are missing and none of them have seen Allen or Ruben. Look, I know their friends might lie for them, but I actually spoke with the parents, so I know they're telling the truth."

"Okay," I said. "Just in case they might've headed in that direction, where is this camp?"

"You know how Main Street keeps heading down the bayou?"

In Chateau Parish, everyone referred to traveling south as heading *down the bayou*, while traveling north was called *up the bayou*.

"Yeah," I said.

"Well, it's probably about fifteen miles that way," she said. "It's not far from the beaches, and it stands alone in the marsh to the right side of the road. They have green walls. It's rough. I don't know what it's made of, but it looks like roofing shingles."

I nodded and jotted the information down in my notebook. "Do you think it's possible they headed there?"

"No," she said. "I really don't. They would need a car to get there and, like I said, none of their friends picked them up."

I shook my head and leaned back to stare up at the ceiling. A thought occurred to me. "Hey, why aren't you in on the interview?"

"Um, Ray thought it would be best if it was just him talking," she said, the resentment evident in her voice. "You know, so I won't say anything *wrong*. Like, what could be said that's wrong in a situation like this?"

I scowled. Ray was a domineering man, that was for sure, but was he also abusive?

"Ma'am," I began slowly, not sure how she would take the question, "has Ray ever hit the boys?"

"What do you mean?"

"Has he ever hit them," I repeated. "Punched them, slapped them, pushed them...stuff like that."

Wendy was quiet for a long moment. Way too long.

"Um, I have to go," she said quickly. "It sounds like they're finished with the interview."

Before I could say another word, she ended the call. I sat there for a long moment seething. She hadn't denied it when I'd asked if he had ever punched his boys. What kind of a father *punches* his sons?

CHAPTER 21

After getting off the phone with Wendy Foret, I did more digging into her husband's past. He didn't have much of a criminal history. There were a few fights dating back to his early twenties, but those only showed up on his criminal history record. I couldn't find any incident reports that would've offered more details.

I went online while it was still possible and searched to see if he had any social media pages. He didn't, but I did find one for Wendy. As I scrolled through her timeline, I was struck by how many messages she posted per day, and all of them seemed to be motivational in nature. I shook my head as I began to imagine what it might be like for two free-spirited boys to live under the same roof with a man as controlling as Ray.

Nothing on Wendy's page offered any insight as to the disappearance of her boys, and she hadn't posted anything in over a month, so I abandoned that search and returned to searching Ray's background. As far as I could tell, he had lived in Mechant Loup his entire life, as did his father and mother. It looked like he had two siblings, but their addresses now showed Colorado and Maine.

I drummed my fingers on my desk. There was no way the boys could've made it to Colorado or Maine by now, but what if that's where they were headed? And if they didn't catch a ride from someone, what if they had stolen a car? A lot of people in town had evacuated and left behind vehicles and RVs and boats, so it would be possible for someone to steal a vehicle and the theft go undetected for days.

With nothing else to go on, I researched his siblings and found contact numbers for each of them. I called his brother in Colorado first, but he said that he hadn't spoken with Ray in years. I didn't get the sense that they got along, but I couldn't get him to say one bad thing about his brother.

Next, I called his sister in Maine, and met with similar results. She last saw Ray and his family two Christmases ago, and had only chatted with him on the phone twice since then. She didn't know much about her nephews, except that they were a handful, and she was glad that she had given birth to only girls.

After ending the call with her, I decided I was lonely for my own daughter. Besides, I had been burying my head in the computer for about two hours now and I hadn't heard anything from my mom in a while, so I called her and asked to speak with Grace.

"Hey, Pumpkin," I said when she was on, "are y'all there yet?"

"We're in a cabin, Daddy!" she said gleefully. "It's a ark and saw. You know, like in the Bible."

"From what they're telling us, we're gonna need an ark and a saw to get out of here," I muttered with a laugh. "How're the dogs?"

"They're being bad." I could tell she was bouncing up and down on something as she talked. "They kissed too much in the car."

I sat there beaming as she told me all about it. I never tired of listening to her talk. Even when I couldn't understand what she was saying, it was like music to my ears. I could be having a bad day at work, but as soon as I'd walk in the door and she would greet me, the day would melt away. Soon, we would have another bundle of joy.

"Hey, Daddy," she began after she'd finished tattling on Achilles and Coco, "did Little Sister come yet?"

"Oh, no, Pumpkin, the baby won't come unless you're here," I said. "And remember, we still don't know if it's a boy or a girl."

Susan and I had decided to wait until the baby was born to find out if it was a boy or girl. It drove some of our family members crazy, but we didn't care. We loved being in suspense.

"I already know it's a baby sister," Grace said absently. She had stopped jumping now, and she seemed to be preoccupied by something else. When she started talking again, her voice was muffled and I couldn't understand a word she was saying. I could tell she was munching on something.

"Don't eat and talk at the same time, Punk," I said. "I don't want you to choke."

She didn't answer. Instead, she must've handed the phone to my mom, because hers was the next voice I heard.

"Hey, what's going on over there?" she asked. "Is everyone okay?"

"We're fine."

"We were listening to the radio on the drive up here and we heard them say that some boys are missing. Lisa knows the mom of two of the boys. The woman named Wendy."

Lisa was Susan's mom, and she had been in town a lot longer than my mom.

"Did she say anything about them?" I asked, suddenly alert. "What does she know?"

"Here, you talk to her."

My mom handed the phone off to Lisa, but before I could ask about Wendy Foret, she wanted to know how Susan was doing.

"Oh, she's fine," I said. "She's out there saving lives in the storm, baby or no baby."

"What?" Lisa was genuinely concerned. "I told her she should've come to Arkansas with us. I didn't want her to stay there, not being pregnant."

"You know Sue," I said with a shake of my head. "Anyway, my mom tells me you know Wendy Foret."

"Yeah, we heard her boys ran away. Are they okay?"

I wanted to remind her that they were missing, so I didn't know if they were okay, but I didn't.

"I sure hope so," I said quickly, wanting to find out if she knew anything. "So, what do you know about Wendy and her family?"

"I mean, I know she's married to Ray and they have two boys. Allen's the oldest, but he's a little immature and he doesn't do well in school. Ruben is more serious, but I know he can be mischievous. I…I can't believe they ran away from home."

"That's the second time you mentioned them running away," I said. "Do you know something I don't know?"

"I know they hate Ray," she said flatly. "Wendy was worried that they would each leave home as soon as they turned eighteen just so they could get away from their dad. He's mean to them. She said he hits them for no good reason. He calls it discipline, but slapping your kid in the face ain't discipline."

"Where do you know Wendy from?" I asked, shaking my head at this new revelation. I could sense that something wasn't right with Ray, and now I had confirmation.

"The library," Lisa said. "We're in the same book club."

I was about to ask another question when Lindsey buzzed my desk phone.

"Clint, we're getting a call on line one from you."

"What?" I scowled. "How in the world are you getting a call from me?"

"It's that lady calling from your satellite phone," she said. "On line one. Pick it up."

CHAPTER 22

Elton White's house

Valerie Verdin stood nervously in the spare bedroom unpacking her clothes. Sure, she and Elton had kissed a few times and they liked each other enough, but she had never dreamed of sleeping over at his place, especially not this early in their—

She scowled. Could she even call it a relationship? She knew that Cory wanted them to be an item. He longed to have a father-figure in his life, but she knew it was more than that—much more. She could see it in his eyes every time he left with his friends. It was guilt. She knew he felt like he was abandoning her every time he left, and he felt downright guilty for it. She had told him time and again that she wanted him to go off and be a boy. To go live life and enjoy his teenage years, but he could see the loneliness in her eyes. No matter how hard she tried to hide it, he could see right through her.

Elton had one of those natural gas generators on his house and he'd told her she could stay here as long as she liked after the storm, so she decided to move her clothes into the dresser that was in the spare room. Once she was done here, she would unpack the suitcase she'd brought for Cory. As soon as he got back home, he would be staying here with her, at least until the electricity would come back on. Inevitably, every time a hurricane blew through the town, they lost electricity and cell service. She was just glad they hadn't lost electricity yet. Of course, by the sound of the wind and rain outside, it might not be long yet.

Valerie had just put away her night clothes when the phone that Detective Wolf had given her began to ring. Thinking it was him and that he had news about Cory, she fumbled with her pocket and tried desperately to get to it before it stopped ringing. Finally, she was able to gain control of it and answer.

"Detective Wolf?" she said in a shaky voice. "Did you find him?"

"Mrs. Verdin?" asked a feminine voice. "This is Laura Cavanaugh. Are you still willing to give me an interview?"

There was a lot of background noise, and Valerie knew that Laura was in her news van in the middle of the storm.

"Um, sure," Valerie said. "I'm at my friend's house now."

"Okay," Laura said. "I just wanted to make sure you're still willing to do the interview. We're going to shoot some footage of the storm on Main Street and then we'll be heading in your direction."

Valerie started to thank her, but the line went dead. She looked up and blinked at herself in the mirror on the bureau. Her hair was a mess. Her face was pale.

"Oh, no," she said, putting the phone down and rubbing her face in embarrassment. She hadn't taken a look at herself since Cory went missing. "I can't believe I let Elton see me like this."

She began looking around frantically for her makeup bag. She knew she had packed it, but she didn't remember seeing it with her stuff when Elton had unloaded everything. As for him, he had gotten drenched from loading her stuff into his truck at her house, so he was now taking a shower and getting into dry clothes.

Normally, she might've given thought to him being in the shower, but she was focused on only one thing at the moment—and that was getting her son back.

Valerie padded toward the master bedroom and paused outside the door.

"Hey, Elton," she called, "do you remember seeing my makeup bag? It's pink."

She paused for a second, but he didn't respond. She put her ear to the door and listened. From somewhere inside, she could hear water running. He was still in the shower. She didn't dare open the door to his room and go farther, because they weren't at that level yet. Not even close.

Having been in his house on a few occasions, Valerie knew the lay of the place and she headed for the kitchen. Once there, she went to the counter, removed his keys from a glass bowl, and hit the unlock button on the key fob. Although he kept his truck parked in a locked garage, she noticed he had hit the lock button when they'd come inside.

Trying not to slip on the damp tile from when Elton had made his wet entrance, she headed for the door that led to the garage. She had helped Elton wipe the water from the floor, but she could tell it was still slick, so she was very careful. The last thing she needed was to fall and bump her head. What an embarrassment that would be.

Once she was in the garage, she went to the rear driver's side of his truck and opened the door. He kept his truck in pristine condition, and it was easy to see that the back seat was empty. She lowered her head to look under the seat, but the makeup bag wasn't there. She cursed under her breath. What if she had forgotten to bring it out of her bedroom?

The thought made her panic. Some might think it foolish to head out into the storm to retrieve a makeup bag, but there was no way she would let Elton see her in the morning without at least putting on a little color.

She hurried to the front passenger's seat, thinking she might've carried it out when she left the house, and opened the door. Although there was no way it could fit under the seat, she checked anyway. Nothing.

"No!" she said, trying hard to retrace her steps. She was certain she had brought it to the door with all of her other luggage, but where could it be? As she tried to remember everything they had done and tried to recall watching Elton grab each of her bags, she noticed that there was a cover on the bed of Elton's truck to keep the rain out. Maybe he had stowed some of her luggage back there, and had forgotten to grab her makeup bag. After all, it was small and could've rolled deeper into the bed, where he might not have seen it.

"Yes," she said in relief. "That has to be where it is. It's the only other place it could be."

She walked to the tailgate of the truck and pulled on the handle. Nothing happened. She pulled again and it moved smoothly, but nothing happened. That was when she noticed a key hole near the handle. It was locked.

She hurried back into the kitchen, grabbed the set of keys, and returned to the tailgate. After unlocking it, she pulled on the handle again and stepped back to lower the gate. It was dark in the confined space beneath the cover, so she fumbled with the latch on the panel to try and open it. She couldn't make it work.

"Damn it," she muttered. "I don't have time for this shit."

She looked around the neat garage and spotted a flashlight hanging from a peg on the wall. Snatching it up, she returned to the bed of the truck and shined the light inside. She scowled when she saw several bags tucked up under the cover, but none of them were pink.

"Where in the hell can my makeup bag be?" she asked out loud, really getting frustrated now. Thinking it might have slid past the other bags in the bed of the truck, she grabbed the nearest one and gave it a tug. When it came free and revealed what was beyond it, she let out an ear-piercing scream.

Valerie quickly clamped her hand over her mouth and stared wildly about the garage. Remembering the satellite phone that Clint Wolf had given her, she reached for it but groaned inwardly when she realized she had forgotten it in the spare room.

"Think! Think!" she whispered to herself, looking around the garage for something—anything that she could use to call for help. That she needed to get out of this house was obvious, and she needed to do it before Elton got out of the shower—

"Valerie?" Elton called from just inside the open door that separated the garage from the kitchen. "Where are you? What's going on?"

His voice was growing stronger as he spoke, which meant he was coming closer.

Oh, no!

CHAPTER 23

As she heard Elton approach the open door, Valerie immediately dropped to her hands and knees and held her breath.

"Valerie, are you in here?" he asked, his voice taking on a suspicious tone.

It was then that Valerie realized the tailgate was still down and that he could probably see it. She looked under the truck and saw his bare feet come into view as he slowly descended the steps. She couldn't hold her breath any longer, so she opened her mouth wide to let it out as quietly as she could.

"I know you're in here," Elton said. "I can hear you breathing. What're you doing? Why won't you answer me?"

Valerie scanned the walls again, searching desperately for what, she did not know, but she needed something to help her out of this predicament. She trembled as she lowered her head again to check his location. He was still standing on the bottom step. She could see that his legs were bare at least up to his knees, so he was either wearing shorts or nothing. Had he heard her scream while he was still in the shower and come running, or had he finished his shower and just happened to see the door open?

Right at that moment, she remembered the garage door opener clipped to the driver side sun visor. If she could crawl around to the passenger side and reach inside to hit the button, she could then escape out of the garage door. If he tried to come into the driver's door to get her, she could simply back out and run toward the opening. If he tried to come around to her side of the truck, she could crawl through to the other side and make a break into the kitchen or out through the garage door. Either way, she was out of here.

Right?

She knew she had to do something and she had to do it quickly, so she scrambled to the passenger side, checked to make sure he was still on the steps, and then jerked the door open. As she reached into the truck to hit the button on the garage door opener, her eyes met his, and she knew instantly that he was involved.

"You piece of shit!" she screamed as she smashed the button and the automatic door rumbled to life.

She immediately jumped out of the truck and turned to race toward the opening. To her horror, the door jerked, rattled, and then settled back down into place. It was then that she realized there was a slide bar with a padlock holding the door down.

"Come inside and let's talk," Elton said soothingly as he began walking toward her. "I can explain everything."

"You get away from me!" she screamed. "I'm warning you, if you touch me—"

"You'll what?" he asked sarcastically. "What'll you do?"

"I'll kill you!" she said with much more confidence than she felt. "I will *kill* you!"

Elton had reached the back bumper now, and Valerie realized he was wearing shorts and a T-shirt. He was still barefooted, so if she could throw something on the ground, maybe he wouldn't be able to chase her. She remembered seeing glass jars filled with nails when she'd first entered the garage, but they were on the opposite side, and she would have to go through him to get them.

"Stay away from me!" she said, easing farther away from him and thinking about making a run for it. She figured she might be able to make it around the passenger side of the truck and into the kitchen before he could turn around, but she couldn't be sure.

Elton's eyes dropped to the tailgate. He scowled. "Val, that's not what you think."

"Don't call me Val!" she said vehemently. "And you'd better let me go. You're already in enough trouble as it is."

He was moving as slowly as she was, and she could tell he was trying to close in on her. She kept pace with him, and by the time he was directly in front of the tailgate, she was back by the passenger side door. She quickly pulled it shut to get it out of her way. He was on her side of the truck now and there was no one between her and the open door to the kitchen. If she could make it to that door, she could get to the front entrance and be gone.

In a flash, she spun and made a break for it. She screamed when she saw him leap into action out of the corner of her eye. He seemed super fast, and she knew there was no way she could outrun him for long. She made it up the steps and through the door before he reached her, and she hurriedly slammed it shut and threw the deadbolt.

Hoping that would slow him down a little, she raced across the living room and threw herself against the front door. She twisted the knob and jerked on it. Nothing happened. She glanced down and saw that there was a deadbolt lock that required a key from the inside.

"No!" she screamed, searching frantically about for some way out of the house.

In that moment, she heard a crashing sound and she saw pieces of wood fly into the kitchen as the door came crashing in. She turned and headed for the spare bedroom just as he appeared in the kitchen. His face was red with rage and he was moving like a tiger stalking its prey. She knew there was no way she could make it to the spare bedroom, so she dipped into the guest bathroom and threw the door shut. She fumbled with the lock and then sat with her back against the door and planted her feet on the side of the tub.

"Open the damned door!" he bellowed, pounding it with his fist as he hollered at her. The door shook each time he hit it, and she jumped with each strike.

"Why?" she cried. "Why are you doing this to me?"

"I want you out of my house!" he shouted. "You're committing a burglary now and I want you gone. If you don't get out of this bathroom and leave my house, I'll call the cops and have you arrested!"

"Do it!" she shouted back in a voice that was stronger than she felt. "I dare you to call the cops!"

Please call the cops, she thought, the tears rolling down her cheeks. *Please call them!*

Elton kicked the door and it slammed against her back, jarring her teeth. She screeched in surprise. He kicked it again and continued to punch against it as he demanded that she get out of his house, but she knew that's not what he wanted. He wanted her out of the bathroom so he could...

So he could do what, exactly? What did he want with her?

"Please call the cops," Valerie said, trying to sound brave. "If you call them, I'll come out peacefully."

"For the love of God, Val," he shouted, punching the door again, "open the door! We need to talk. This is not what it seems. I swear to God you're overreacting."

"Bullshit!" she screamed back. "I know what I saw. Now, call the cops or I'm never getting out of this room!"

He kicked the door again and she heard the locking mechanism shatter. Pieces of metal sprang into the air and clanked to the floor, and one piece even hit the opposite wall. She straightened her legs and clutched at the floor with her hands, desperately trying to keep him from getting the door open.

And then, all of a sudden, everything went quiet except for the rumbling of thunder and the beating of wind outside. Her chest heaved as her breath came in gasps. She was confused. She cocked her head to the side and tried to slow her breathing so she could hear what was going on. She couldn't be positive, but she thought she heard his footsteps padding away from the door and down the hall.

A trick, perhaps?

She felt like she was hyperventilating. She grabbed at her chest as she put her ear to the door. That's when she heard it. Above the howling of the storm outside, there came a sharp rapping sound on the front door. She suddenly remembered the interview. It was Laura Cavanaugh!

Her brief moment of excitement turned to reality. Laura was a reporter. She wasn't a cop and she wouldn't have a gun. If Valerie ran out now and tried to get Laura's help, she might be putting the reporter in danger, as well.

"Hello, I'm Laura Cavanaugh," she heard a sweet voice say. "And you must be Elton White?"

"Yes, ma'am," he said, sounding very smooth and calm for a man who had just tried to beat down the door to get to her. "What can I do for you?"

"I'm looking for Valerie Verdin," she explained. "I was supposed to meet her here for an interview."

"Oh, she's in the bathroom right now," Elton said. "How about you wait out here and I'll see if she's ready?"

Valerie wasn't waiting. Scrambling to her feet as quietly as she could, she made a mad dash for the spare bedroom. Once inside, she quietly closed the door, locked it, and dashed across the room to grab Clint Wolf's satellite phone.

In her haste to call for help, she fumbled the phone and it clattered to the floor. She cursed under her breath and paused to listen. She heard Elton's voice from down the hall, and that spurred her on. She picked up the phone again, trying to remember how to use it.

"Valerie, get out of the bathroom, there's someone—" Elton's voice stopped dead. "Valerie? Where are you?"

She was beyond desperate now. Elton would know that there was only one other place she could be, and that's exactly where he was heading now.

"Come on, Val," Elton called in a soothing voice, the anger seemingly gone. "The reporter's here to interview you. Stop doing this."

Valerie didn't know what kind of game he was playing, but she finally settled down enough to pull up the preprogrammed number to the Mechant Loup Police Department.

CHAPTER 24

Mechant Loup Police Department
Two hours before landfall

I snatched up my handset and punched the button for line one. "Valerie, are you okay?"

"No!" came a terrified cry. "I'm not okay! It's Elton—he's the one who kidnapped the boys, and he's got me trapped in the back bedroom!"

"Stay on the line!" I was out of my chair in a flash. As I raced through the radio room, I hollered at Lindsey to pick up line one and to keep Valerie talking. Without slowing down, I headed for the rear entrance to the police department, and out of my peripheral vision I saw Amy, Regan, Takecia, and Baylor leap into action. Shade and Melvin were still resting, because they had been out the longest during the day, and we would need them fresh once the storm blew through town.

Susan also jumped to her feet, but I noticed she hesitated. I knew she would do the right thing and stay put. She might be strong-willed, but she was also very intelligent. While I could admit to being overprotective when it came to her being pregnant, I also knew she was sensible.

I made my way rapidly down the rear stairs and burst out into the bay area under the building in time to see a large metal garbage bin go flying down Washington Avenue. It came to a thunderous stop when it crashed into the side of a building. I stopped for a brief moment and stared. The wind was screaming. Street signs whipped furiously in place. Trees bent almost to the point of breaking.

Somewhere in the distance, a car alarm sounded.

Amy, Regan, Takecia, and Baylor had just thundered down the stairs and they stopped to gawk at the awesome display of Mother Nature's fury. The police department was built so soundly that we could barely feel the effects of the storm from the inside, and we hadn't realized the weather had dissolved so quickly into all-out war.

I turned to them and saw the determined expressions on their faces. Every last one of them would venture out into this weather—and worse, if it could get any worse—to do their jobs, but I couldn't risk getting everyone hurt for this case.

"We can't all go out there," I said. "Some of us have to stay behind to be available for when the storm passes. I'm going and I could use one volunteer as backup."

Just like I'd figured, they all raised a hand. Our response was time-sensitive, so we didn't have the luxury to pull straws. I quickly pointed to Amy. "It's your case, too, so let's go, and we're taking my truck."

As we jogged to my truck and climbed inside, I asked Amy to get Lindsey on the phone.

"Valerie claims Elton White is the one who kidnapped the boys, and she says he's got her trapped in a back bedroom at his house," I explained hurriedly as I paused at the edge of the building's overhang to search for danger. "I want live updates so we know what we're walking into."

I looked up and down Washington Avenue, but could see no other projectiles flying down the street, so I took a right and headed for Seventh Street.

Amy was already on the phone with Lindsey. "Hold up, Lindsey, I can't hear you," she said, cupping a hand over one ear to block out the screaming wind that threatened to push my truck off the road. "Say that again."

It was almost impossible to see out of my windshield. I was forced to drive slower than I'd liked, and even then the drive was precarious. I saw a number of vehicles parked along the street, and some of them appeared to have busted windshields. I wondered briefly how the tourists who stayed behind felt about hurricanes now.

"Clint, Laura Cavanaugh is reporting live from Elton White's house!" Amy said incredulously. "Lindsey and all are watching it on TV right now. Elton's talking to Laura under his carport and he's saying the mother of one of the missing boys is in his house and she's refusing to come out."

"Are you kidding?" I dared not take my eyes off the road to look at Amy. "How in the hell did that happen?"

"According to Lindsey, the news anchor was talking about the storm and then suddenly said they had breaking news from Mechant Loup," she explained. "When they switched to a reporter on the ground, it was Laura and she said she was there to conduct an interview with the mother of one of the missing boys, but the mother was refusing to do the interview."

"Is Lindsey still on the phone with Valerie?" I asked, trying to think ahead to what we might find once we arrived at the house. While it was good that Elton was outside and we weren't driving up on a potential hostage situation in the middle of a hurricane, it did seem odd that he was talking to the media. Was he pro-actively trying to sway the public's opinion in his favor? And if he was, indeed, the kidnapper like Valerie had claimed, then where were the boys?

"Lindsey, are you still talking to the victim's mom?" Amy asked in a raised voice, herself trying to be heard over the storm. "Okay, ask her what's going on." After a brief pause, Amy turned to me. "Yeah, they're still communicating. Valerie's hiding behind the bed in the spare room waiting for us to arrive. She says she doesn't know where Elton is at the moment, but she's afraid to come out. She says she tried to hide in a bathroom and he busted the door down."

"Did he threaten her?" I asked.

Amy relayed the question to Lindsey, there was a brief pause, and then she said, "No, he never threatened her, but he started acting aggressive when she found Cory's bag in the back of his truck."

I was on Seventh Street now and two blocks from Green Grove. On a normal day, I could've seen Elton's house by now, but this storm had limited our visibility to about ten feet.

When I took the sharp turn onto Green Grove, I had a blurry visual of Elton's carport. The bright light from the news camera was shining on him and I recognized Laura standing off to one side as she pointed a microphone in his direction. She and her cameraman wore rain suits with her news station's logo, but Elton was in shorts and a T-shirt.

"Let Valerie know we're here," Amy told Lindsey. "We're getting out now."

CHAPTER 25

Before stepping out into the storm, I snatched my raincoat from the back seat of my truck and shrugged into it. Amy was already wearing hers, and we quickly made our way to the carport, where Laura was still filming live. Even under the metal overhang, she and her cameraman were getting peppered with rain.

"Mr. White?" I asked, extending a hand to the man in the T-shirt and shorts. He was backed up against the wall of his house, but he was wet from the driving rain. "I'm Clint Wolf. Can I speak with you inside?"

He hesitated, glanced from me to the camera, and then finally nodded. I turned to Laura and told her it would probably be best if she and her cameraman got out from under the carport.

"It's dangerous out here," I said, yelling to be heard over the thunderous sound of the rain beating down on the metal roof. "If y'all need a place to hunker down, head to the police department. We've got room."

"I still want my interview with the mom," she hollered back.

I lifted a thumb and told her we'd bring the mom to the police department shortly. When she and her cameraman were walking to her van, I turned to approach Amy and Elton when a sudden gust of wind swept through that nearly knocked me off my feet. I caught myself, but not before a portion of the metal roofing was ripped from the carport and sent soaring into the night air.

"Let's go," I said, waving for Elton to lead the way into his house. He didn't have to be told twice.

Once we were inside, I asked him if Valerie Verdin was in his home.

"Yeah, she is." He wiped some rain from his face. "I invited her over to spend the night, I went to take a shower, and then when I came out, she threatened to kill me."

"For no reason?" Amy asked with a smirk.

"None at all," he said. "I found her in the garage acting frantic. I think she's just stressed out."

I indicated the rear of the house. "Is she back there?"

He nodded.

"I'm going get her." I said it as a statement and not as a question, and he didn't object. As I headed down a hall that led to the back of the house, I came upon a bathroom that had a busted door. I glanced inside. Other than the splintered frame and pieces of the lock on the floor, there was nothing to see.

"Valerie Verdin," I called as I continued down the hall. "It's Clint Wolf."

Before I reached the end of the hall, a door opened and Valerie came running out. She wrapped her arms around me and cried as she held on tight.

"Thank God you're here!" she wailed. "I thought he was gonna kill me!"

I patted her back to calm her, but I didn't waste any time. I gently pushed her away and stared down at her.

"Look, we need to get out of here," I said. "Tell me exactly what you saw."

"I had lost my makeup bag and I went into his truck to look for it." Her entire body was trembling. "I couldn't find it inside the truck, so I went into the bed. It's got this cover on it and the tailgate was locked, so I had to use his key. Anyway, when I opened it, I saw some backpacks, but I didn't think anything of it. I thought my makeup bag might be behind the backpacks, so I moved one of them to look behind them, and that's when I saw Cory's backpack."

"Are you sure it's Cory's backpack?"

Her head bobbed up and down. "It has his name on it. We flew to Houston last summer and it still has the airline tag with his name and address on it."

I pursed my lips. "Can you think of any reason he would have for kidnapping the boys?"

"No, none at all." She threw her hands up. "I don't know what's going on. I'm freaked out right now."

"I saw the bathroom door busted open." I shot a thumb down the hall. "What happened?"

"He...well, he chased me from the garage and I locked myself in the bathroom," she explained. "I put my back against the door and was trying to keep it closed, but he broke it open. I don't know what he was gonna do to me, but I was scared to death."

"What happened after he busted the door open?"

"Well, I was able to push it back closed, and that's when someone started knocking on the door." She paused to take a nervous breath. "It was that reporter and she was asking about me. That's when I took the chance to run back here and lock myself in the spare bedroom. I...I had left your phone in here, so that's why I ran back here."

I was about to ask another question when she reached up and grabbed my hands. "Can you please make him tell you where Cory is? Please get him back!"

I didn't want to commit to anything, because I hadn't even seen the evidence for myself at this point. Even if what she was saying was true, it didn't mean he kidnapped the boys. He could've merely been the one to give them a ride somewhere.

"Did Elton put his hands on you?" I asked.

"No."

"Did he threaten you?"

She was thoughtful. "No, he never did, but…"

"But what?" I asked when she let her voice trail off without finishing her sentence.

"I might've threatened him," she finally said. "I mean, yes, I definitely threatened him."

"Tell me about that."

"Well, when he caught me looking through his truck in the garage, he got real aggressive," she explained. "So, I told him not to touch me or I would kill him, but I never would. I was just saying that to make him leave me alone."

"What did he say about the backpacks?" I asked.

"He said it wasn't what I thought it was and that he could explain everything." She smirked. "But isn't that what they all say? Anyway, I even tried to escape out of the garage, but he had the big door locked. It was like he had me trapped inside this house for some reason. I mean, Cory could be in this house somewhere. I didn't have a chance to look everywhere."

I gently pulled my hands from her grip and indicated the front of the house.

"I'm gonna walk you to the front door," I explained, "and Detective Cooke's gonna take you to the police department, where you'll be safe. While we're walking to the door, I want you to focus on me and not say anything to Elton, okay?"

She nodded. "Just don't let him come after me again."

"He won't."

"Will you arrest him for what he did?"

"At the moment, we don't know anything except that he has Cory's bag in the back of his truck." I scowled. "If he doesn't admit to anything, I'm afraid we won't be able to charge him with a crime."

"But he broke down that door," she insisted. "Doesn't that amount to something?"

"It's his door, so I can't charge him with destruction of property, but I can get him with assault if he threatened you." I leaned forward and looked her right in the eyes. "Did he threaten you?"

She frowned and shook her head. "He just kept saying he wanted to talk to me and that things were not what they seemed."

I shook my head slowly. "Okay, I'll see what I can come up with when I talk to him."

"What about my bags?" she asked.

"Bring what you need now, and we'll come back for the rest later, after the storm blows through."

She hurried into the room and grabbed a bag that had wheels, and she pulled it into the hallway. When she was ready, I walked toward the front of the house with her falling in right behind me. She was so close to me that I could feel her feet bumping mine as we walked.

When we reached the living room area, I nodded for Amy to take her out of there. I noticed Elton following Valerie with his eyes, but I could detect no animus. He actually looked sad.

CHAPTER 26

Once Amy and Valerie had left Elton's house, I informed him that he was not in custody, and I asked if he was willing to voluntarily speak with me about Cory and the other two missing boys.

"Sure," he said, a little nervously. "I've got nothing to hide."

"Is it true what Valerie said," I began, "that you have Cory's backpack in the bed of your truck?"

"Yes, sir, I do, and I can explain it."

"Mind if I have a look inside your truck first?" I asked, wondering what kind of explanation he might offer, and also wanting to see if there was any trace of blood in the bed of his truck.

"Don't you need a warrant?"

"Yes," I said. "I either need a warrant or your permission. In this situation, I can easily get a warrant. We're working a case where three boys are missing under suspicious circumstances, and the mother of one of the boys found her son's backpack in the back of your truck. A judge would sign that warrant in a heartbeat, but I'll be honest, I don't want to wait to get a warrant. The worst of the storm is almost upon us, and the longer it takes us to get down to the bottom of this, the more danger they'll be in."

"Yes, then of course, search my truck," he said. "I don't want anything to happen to them and I'll do whatever I can to help you find them."

Having said that, he was already indicating that he didn't know where the boys were. I wasn't sure if I was buying it.

"If you don't mind," I said, remaining very aware of my surroundings and his every movement, "lead the way to the garage."

Elton nodded and headed for the kitchen. Before we even crossed the kitchen to the garage entrance, I could see that this doorframe was also splintered and the door hung ajar.

"What happened here?" I asked casually.

"She locked me out of my own house," he said indignantly. "Can you believe that? I had to kick open the door to my own house, thanks to Val overreacting. If I didn't love her, I'd make her pay for the damages."

"Oh, you love her, do you?"

He stopped walking down the steps that led into the garage and twisted around to face me. "I adore her and Cory. They're like family to me."

I nodded and indicated the truck. "Can we get on with this?"

He continued down the steps and walked to the rear of the truck. I noticed that the tailgate was already down, which supported Valerie's claim about what had happened in the garage. Keeping an eye on Elton, I pulled a flashlight from my back pocket and aimed the beam into the bed of the truck.

"Does this cover come off?" I asked.

"Yeah, it folds up and over in sections."

I saw a wire hanging down under the edge of the first panel, and I pulled it to release the locking mechanism. With the back of my palm, I then folded that panel over and was able to see better into the back of the truck. Sure enough, there were three backpacks. One of them had been pulled onto the open tailgate, exposing the one that had an airliner tag with Cory's name on it.

I visually inspected every inch of the bag that was visible, but I didn't see any blood or markings on the bag that would indicate there had been a fight or struggle over the bag. The bed of the truck was also clean.

"So, how'd you come to be in possession of these backpacks?" I asked, turning to face Elton.

"Cory called me yesterday and said he and his friends were done with baseball practice and they wanted to go camping," he said smoothly, "so they asked me to meet them in the back of town to pick up their bags from them, because they didn't want to lug their baseball gear everywhere."

"What do you mean by back of town?"

He shot a thumb toward the west. "Over on Jezebel. I met them near the water tower."

"What time?"

"Oh, it was right around seven o'clock," he said without

hesitation. "They said they left practice early because they wanted to get to their campsite before it got dark. They said the mosquitoes got really bad after dark, and they hated setting up the tents while getting eaten alive."

I heard a door slam from inside the house, and then Amy's voice was calling out to see where I was.

"We're in the garage," I hollered, and waited for her to get there. When she walked up, I asked if she had some latex gloves. She dug a folded-up pair from her back pocket and handed it to me. Once they were on, I reached for the first bag and opened it. Inside, I found a baseball glove, a bat, a flashlight, a sleeping mat, and some flexible tent poles. In the second bag, I found similar items, including more tent poles and some stakes. In the third bag, which was Cory's, I found a glove, a bat, a sleeping mat, a flashlight, and the actual tent, which was balled up into a tight bundle.

"If they were going camping," I began slowly, turning to face Elton, "then why's the camping gear still in their bags?"

"Look, all I know is what they told me," he explained. "I didn't look in the bags and I didn't ask them what was inside. Cory just called me to pick up their bags, and I did."

"Where were they when you saw them?"

"Like I said, they were near that water tower."

"Where, exactly?" I pressed. "Were they on the road near the water tower? Were they in the shell parking lot? Tell me exactly where they were when you met them there."

"Um, they were on the down-the-bayou side of the building," he said, "like, between the water tower and that metal building."

"Did they have anything else with them?" I asked.

"Yeah, they had their bicycles."

I nodded, studying the man. "Where were their bikes when you saw them?"

"Uh, they were right there in the shell parking lot."

"Are you sure?"

He nodded, but I could tell he wasn't being honest. He had seen the bicycles all right, but they had been in the tall grass on the side of the building where the boys had hidden them. Elton might not have kidnapped the boys, but I was sure he had given them a ride somewhere.

"Where'd you take the boys?" I asked suddenly.

He opened his mouth to answer, but then quickly clamped it shut. "Um, excuse me?"

"Where'd you bring them?" I repeated.

"I didn't bring them anywhere."

I nodded, moved toward the passenger side of the truck, and peered in through the window. "If we were to swab the seats and handles in your truck, would we find DNA from Cory, Ruben, and Allen?"

"I'm sure you would," he said. "I've given them rides before—a few times in fact—but I didn't give them a ride yesterday."

"When was the last time you gave them a ride?"

His eyebrows formed a V above his nose. "Let's see, it was probably two weeks ago. It was raining and his mom was working, so Cory called and asked if I could bring them to the library. And Cory's been in my truck many times, because he does work for me."

"What kind of work?"

"He cuts my grass here at the house and he trims the trees," he explained. "He pressure-washed my house last spring, and he even cleaned out my gutters. I also pay him to help out at my shop from time to time."

"Where's your shop?" I asked.

"It's on East Main."

"What goes on over there?"

"I build cabinets and other furniture," he said, his voice losing some of its confidence from earlier. "At first, I hired him to clean up the shop, but then I started teaching him how to use the tools. He's a natural. He really is. I...I really like him and his mom. I've been divorced for a while and I never had kids of my own. He's...look, I don't want to sound corny or anything, but he's like a son to me. The one I never had."

I moved closer. "You love him like a son?"

He nodded, shifting his feet and lowering his eyes under the weight of my stare.

"Then you need to help me find him before this storm hits," I said. "He could die out there. We already almost lost two of our officers trying to find them—"

"Three," Amy corrected. "We almost lost three officers trying to find them."

"I...I'm real sorry about that," Elton said. "If I knew anything, I'd tell you. Like I've already said, I love Cory and I love his mom. They treat me like family. Val cooks for me on a regular basis. Um, I'm always doing things with Cory. You know, teaching him stuff. I would never do anything to put him in harm's way."

"Did Cory tell you where they were camping?" I asked.

"No, but I know they usually go on the east side of town," he said. "I've been there once."

"You went camping with them?"

"No, I helped bring some wood there to repair a tree house," he said. "Ruben and Allen's dad had helped them build the tree house, but it was falling apart, so I gave them the scrap wood from my shop. I told him that he could borrow my tools to repair it, but I don't think they fixed it yet. I know he's been really busy with baseball when he's not working, so I doubt he's had time to do much back there."

As I nodded, trying to figure out this man's angle, the garage door on his house suddenly rattled and I heard a tearing sound from outside.

"There goes the rest of your carport," Amy said wryly.

I muttered a silent prayer that it hadn't landed on my truck. Things were deteriorating even more out there, but I needed to search the rest of Elton's house and I needed to know if the boys were in his shop—provided, of course, he would grant us permission.

"We're taking these," I said of the backpacks, "and I'd like permission to search the rest of your house."

"Of course, the bags don't belong to me." He raised his hands. "As for the house, feel free. I'll do whatever I can to help."

I gave Amy a nod and she headed off to search. I turned back to Elton. "Do you mind if I search your shop?"

"You can, but you'd be wasting your time. I give you my word—the boys aren't there."

"Well, considering you've already lied to me once, I'll have to see for myself."

Elton's mouth fell open. "What do you mean? I didn't lie to you."

"You said Cory called you and asked you to go pick them up from the back of town," I said, "and you claimed that call came in around seven o'clock yesterday evening."

"Yeah, give or take a few minutes."

"Then how do you explain the fact that his cell phone was turned off during that time?"

Elton gulped, but didn't respond.

"You see, we've been investigating this case since early today," I said. "We already know a lot, and we know that the last time Cory used his cell phone was at five in the afternoon, and his last known location was the ballpark. Since then, it's been out of service or turned off. Do you still contend that he called you at seven, or are you ready to admit it's a lie?"

"I...I know he called me at seven," Elton said weakly. "It was almost exactly seven o'clock. I even looked at my watch."

"Can I see your cell phone?"

"Why?"

"To check the radar and see where the storm's at," I deadpanned, cocking my head to the side.

There was a blank expression on his face, but he didn't respond.

"I want to see if he really called you," I said. "If you're telling the truth, then his number should show up on your phone."

Elton hesitated, and then pulled out his cell phone. He stared down at it for a long moment before speaking. "Do I have to let you look at it?"

I shook my head. "I can't make you show it to me without a warrant."

"Then I'd rather you not."

I sighed. I knew he was lying about the phone call, but I didn't understand why. I had to consider the possibility that Elton could be telling the truth about some things, while lying about others. For instance, it was possible that Cory had asked Elton to pick up their gear after practice, because they wanted to go for a ride with someone. Perhaps some girls? If that was true, then it would mean that Cory had lied to Elton about going camping.

At that moment, Amy came into the garage. "All clear," she said. "No signs of the boys anywhere."

I was about to suggest we leave for the shop when I heard a rumbling sound over the whistling wind and clapping thunder. It was followed quickly by the sound of screeching tires. Whoever it was, they were right outside the garage door.

CHAPTER 27

I asked Elton if he was expecting company, but he shook his head. A door slammed outside and it sounded angry. I remembered the live news broadcast and suddenly knew what was going on.

"Keep Elton in here," I said to Amy, and rushed up the steps and through the kitchen to the living room. Before I reached the front door, Ray Foret was already banging on it.

"Come outside, you piece of shit!" he bellowed. "I know you kidnapped my boys!"

Ray banged on the door with such force that I thought he would knock it from its hinges.

I opened it and rushed out into the rain, not wanting to give him a chance to get inside.

"Let me at him, Clint!" he roared. "I'll make that son of a bitch talk!"

"Ray, you need to go home!" I said sternly. "Your wife needs you."

He leaned back to take a swing at me—probably thinking if he could knock me down, he could get inside to attack Elton—but it was a telegraphed blow and easily avoidable. I simply bent at the knees and rolled to my left, while his arm swung in a wide arc over my head. Once his momentum had carried him around and off balance, I hooked my right foot around his ankle and tripped him to the ground. I landed on top of him for two reasons. One, so I could control him, and secondly, so I wouldn't get mud on my rain suit.

"Ray, I'm gonna tell you this only once," I said loud enough to be heard over Hurricane Ursula, "if you don't get up and get your ass out of here, you'll be spending the night in a jail cell. Do you understand me?"

"For what?" he bellowed from beneath me, struggling to buck me off of him. "I did nothing wrong!"

"You took a swing at a cop," I said. "That could land you fifteen days in jail."

I heard a *swooshing* sound behind me. I turned to see what it was, but was blinded by the rain. Whatever it had been, it came to a crashing stop against someone's car, causing another alarm to go off.

"Ray, we're gonna get killed out here if you don't stop your foolishness," I hissed. "I'm giving you one chance to calm down and leave. Otherwise I'm dragging you out of here in cuffs."

The large man sagged beneath me. When he spoke, water sprayed from his mouth. "Fine! Just let me up."

I rose cautiously to my feet, ready to knock him out if I had to. The storm was getting closer to hitting our southern coast, and things were getting crazier by the minute. I didn't have time to play with him.

Once I'd backed away, he staggered to his feet and hurried to his truck. He was drenched and beaten. He yelled something over his shoulder, but I couldn't make out a word of it, thanks to Mother Nature's wrath.

I turned and hurried into the house, where I found Amy and Elton waiting by the door.

"Ready?" I asked.

He took a nervous glance outside. "Do we have to?"

"I've got to know you're not hiding the boys in your shop," I said, not wanting to venture out there any more than he did.

"I swear to you I'm not!"

I shook my head. "You're already lying to me, so I can't trust anything you're saying."

"But I can refuse to let you search it, can't I?"

"Yeah," I said begrudgingly, "but I have enough to get a search warrant. So, you'll only delay the inevitable."

"And you're only searching for the boys?" He asked. "Nothing else?"

"That's correct."

"Okay, I'll go."

I gave Amy a nod and she kept an eye on Elton while I ran to my truck and drove it closer to the house. Once I was near the front steps, she and Elton hurried to my truck, with her getting in the back seat and him jumping in the front.

Based on the description he'd given, I already knew where his shop was, so I didn't need his input, but it took about fifteen minutes to reach it. We dodged a number of flying objects, barely avoided a falling tree, and ran over someone's garbage can before we finally stopped in front of the shop.

"The awning's gone," he said, peering through the side window. "I just put that thing up."

I glanced toward the front door and saw a metal framework where the awning must've been. One of the bars was dangling and flapping precariously in the wind. I made a mental note to avoid that corner on our way into the place.

"Ready?" I asked.

His hair and clothes were drenched. "As ready as I'll ever be, I guess."

We all stepped out at the same time, and Amy and I kept an eye on him as we made our way to the entrance. After the door was unlocked, we quickly stepped inside. It was a metal building, so the sound of the rain was thunderous, but at least we weren't getting pounded on anymore.

Elton flipped a light switch and the entire room lit up like the daytime. Before we could begin walking around, the lights blinked a few times.

"We're about to lose electricity," Amy said, whipping out her flashlight and aiming the beam at Elton. "I would advise you to stay very still if that happens."

Elton gulped and nodded. He raised a hand. "I've got an automatic generator attached to the building," he explained in a shaky voice, "so if the lights go out, it'll only be for a second."

The metal building was large and open, except for two rooms off to one side. I told Elton to stay near me while Amy went to check out the rooms. I surveyed the open space while Amy moved toward the first room. There were several piles of wood neatly stacked and positioned to one corner of the building, and there were two large work tables nearby. On one of the tables, a planer had been dropped into the middle of it, and within the other was a table saw. Three large roller bins were filled with sawdust, and ductwork snaked from the table saw to the one nearest it.

I could hear Amy's movements, and I turned to look when her boots stopped shuffling across the floor. She had reached the first door and was standing to one side. With her left hand, she reached for the knob, and she kept her right hand near her pistol. I glanced over at Elton to judge his expression. He didn't seem concerned, but I realized it could be an act. He had lied to me about Cory's phone, so what else was he lying about—and why?

Amy opened the door and aimed her flashlight into the room. She disappeared for about a minute.

"What's in that room?" I asked.

"It's storage, mostly," Elton said. "I've got some old tools and some engine parts from an old truck I had. The riding mower's in there, too, and there's a garage door that leads to the back of the building."

"What's in the back of the building?"

"I've got about 1200-feet of bayou side property, and a wharf where I dock my boat," he said. "The boat's not there, though. It's getting worked on. I guess that's a good thing, otherwise it would probably be gone by now."

Amy reappeared in the doorway and shrugged. "There're mostly junk parts inside," she said. "No boys."

She approached the next room and I glanced at Elton. He was looking down at his phone. If he was worried, he sure was playing it off like a champ.

I was about to ask him what was in that room when my cell phone rang. Before I could look down to see who was calling, Amy suddenly hollered, "Clint, grab Elton and get over here! I might've found something!"

CHAPTER 28

Mechant Loup Police Department
One hour before landfall

Melvin felt refreshed as he sat up on the cot in his office. After stepping out of the shower earlier—and knowing that things might get dicey once the eye of the storm made landfall—he had come to his office to take a nap. Now, having slept longer than he'd intended, he was ready to tackle the evening.

He stood and padded across the room in his bare feet. He pulled on dry BDUs and socks, dropped to his chair to pull on his spare boots, and then paused for a second to stretch. His neck, back, and ribs were sore from getting battered by the flying debris earlier before going into the ditch. They had only been exposed for a quick second, but that brief beating had been relentless.

After he had tackled Shade into the ditch, they had huddled there for what seemed like forever as the tornado thundered by overhead. Thankfully, they had been below the level of the tornado and out of its direct path, but it hadn't been all rainbows and picnics down there. Several tree limbs and a fence post carrying a chunk of concrete on one end had rained down on them. Luckily, the concrete end hadn't hit either of them in the head, but part of the post had landed across the back of his neck. He'd felt a shock down his right arm, but he'd been able to move it, so he wasn't much worried about a serious injury.

He could hear the storm intensifying outside, and he was glad his wife and daughter had left town. Even if his family had hunkered down in the building with them, he would've been worried sick about their safety. This building had survived a few storms since it had been built, but all it would take was for the storm to find one weak spot in the construction, and then it was all over. With hurricanes, if you gave them an inch, they blew the whole damned roof off.

"What's going on?" Melvin asked when he entered the radio room and saw Laura Cavanaugh standing in one corner with a cameraman. They were both dripping wet. Regan was walking Valerie Verdin, who was also wet, to the women's bathroom. Shade must've heard the commotion, because he was in the radio room with Susan, Lindsey, Takecia, and Baylor. Clint and Amy were nowhere to be seen.

Susan's face was tight, and he could tell she was worried about something. She moved close to him and lowered her voice so the reporter wouldn't hear.

"There's been some trouble out at Elton White's house," she explained. "Valerie found her son's backpack in the bed of his truck. Clint and Amy went out there and they're investigating his possible connection to the missing boys."

"Amy texted me a few minutes ago to say they were heading to the east side of town to search Elton White's shop," said Baylor, who had walked over. "That's the last we heard from them."

Melvin scowled. "They must think there's a chance the boys are there. Otherwise they wouldn't risk it in this weather."

Susan nodded, one hand resting on her belly. "The eye wall is scheduled to make landfall in an hour, and it'll reach us within two," she said. "They need to search that building and get the hell out of there."

Shade also joined them. His brown hair was still damp around the ears from his shower, and Melvin wondered if the kid had slept at all.

"Are you sore, Mel?" Shade asked. "I feel like a refrigerator fell on top of me."

Melvin nodded, but didn't have a chance to respond. The phone rang and they all turned their attention to it. It was an ominous sound. They knew that any call they received at a time like this would spell trouble. Melvin noticed Laura Cavanaugh watching intently.

"Police Department," Lindsey answered, "how can I help you?"

As the person on the other end spoke, Lindsey's eyes widened in horror.

"Sir," she said, "hang on a second. I'm putting Lieutenant Saltzman on the line. I don't want you to have to repeat yourself."

She quickly handed the phone to Melvin with an explanation.

"It's Red McKenzie. He said it's an emergency."

Melvin took the phone. He was familiar with Red, and if he said there was an emergency, it was an emergency.

"What's up, Red?" Melvin could feel everyone moving closer. He wondered for a brief moment if the cameraman was filming, but quickly dismissed the thought. He was familiar with Laura, and she wouldn't allow something like that to happen inside the police department.

"Hey, Melvin, what the hell's going on with this storm?"

"It turned," Melvin explained. "It's gonna hit us head-on within thirty minutes. You've got an emergency?"

"Yeah, Paulie and me, we found a body."

"What?" Melvin was careful not to echo Red's words, considering members of the media were a few feet over his shoulder. As he waited for Red to answer, he tried to think ahead to his plan of action. Recovering a dead body was important, especially if that person was the victim of a homicide, but it wasn't important enough to risk getting another person killed. Now, if there was a chance the person was still alive, that would change things, but only a little at this point. The policy of the police department was not to deploy any officers for a rescue mission once a storm of this magnitude had made landfall. It was just too dangerous and counterproductive. While the eye wall hadn't reached the coast, the deadline to hunker down was quickly approaching.

"We found a body," Red repeated.

"Where?" Melvin reached over Lindsey's shoulder and grabbed an ink pen and a notepad that was resting on the desk.

"On Lake Berg," Red said, his voice strained. There was some creaking and groaning noises in the background, and it sounded like Red's camp was falling apart around him. "The last we had heard on the news, the storm wasn't coming here, so me and Paulie went fishing. All of a sudden, the weather got bad. We started heading back home. We hadn't even left the lake when we saw a tornado touching down somewhere to the north of us. That's when I knew we were in trouble, so I sped up the boat."

Melvin scowled. Had there been more than one tornado? Certainly that was possible, but there would've been other reports. Right? There was a sinking in his stomach. There were camps out on the remote lakes and bayous, and he was certain a lot of those residents had remained home to ride out the storm. If an entire section of camps was wiped out by a tornado, there might be no one left to call for help.

"How long ago was the tornado?" Melvin asked.

"Oh, it was much earlier in the day," Red explained. "It was heading north and it was a big one. I'm surprised you didn't know about it. It was heading right for the west side of town."

Melvin sighed. It would be the same one they had encountered. As luck would have it, no homes had been damaged and there had been no reported injuries, other than him and Shade getting a little banged up.

"Continue," Melvin said, maintaining his media discipline.

"When we reached the mouth of the lake, Paulie saw what looked like a body on the edge of the shore. He pointed it out. It looked like a man at first, but when we got closer, I saw that it was a young boy, maybe seventeen or eighteen. I started heading to the shore, but the wind picked up and a big tree limb fell across the stern of our boat. It ripped the motor off and threw Paulie and me into the water. I told him to swim to the shore while I went to the boat and grabbed the life jackets. Afterward, I met him on land."

"Was the body of the boy still there?"

"Yeah, he was tangled up in this big tree, so it was hard to get to him," he explained. "Trees were falling all around us and the water was rising. I thought we were goners. I wasn't worried about the body. I was just gonna leave it where it was and try to get me and Paulie out of there, because I knew it was too dangerous, and it would've been impossible to carry the body all the way to our camp in that weather."

Melvin cursed under his breath. Even though they had a little time to act, it would be impossible to get a boat out on the lake in this weather. But what if the boy wasn't dead? It had to be one of their missing teens, and if one of them was alive, he would have to do something to try and save him.

He shot a glance over his shoulder, and then lowered his voice. "Are you sure the boy was dead?"

"Yeah, I'm positive," Red said. "He was ate up by an alligator. Me and Paulie were leaving the area, heading along the edge of the lake, when I noticed something else floating in the water."

Melvin's heart sank. Was it one of the other boys?

"When we got closer, I saw that it was a boat," Red said, raising his voice even louder, trying to be heard over the rattling of tin that had just begun in the background. "I figured it had to be the boy's boat, because we hadn't seen nobody else out there on the water. Since our boat was down, I knew I would have to use it to get us out of there, but that's when I decided I had to bring the boy back with us. If I was gonna take his boat, it was the least I could do. It would've been wrong to take his boat and leave him behind, you know?"

"Yeah, I hear you."

"Anyways, with Paulie's help, we managed to pull the body out from where it was entangled in the tree, and we dragged him to the boat," Red explained. "It was hard to get him inside. I've never moved a dead body before. I didn't realize how awkward they were to move around. He kept bending and flopping over. I...I don't envy what you have to do in your job. But, anyway, we took the boat and brought him to the house. You can come get him and the boat. I don't want neither one of them hanging around."

Melvin scowled. The bikes for the missing boys had been located on the west side of town, and nowhere near the water. The tire tracks behind the metal shed indicated they had left by vehicle. There had been no evidence connecting them to a boat. The body that Red had found must be unrelated to their case.

"Can you describe what you found?" Melvin asked, careful not to give anything away to Laura and her cameraman. He could feel the eyes of his chief and fellow officers on him, as they tried to understand what was going on. They knew him well enough to know what he was doing, but he could tell they were trying to decipher from his comments exactly how bad it could be.

"Like I said, I found the boy and we loaded him in his own boat—at least, I think it was his boat—and we brought him to my house." Red paused to take a haggard breath. "He's still in the boat. I didn't take him out. I just tied it to my wharf. If you don't hurry and come get him, I'm afraid the rough waves and wind are gonna snap the line and we'll lose it forever."

"Describe the boy," Melvin finally said, trying to keep his voice low.

"Say again?" Red hollered.

"What does the boy look like?" Melvin hollered back.

"Oh, he's a thin kid. Looks athletic." Red was thoughtful. "Oh, yeah, and he's got freckles all over his face and orange hair. Carrot-top is what we used to call them when I was in school a hundred years ago."

Melvin glanced at the clock on the wall. "How's the road to your house?" he asked. "Is it flooded yet?"

"No, the water's not coming up over the levee over here yet, but it won't be long. If you're gonna come, you'd better hurry."

Melvin told him to keep his SAT phone handy and then ended the call. He waved for Susan and the other officers to follow him to the break room. He saw Laura frowning from the corner of the dispatcher's station, but he wasn't about to let her know what was going on.

Once they were behind closed doors, he told Susan what Red had said, and—for the newer officers in the discussion—he explained the difficulties of reaching Red's camp by either boat or vehicle.

"I need to leave now and retrieve that body," Melvin said. "If we wait until after the storm blows through, it might be gone. If I wait another fifteen or twenty minutes, it might be impossible to reach the camp."

Susan nodded and turned to Shade. "Do you want to go with him?"

"Absolutely," he said with a nod of his head. "We can take my POV. I've got mud tires on my four-by-four."

"Then get out of here," she said. "I'll call Clint and let him know what's going on."

CHAPTER 29

Elton White's Shop

"Walk in front of me," I told Elton, "and keep your hands where I can see them."

Elton walked slowly toward the back of the shop, where Amy was standing just inside the doorway of the second room, and I could tell he was worried about something. When we reached Amy, she pointed first into the room with the flashlight, and then shined it in Elton's face.

"What in the hell is that?" she asked.

I sucked in my breath when I saw a large upright tank taking up the larger portion of the room. The tank was so large that it appeared the room had been built around it, because there was no way it would fit through the door, and it was plugged into a power outlet. There was a digital thermostat attached to the exterior wall and an LCD screen displayed the temperature and humidity inside the tank.

"It…it's nothing," he said. "It's just an incubator."

Amy turned back toward the incubator and reached for the door latch. I kept my eyes on Elton and waited for her to pull it open, a million thoughts going through my mind. What if the boys were alive and well inside? It would bring an end to this case just in time to get everyone to safety before the storm hit, but it would also present a number of questions, the foremost being, why in the hell had this man kidnapped these three boys?

I heard metal clank against metal as Amy unlatched the door, and then the door creaked open. Elton didn't appear ready to make a move, so I glanced into the incubator.

Amy grunted. Although the tank was big enough to fit four or five people, it was empty. Well, except for a row of metal shelves lining the right side. Atop these metal shelves were over a dozen plastic bins with lots of holes for ventilation.

"What's going on in there?" I asked.

"I was gonna buy some emu eggs and hatch them in here," he said. "He pointed behind us to another corner of the shop, where large rubber bins were lined up. "Once they hatched, I was gonna raise them in the shop and then sell them. I…I heard a lot of people are doing it and it's a pretty lucrative business."

"Where were you planning on getting the eggs?" I asked.

"There are a few shops online that sell them," he said. "I've been in contact with one of them. They have the best prices on the eggs and I was gonna pull the trigger on the order, but I've been watching the news about the storm. I was around for Katrina and a couple of the other big ones, so I know how bad things can get. I figured if the storm hits this area and shuts everything down, then we won't be getting mail for a while. I was afraid to pay for the eggs only to have them get stuck in transit and go bad in the back of a mailroom."

I cursed under my breath as the storm seemed to be intensifying even more outside. I remembered my ringing phone and checked it. It was a missed call from Susan. Instead of calling her back right away, I decided to get out of there.

"Let's go," I said with a wave of my hand. "I'm bringing you to the police department."

"For what?" Elton asked. "Am I under arrest?"

I studied the man. As much as I felt like he was involved, I had no real evidence to prove he had done anything to the boys and I wasn't in the business of arresting people who were potentially innocent, so I finally shook my head.

"You're not under arrest yet," I said, "but if I find out you lied about the boys, you're definitely going to jail."

He gulped, which made me even more suspicious, but that wasn't evidence.

"Well, then, if I'm not under arrest, I'd like to go home," he said. "I know for a fact that I didn't do anything to Cory, Ruben, or Allen, and I'd rather be home to protect my property."

I sighed and led the way toward the entrance to the shop. When I opened the door, I almost lost it to the wind, but somehow managed to hang on. I flipped the lock on the knob and waved for Amy and Elton to head to my truck. Once they were in it, I forced the shop door closed and joined them.

The drive through town was painstakingly slow, but we managed to reach Elton's house without incident. I reminded him what I'd said about him going to jail if he was involved, and he again swore that he had not—and would not—hurt anyone, especially Cory and his friends.

After making sure he made it into his house alive, I backed out of his driveway and headed for the police department. I was too busy dodging airborne debris to take my eyes off the road, so I waited until we made it to the police department to call Susan.

CHAPTER 30

"Hey, where are y'all?" Susan asked when she answered my call.

"I'm underneath you," I said, stepping out of my truck and heading for the stairs that led to the rear entrance of the building. "The boys weren't at Elton's house or shop, and, besides what Valerie located, we didn't find any evidence that they had been at either place."

Susan didn't answer and I was about to pull the phone from my ear when light shone from the open door at the top of the stairs above me. It was Susan and she was waiting for us at the landing. Even before we reached it, she began telling us that Melvin and Shade had gone out into the weather to retrieve a body from Red McKenzie's place.

I was in shock as we followed her through the corridor and into one of the interview rooms.

"Are we sure this is one of our boys?" I asked. "I mean, with this storm, it could be anyone."

"He said the kid was young and had red hair and freckles," she said with a frown. "It's either Ruben or Allen."

I sank into one of the chairs. This was not how I'd wanted the search to end, and I was confused about this discovery. What in the hell were they doing out on the lake? And how had they gotten there? As I pondered these things, something I'd heard recently began to gnaw at me. It had meant nothing earlier, but with this new revelation, a picture was starting to form.

"And there's no sign of the other boys?" I asked after a moment.

Susan shrugged. "Not so far. I'm waiting for Melvin to call when he gets there."

I pulled out my cell phone and glanced at the time. "How long has he been gone?"

"Thirty minutes."

"And what's the latest on the storm track?"

"The last I saw, it'll make landfall within the hour," she said, "and it'll reach us an hour later. Unless it slows down, and they are predicting it to do that once the eye wall starts interacting with the land."

I stood to my feet. "What'd you do with Laura, her cameraman, and Valerie?"

"Laura and her cameraman are in the lobby. They want to keep an eye on what's going on outside." She shot a thumb in the direction of the opposite side of the building. "I put Valerie in my office. When I left her, she was lying on the cot. I think she was crying."

I nodded my understanding and stepped back to allow Amy and Susan through the doorway first. I then followed them to the radio room.

"Any word from Melvin?" Susan asked Lindsey.

Baylor, Takecia, and Regan were huddled around the radio, waiting for their turn to head out into the weather for something—anything.

Lindsey shook her head. "Nothing yet."

I joined the others in waiting, but it wasn't long before Melvin was trying to call Lindsey over the police radio. The reception was scratchy and she couldn't make out anything he was saying. I figured my cell phone was probably useless by now, so I glanced around the room.

Knowing what I wanted, Susan reached in her pocket and pulled out her SAT phone.

I took it gratefully and called Melvin.

"Clint," he hollered, "I need to run a registration on a boat. I think this is our boy, but he's chewed up bad. I can't get a good look at his face, but he's got big ears and red hair, so I think he's the youngest of the Foret brothers. Red believes he was in this boat, so I need to run it to figure out who the registered owner is."

I had a sinking suspicion I knew what the results would be, but I told him to hold on and I handed the phone to Lindsey. As Melvin talked in her ear, her fingers danced across the keyboard.

"Got it," she said, and stopped to stare at the monitor, using her left shoulder to keep the phone pressed against her head.

I was standing over her staring too, along with Susan and Amy, as we impatiently waited for the NCIC computer to do its job. When the results came up on the screen, there was a collective gasp from Susan and Amy, but I only shook my head. This was what I had begun to suspect.

"The boat belongs to Elton White," Lindsey said to Melvin. "Okay, got it."

She continued speaking with Melvin—jotting things down in the radio log—but I was barely listening. I was trying to remember everything Elton had said about his boat. It hadn't been much. He had said he kept his boat docked along the bayou side behind his shop, but he said it wasn't there because it was getting serviced. I hadn't bothered to ask where, because it hadn't seemed important at the moment. Even now, the information wouldn't do much good, because we had found the boat. We could already prove he was lying about it. However, like everything with him, I couldn't figure out why he might be lying or what he might be up to.

But what if he wasn't lying? Was it possible the boys knew where the boat was being serviced and had stolen it from that location without his knowledge? I might've been open to that idea if Valerie hadn't found the backpacks in the bed of his truck. No, Elton was lying about something, and I needed to find out what it was. This time, though, the conversation would take place at the police department.

Lindsey eventually turned from her computer. "Melvin wants to talk to you."

I took the phone and said, "Well, it seems like Elton White has some explaining to do."

"Yeah, do you know how the boys got their hands on his boat?"

"I've been thinking about that," I said. "We know for certain that he met the boys near the water tower, so I'm guessing he picked them up from there and dropped them off behind his shop, where his boat was docked. If he loaned them the boat and everything was above board, they would've simply driven to his shop and jumped in. Since that's not what happened, I've got to think something shady is going on and he's involved."

"Is it possible they stole the boat?" Melvin asked.

"I doubt it, especially since he had their backpacks."

"What if he took them out here to murder them?"

The question was one I had not considered. I quickly ran over the timeline in my head. While he would've had enough time to do it all, why would he have left his boat at the scene of the crime? And how would he have gotten back to town? Also, it seemed unlikely that he would've held onto the backpacks of the boys he killed.

"I don't think so," I said, and explained my reasoning. "He does know more than he's saying, though, and I've got something to squeeze him with now. He can't explain this away, especially since he lied about his boat being at the repair shop."

I took a breath as I scanned the faces in the room. I would have to notify Ray and Wendy Foret, and I knew that wouldn't go over well.

"Hey, Melvin," I said, "did you check the boy's pockets?"

"No, I didn't want to disturb anything until you had a chance to look at the body."

"Go ahead and see if he's got some identification on him," I said. "Before I notify the Forets, I'd like to be positive it's him."

When Melvin pulled the phone away from his ear, it allowed me to hear the unadulterated force of the wind swirling in the background. A moment later, the distinct sounds of a boat banging against a wharf could also be heard, and I knew he was near the body.

After what seemed like an eternity—during which I regretted asking him to check for identification—the sounds of the storm subsided just a little, and I knew Melvin was back inside Red's camp.

"It's the youngest boy," he said. "It's Ruben Foret. I found his wallet with his library card, school ID, and driver's permit inside."

"Shit." While it sucked that it had happened to anyone, I would now have to bring the bad news to Wendy and Ray. Something I'd heard earlier suddenly came to mind. "Hey, Mel, Red said it looked like the boy was killed by an alligator. Is that accurate, or is it possible he drowned first and an alligator just fed on him?"

"Remember how you once explained the differences between antemortem and postmortem injuries, and how the postmortem injuries don't have blood in them?"

I said I remembered.

"Well, most of these injuries happened while he was still alive," he said. "This kid was eaten to death."

I winced. That was a detail I did *not* want to share with Wendy Foret. While it would be difficult for Ray to handle, it would absolutely destroy Wendy.

"There's another thing that's weird," Melvin said. "The teeth marks are different sizes. The weather's crazy out here, but Shade held the light for me while I looked over the body, and there seemed to be several different bite marks. It looks like a few alligators fed on him."

"That's it!" I snapped my fingers. "Mel, those boys were out there messing with alligators. When Regan dug through Cory's computer, she found search results relating to wrestling alligators, owning alligators, and whether or not it was illegal to keep one as a pet. They were either wrestling them or trying to capture one."

"If that's true," Melvin said, "there's a good chance the other two boys are dead, as well."

"I'm afraid of that." I was thoughtful. If that had been their plan all along, and Elton had known about it and loaned them his boat for that purpose, then he could be charged with contributing to the delinquency of a juvenile, because in Louisiana it was illegal to harass, molest or attempt to move alligators, and it was equally illegal for an adult to help facilitate a juvenile's delinquent behavior.

On the other hand, I had to be open to the idea that Elton knew nothing about the alligators—if, indeed, that's why they had gone out there. It was possible they asked to use the boat to go fishing, and that he had kept their secret because he was protecting them. Even if his intentions had been honorable at first, things had turned deadly for the boys, and I was going to see to it that Elton was held responsible for any part he might have played in this whole scheme.

"Okay, thanks a bunch, Mel," I finally said. "Be careful coming back."

"Oh, Clint," he said hesitantly, "we're not coming back."

"What?" The tone of my voice caused everyone in the room around me to stiffen up. "What do you mean?"

"Those other two boys are out here and they need us," he explained. "I've already talked to Shade about it. We're gonna look around until it gets too dangerous to be out—"

"It's already too dangerous to be out there!" I protested. "Come on, Mel, get back here."

"Clint, you know good and well that you'd do the same damned thing if you were out here," my friend said slowly. "At the moment, the wind's not too bad. I've seen worse. When the worst of it comes ashore, we'll hunker down at Red's camp. That way, we'll already be close to the water when everything passes and we can start searching immediately."

I sighed, knowing I wouldn't win. "Just be safe."

"You, too."

I ended the call and explained to Susan what was going on. I could tell by the line in her jaw that she didn't like it, and I knew she would like it even less when I told her I was going after Elton White.

CHAPTER 31

As hard as I had tried to convince Amy to stay behind, she had insisted on coming with me. We had gotten lucky and made it to the Foret home without running into any debris in the roadway. While the wind didn't seem as strong at the moment, we both knew that the worst was yet to come.

As I pulled the zipper on my rain coat all the way up, I couldn't help but notice that something was missing from the home in front of us, but I couldn't put my finger on it until we had almost made it to the steps and the front door burst open.

"Oh, no," Wendy wailed. "I thought it was Ray."

I stopped and scanned the front yard and driveway, finally realizing what had been missing—Ray's truck.

"Where'd he go in this weather?" I asked.

Wendy just stood there squirming, oblivious to the rain that was pelting her.

"Wendy!" I hollered. "Where in the hell is Ray?"

"He left to confront Elton," she said. "He thinks he can make him talk."

"Shit!" I turned and raced back to my truck, my boots kicking up water as I ran. Once Amy and I were back in my truck, I sped toward Elton's house, praying we would get there before Ray did.

We didn't.

The first thing I noticed when we arrived was that the entire metal roof of the carport was now gone. The second thing I noticed was that the front door was flopping in the wind. Ray's truck wasn't there, so it meant he had come and gone, but what kind of damage had he done while he was here?

Amy made it to the front door before I did, and she immediately headed for the garage. I went in the opposite direction, both of us calling out to Elton as we searched the house. I had made it to the guest bedroom when I heard Amy's boots approaching me hastily from behind. She ducked into the master bedroom, reappeared a second later, and huffed.

"He's not here!" she said. "Ray took him!"

I cursed out loud. "I should've forced Elton to come to the police department with us."

"You couldn't," Amy said. "It would've violated his rights and you're not into that, but now we've got to figure out where Ray brought him."

I was thoughtful, immediately remembering the camp that Wendy had spoken about. While it was a long shot, it was all we had—unless Ray had taken Elton back to the water tower where the bikes had been found.

"Let's go," I said, heading for my truck. "We've got two places to check, and we might not make it before the storm gets here. In fact, one of those places will take us closer to the storm."

As we headed across town to the water tower, I explained about the camp and how it might be our only chance. She didn't hesitate for a second.

"I wouldn't miss this for the world." She grabbed onto the *oh, shit* bar and held on tight as I swerved left to miss a tree branch in the road and then right to avoid a shopping cart. She laughed. "Where in the hell did that come from? Mechant Groceries is on the other side of town."

I didn't answer. I just kept maneuvering to the opposite side of town and didn't stop until we'd reached the water tower. There was no one around.

"Shit, here goes nothing," I said, and whipped my truck around. There were lots of trees and power poles along Old Blackbird Highway between us and the camp, and they were always the first to go during a hurricane. I knew there was a good chance we might not make it to the camp, and if we did, we might not make it back, but we had to try. I was certain Ray would kill Elton if he didn't tell him what he wanted to hear, and he might even kill him if he did.

"If Ray beats Elton's ass and gets him to confess to feeding the boys to the gators, can we use that in court?" Amy asked after a while. "I mean, it's not like we did it, so why should we be punished for Ray's sins?"

"I just hope he's still alive to take to court," I mumbled, staring in awe as we rounded the corner on the southern end of town.

The parking lot of Mechant Groceries looked like a jailbreak. There were shopping carts scattered all over the parking lot and across the highway. There was even one flying through the air. When we drove past the store—dodging carts like a running back picking his way through the defensive line—I understood what had happened. Either a strong gust of wind or a small tornado had blown the roof off the overhang, busted out the windows and doors to the vestibule, and sent the buggies scattering. It looked like someone had tossed a handful of grenades inside and walked away.

We had barely made it past the store when everything went black around us.

"Aw, shit," Amy said, "there goes the power. As soon as this thing blows through, either me or Baylor will have to head home and run the generator so we don't lose everything in our freezer."

I nodded. I'd have to do the same thing. In southeast Louisiana, not everyone could afford an automatic generator to power their entire home, but nearly all of us had a gasoline generator. While they were life savers, they could also be deadly, and we were always reminding our citizens to run them outdoors in well-ventilated areas. While most people knew that, some didn't, and I'd worked more than one storm where carbon monoxide from generators had killed more people than the storm itself. Those tragedies were a little harder to stomach, because they were completely avoidable and they usually involved the loss of entire families.

I picked our way south along Old Blackbird Highway for more than thirty minutes, and I didn't need a forecaster to tell me that the storm had made landfall. While the eye wall was still about an hour from us, we knew that we were close to the belly of the beast.

My truck rocked violently in the roadway with every other gust that blew through, and trees were snapping like toothpicks all around us. I had been forced to get out once to cut the top of a fallen tree from our path, and the wind had nearly knocked me off my feet.

The closer we got to the coast, the closer the water came to the sides of the road. The highway had been raised years earlier because of the constant flooding issues we'd had during storms, and I was hoping they'd elevated it enough to account for a storm such as the one breathing down on us now.

Finally, our destination loomed ahead, but we still couldn't see the camp. What gave it away was the red glow my headlights made as it reflected off of the rear taillights of Ray's truck. Although I figured Ray would be too busy and the storm too distracting for him to see us approaching, I switched off my headlights.

"We might have to kill this prick," Amy said as I turned off of the highway and parked my truck in the middle of the wooden bridge that connected the property to the road. "Once he gets an idea in his head, it's hard to redirect him."

I nodded and eased my door open. While we were in the open and vulnerable out here, it was too dark and the rain was falling too hard for him to see us. Even if he was aware of our presence, it would be impossible for him to track our progress through the yard.

I had to hold onto the side of my truck to keep from being blown off the bridge and into the churning water beneath my feet, and I hollered a warning to Amy as I made my way to the front of the truck. I was happy to see her when I rounded the front quarter panel. Huddling close together, we pushed our way forward. At one point, I felt Amy's hand on the outside of my rain suit. She grabbed my collar and pulled my ear toward her.

"I see a flashlight," she said. "It's moving around to the right side of the camp."

I looked up to scan the windows of the raised camp, and I saw what she was talking about. I nodded and drew my pistol. It appeared that we'd been undetected, so the element of surprise would be on our side. I was just hoping we weren't too late.

The water was up to our knees by the time we reached the wooden staircase leading up to the camp. My feet swished in my boots as I made my way up the stairs. I groaned. I hated wet socks and cursed myself for not pulling on my hip boots.

Once I reached the landing, I crouched low and made my way toward what looked like the main entrance. A length of gutter had broken loose and was banging loudly against the fascia, and I used this to our advantage. Even if our boots were making noise on the wooden deck, it would be impossible to hear in this weather.

I stopped on one side of the door and looked for Amy. Although she was inches away from me, it was impossible to see her. I felt for her and pulled her close.

"We'll count slowly to three in our heads," I said, "and then I'm gonna open the door and head to the right. You take the left."

She squeezed my arm to let me know she understood, and then I turned back to the door. Once I'd done the countdown, I twisted the knob and rushed forward. Immediately upon entering the building, I could tell how well it was built, because most of the roaring noise from the storm was instantly reduced to a low rumble, and I could also see that it had an open floor plan. We found ourselves in a living area, across from which was a kitchen, and then to the right there were what appeared to be sleeping quarters. It was from the door to one of these sleeping quarters that the flashlight was shining.

While I was pleased to be in such a secure building, it only took me two steps to realize we were in trouble. The echoing of our boots would surely give away our element of surprise, so I had no choice but to rely on our next best weapon—and that was speed.

CHAPTER 32

Red McKenzie's Camp
Landfall

After ending the call with Clint, Melvin waved for Shade to help him carry Ruben Foret's body into Red's camp. Once they were inside where it was dry, they set the boy down just inside the doorway and Melvin asked Red for a large towel and a paper bag. While Red headed for the bathroom, Melvin slipped back into the storm and stumbled toward Shade's truck. They had loaded some gear before leaving the police department, and—in addition to chainsaws, rope, and life vests—part of what they'd grabbed included three body bags. He was hoping they'd only have to use one.

Once Melvin had retrieved the body bag, he returned to the camp and helped Shade remove the boy's clothes. They weren't about to put a body covered in wet clothes into a body bag for an undetermined amount of time, because that would only invite the growth of mold and other bacteria.

After removing the clothes and placing them in the paper bag Red had provided, they dabbed at the body with the towel, wiping away what was left of the blood. Using his flashlight, Melvin then inspected the body carefully. He was able to get a better look at the wounds and, as hard as he searched, he could find nothing but alligator teeth marks on the boy's flesh. When he was satisfied there would be no surprises at an autopsy later, he and Shade loaded Ruben into the body bag and zipped it up.

Paulie, who was Red's fourteen-year-old son, was standing

nearby but had averted his eyes during the entire process.

"I would put the body in Shade's pickup," Melvin explained to Red, "but I'm worried the truck might get blown away or a tree might fall on it. Do you mind if we store it somewhere in here?"

"You can put him in Zeke's room. No one goes in there anymore," Red said, and then hesitated. After a long moment, he continued in a somber voice. "You know tomorrow's the anniversary of when we lost him? It's been two years, but it still feels like yesterday. I can still hear his voice around this place when things get real quiet. I called Sister Mildred to come over to the house and do a trance, and she said his spirit is still hanging around the place."

Melvin nodded and frowned as he bent to lift his end of the body bag. While he didn't put much stock in what Red had said about Sister Mildred, he did remember quite vividly the case that had involved the disappearance of Red's two boys. It had ended in tragic fashion—not just for Zeke, who had been killed, but also for the boy's father and brother. Red and Paulie had never been the same since, and neither had many other people in town. Melvin only hoped that they would find the other Foret brother and Cory alive, just as they had found Paulie alive.

Once Melvin and Shade had carried the boy's body into Zeke's room, they returned to the living area and Melvin asked Red for the keys to Elton's boat.

"Wait a minute," Red said, "you're not going out in that weather?"

"We've got two other boys missing," Melvin said. "We have to try to find them before the eye wall gets here."

"It's already here! It's upon us. If y'all go out there, y'all are gonna die." Red pointed upward. "I've never felt something so powerful. This camp is built so strong that I can't even hear a heavy rainfall on the roof, but this is crazy. To be honest, I wish we would've left."

"Are you serious, Dad?" Paulie asked from the other side of the living room. "You always swore you'd never leave for a storm."

Red lowered his eyes. "I did say that, but this one's got me scared."

Melvin dug out his SAT phone and called Susan to find out if Red was right about the eye wall being upon them. Based on what he could remember, the storm should be making landfall right around now about an hour to the southeast of them. If the pounding they were taking right now wasn't the eye wall, then they were in for a rough night.

"Melvin, please tell me you're someplace safe," Susan said immediately. "The storm's picked up speed."

"Yeah, we're at Red's camp," he said. "It's as solid as they come."

"Thank God!" While he could hear the relief in Susan's voice, he could tell there was still something bothering her. "The eye should pass a little to the west of us, but we're gonna get hammered in the process. You need to stay inside. This is a dangerous storm."

"Will do," he promised. "How's Clint?"

"I don't know." She took a deep breath and exhaled. "It seems that Ray Foret has kidnapped Elton White. On a hunch, Clint headed to this old camp that Ray's wife mentioned earlier in the day. Amy texted me to say they'd made it and found Ray's truck, but I haven't heard anything since then."

Melvin stood straighter. "Where's the camp?"

"You'll never make it there," Susan said. "You're too far away and it's too dangerous. I'm sure I'll hear from them soon."

The walls to the camp suddenly rattled and shook and Melvin heard Red let out a gasp. He asked Susan to let him know once she'd heard from Clint and Amy, and then he ended the call.

He stood there pondering everything he knew. He had a strong urge to get out there and search for the boys, the storm be damned. With his gear and experience, he had a much better chance of surviving than they did, so he felt obligated to get out there and help them. However, he knew that if he did go out there, he would not only be putting his own life at risk, but also Shade's life, because there was no way the young officer would let him go it alone. Besides, he had no way of knowing where the boys were, and visibility would be nil.

A flame from an oil lantern was flickering and it cast an eerie glow about the room as Melvin's eyes turned from Red to Shade and then, finally, to Paulie. The younger McKenzie didn't seem to be bothered by the storm, and neither did Shade. Red, on the other hand, was visibly concerned. Melvin was sure all of that concern was aimed at his one remaining son.

"Okay," Melvin finally said, "we'll stay put until the eye wall pushes through. Afterward, we're taking Elton's boat and we're going search for the boys."

"And I'll be coming with y'all," Red said. "Me and Paulie. We'll do everything we can to help y'all find those other kids."

Paulie nodded and said, "I'd go out there right now if my dad would let me."

Melvin was about to respond when the front door of the camp burst open and two dark figures rushed inside carrying rifles and wearing pistols and large knives on their belts.

CHAPTER 33

Old Blackbird Highway

I was running as fast as I could toward the light and had almost made it to the doorway when a shotgun blast exploded from somewhere inside the sleeping quarters to the right. I threw myself to the left and began rolling until I was behind a thick wooden coffee table. I quickly flipped it onto its side and hunkered down behind it.

I had barely settled in when I felt something drop on top of me. Before I could react, it scrambled furiously and rolled off. I turned and—from the faint glow of the flashlight in the opposite room—saw that it was Amy. I heard a voice hollering from the sleeping quarters, but I could barely make out what was being said thanks to the ringing in my ears. A shotgun blast was loud enough on its own, but within a confined space it was ear-piercing.

"Ray Foret, put down that damned gun!" I hollered back. "This is not the way to get your boys back!"

"Oh, I'll get them back," he bellowed, "just you wait and see! I got more out of this man than you did, and I won't stop until I get my boys back home. You can arrest me later, but I'm not going in until they're safe at home."

"Ray, you've got to let Elton go," I said. "You're screwing up our case."

"I don't give a shit about your case," he said. "I want my boys back. That's all I care about. As a dad yourself, you should understand that."

"I do, and I get it, but can't you just release Elton?" I pleaded. "Let me finish interviewing him. Once he tells us what he knows, we can go out there and get them."

"He doesn't know where they are, but he knows where they were and he has an idea about what happened to them," Ray said. "You couldn't get that out of him, but I did, so I'll be damned if I let you or anyone else screw this up anymore. I'm their dad and it's my job to get them back—no one else's!"

My hearing was slowly coming back, but there was still an intense ringing in my ears. I could feel Amy moving to my left, and I knew she was trying for a more advantageous position. As things stood now, Ray could simply move to the far right side of the room and launch some shotgun pellets in our direction. If he was loaded for squirrels, then we should be fine. If he was loaded for bear, we were screwed. There was no way this wooden table would stand up to buckshot or slugs.

"Look, Ray, you said you've got your information and that's great," I said, not wanting to hurt the man. "Why don't you just release Elton into my custody and leave? We won't try to stop you. You can go find your boys without any interference from us."

"That sounds like a plan, but first, I need you to throw down your gun."

I cursed under my breath. "Sorry, but that's not gonna happen."

"I don't want to have to hurt you, detective," he warned, "but I mean it when I say that nothing and no one will stand between me and my boys."

"We're on the same side here," I said, realizing everything I said was in vain. "Why don't you just leave Elton back there and walk out of here. I won't try to stop you. I give you my word."

"You won't try to stop me until you have Elton safe and secure in your possession," Ray said in an evil tone. "I'm not stupid. You're not getting him."

I propped up on my elbows. "Ray, what did you do to him?"

Silence.

"Elton, can you hear me?" I asked loudly. "Elton White, are you back there?"

"Oh, he's back here alright," Ray said, "but he won't be doing no talking ever again."

Shit!

"Ray, did you hurt him?" I gripped my pistol firmly in my hand and waited, but the man didn't answer. As I waited for him to respond, a thunderous boom shook the camp and something could be heard ripping away from the roof. It was almost immediately followed by the sounds of water dripping on the wooden floor.

Lightning flashed intermittently, but it did no good. I was huddled behind the thick coffee table and couldn't see into the room.

"Look, Ray," I said, "if you share what Elton told you, we can go out there together and find your boys."

I felt Amy's presence more than heard her, as she crept closer to me, and then her breath was hot against my ear as she spoke.

"I think he's trying to circle around to the front of the camp," she whispered. "There must be a door that connects the two sleeping quarters, and it has to lead to the front entrance."

I shoved my hand into my slicker suit, grabbed my flashlight from my back pocket, and nodded. I turned my face in her direction and whispered my plan. Once she was ready, I turned on my flashlight and slid it across the floor, with the beam aiming at the doorway to the sleeping quarters. As it rolled away, I inched out from behind the coffee table and scanned the room in front of me.

Suddenly, I heard Amy holler a warning. I whipped around toward the door that led to the other sleeping quarters as lightning flashed, and there stood Ray Foret, the butt of his shotgun pulled into his shoulder and the muzzle pointing right at our location.

Before I could bring my pistol around, the shotgun boomed thunderously, spitting fire and lead in our direction. The brief glow from the fired cartridge illuminated Ray's face and I noticed his expression was odd. I was about to pull the trigger on my own pistol when I heard the shotgun clank loudly to the wooden boards at his feet. It was dark again and I couldn't see anything, but the sound of Ray's large body hitting the floor was unmistakable.

I scurried across the room to retrieve my flashlight. Once it was in hand, I jumped to my feet and aimed it first at Amy and then at Ray. Amy was standing and approaching the downed man, her flashlight in one hand and her pistol in the other, but Ray was a different story. There were three bullet holes in his face. One had blown out his two front teeth, another had punched a hole through his forehead, and the third had sprung a leak in his throat.

The smell of gunfire hung heavy in the room, as Amy continued her approach to the large man. I glanced at her face once on my way to the sleeping quarters, and saw it relax when she realized Ray was dead.

My light stabbed the room and there, in the far corner, I found Elton White. He was strapped to a wooden chair by a leather belt, his wrists and ankles bound with gray tape. His left foot had been blown to bits, and so had his right knee. The blood on the floor was thick, and there was a lot of it.

Making sure not to step in the puddle at his feet, I reached two fingers under his dangling head and felt for a pulse. There was none and he was cold to the touch.

"Shit!"

"Is he dead?" Amy asked from behind me.

Thanks to the relentless beating the camp was taking from Hurricane Ursula, I hadn't heard her approach.

"Yep, and his secrets died with him." I shone my light around the room. There were two spent shotgun shells on the floor several feet from Elton's body. A duffle bag filled with tools and two rolls of gray tape were resting atop one of the bunk beds. A picture of Ruben and Allen was in a frame and propped up on a night table facing Elton's chair.

I shot a thumb toward the front room. "I guess Ray ain't talking either, eh?"

In the glow from our flashlights, I saw Amy frown.

"No," she said. "I'm sorry. I know we needed him alive, but I had to make the head shot to stop him as quickly as—"

"Don't apologize for taking swift and decisive action that saved our lives," I said quickly. "Had you aimed for center mass, he could've gotten off a few more shots, and he might've killed one of us."

I was about to head back toward the living quarters when there was another thunderous booming sound and I thought I felt the floor move.

"What the hell was that?" I asked, spreading my legs to achieve maximum balance.

Amy had holstered her pistol and was now holding onto a nearby wall. "I think we just lost one of the pilings."

When we'd first driven up, I'd seen that the camp was elevated on large creosote pilings. While there were plenty of them and they were spaced out evenly, I knew it would only take one or two of them to go down before the rest fell like dominos.

"We need to get the hell out of here!" Just as the words left my mouth, the building shivered and the floor beneath my feet seemed to drop a few inches. Pushing off as hard as I could with my legs, I lunged toward Amy. The floor gave way beneath me, but I got enough of a push-off to launch myself into the air.

Amy was waiting for me and pulled me to her side of the room just as the front half of the building collapsed and disappeared into the darkness beneath us.

"Come on," Amy said, grabbing me by the arm. "I saw a

bathroom in this direction!"

She hurried past Elton's body and disappeared through a narrow doorway. I followed close behind her as the rain and wind battered the room we had occupied seconds earlier. Once inside the next room, I turned and tried to close the door, but the wind was too strong. Amy suddenly hurled herself into me, and her momentum was enough to get the door to shut.

Once that was done, we shone our lights into the room and found that we were standing in the second sleeping quarters.

"It's this way," Amy hollered, and she led the way.

The sounds of the storm were deafening now. The walls rattled and the floor swayed beneath our feet. I just knew the entire building would collapse with us in it, and I doubted we could survive being dropped to the ground and then buried under the thick and splintered wood with which the camp was constructed.

Amy slipped through another doorway and stopped in a tiny bathroom. We closed and locked the door and surveyed the room. There was a toilet, a cast iron bathtub, and a small closet. Without hesitating, we both jumped into the tub and sat across from each other, our legs curled up and our hands gripping the sides. If the floor under us collapsed, it would be one hell of a ride, and we might not make it out alive.

CHAPTER 34

Red McKenzie's Camp

Melvin and Shade watched the two dark figures warily as they slammed the door to Red's camp and shook the rain from their faces. Each man carried a lever-action rifle, but they weren't holding them in a menacing way. When the first man looked up, Melvin relaxed.

"Brennan, what in the hell are you doing here?" he asked. "Don't you know there's a storm coming?"

"It's already here, Mel," said Brennan Boudreaux, pushing the dark hood from his head, "and she's bringing hell with her."

Brennan was brother to Dexter Boudreaux, who used to be an alligator trapper before he became mayor for the town of Mechant Loup. Dexter and his wife had been killed during a gun battle with the Parker Brothers nearly seven years ago, and Brennan and his friends had readily joined forces with the police department to help track down his brother's killers.

Melvin introduced Shade to Brennan and his friend, who was a crusty old coot named Sid Punch. The last time Melvin had seen Sid was when they'd organized a search for a missing girl. That had only been two years ago, but it looked like Sid had aged ten years.

After Brennan and Sid leaned their rifles against the wall in the corner near the door, Shade shook hands with both men. They all then moved to the kitchen table, where Red was busying himself clearing off a spot for everyone to sit and talk. It was obvious that Red and his son didn't get many visitors, and Paulie seemed happy for the company.

Melvin and Shade each grabbed a stool and sat opposite the new arrivals.

"Are you heading to your place or leaving it?" Melvin asked Brennan. In addition to being Dexter's younger brother, Brennan was the owner of Brennan's Seafood and Swamp Tours, which was a popular tourist attraction that was located out on the water.

"I hate to admit this, but we're abandoning the place," he said. "We were trying to get back to town, but my boat started taking on water. This was the closest camp to us, so we headed here to get out of the weather." Brennan paused and looked at Red. "Is it okay if we ride out the storm with y'all?"

"Absolutely," Red said. "Paulie and I would love the company."

Usually a tough-as-nails man, Red appeared more vulnerable in his later years—especially since he'd lost his elder son—and Melvin felt sorry for him.

Brennan indicated Melvin and Shade with a nod of his head. "What are y'all doing so far from town in this weather?"

"We're looking for some missing boys," Melvin said. "Red and Paulie found one of them dead, but there're still two of them out there."

"Hold up a minute." Brennan shot a thumb over his shoulder. "Y'all found one boy dead, but there're two more boys still out there?"

Melvin nodded.

"In this weather?"

Melvin nodded again. "We're gonna start looking for them as soon as the storm lets up."

"How'd the boy die?" Brennan asked. "Did the storm get him?"

"No." Melvin shook his head. "He was killed by alligators."

"Oh, shit," Brennan said with a shake of his head. "That ain't good."

"No, it's not." Melvin went on to tell Brennan how it looked like Ruben had been killed by multiple alligators. He went on to describe the wounds on the boy, while also telling him everything else he knew about the disappearance, including what Amy and Regan had found on one of the boy's computers regarding wrestling alligators.

Brennan scowled and rubbed his beard thoughtfully. In addition to his restaurant and swamp tour businesses, Brennan Boudreaux also owned an alligator farm, so he was well-versed in all aspects of alligator handling. Since Brennan was a bit of an expert on the matter, Melvin figured he could rely on the older man's knowledge now.

"Have you ever heard of multiple alligators attacking a human in the water?" Melvin asked.

After a long moment, Brennan shook his head. "While I think it's possible, I've never heard of it happening. Now, you say these kids might've set out to wrestle alligators or something?"

Melvin nodded and explained what Regan had found on Cory Verdin's computer. "Just because he was researching capturing alligators and wrestling them," Melvin acknowledged, "it doesn't mean they tried it, but I don't think it's a coincidence."

"Gators are like any other wild animal," Brennan explained, "they're naturally afraid of humans and—considering how many of them there are—attacks on humans are rare. But, if you've got people feeding them at a certain location, the gators in that area would be conditioned to associate humans with food. I don't need to tell you that it ain't a good thing, because you already know it, but it ain't good."

Melvin was thoughtful, trying to think of an area along Lake Berg where people would be most likely to feed the alligators. Based on what he knew about the case, the three missing boys hadn't been frequenting the swamps, so it couldn't have been them who were conditioning the alligators to associate humans with food. They were most likely a victim of someone else's folly.

"Do you think a large population of alligators would congregate at a place where people are known to feed them?" Melvin asked. "There's no evidence that the boys have been coming out here on a regular basis, but there are a few spots along the lakeshore where tourists have been regularly caught feeding alligators. Could the alligators around that area associate the location with food and hang around waiting for more?"

"Absolutely." Brennan nodded his head. "Not only that, but that type of behavior will help to create a feeding frenzy in those areas. I mean, you can tell where alligators are being fed. As soon as something hits the water, they all start heading for the sound. If one of the boys fell into a fed area like that, then they could have a bunch of gators attacking him and mistaking him for whatever food was thrown to them over time. Once they bite into him, it's over. They won't just taste the human flesh and spit it out. By then, nature kicks in and they start to eating him."

Outside—and above the howling of wind and driving of rain—came a loud and sharp cracking sound of a tree snapping in half. It was obviously nearby, and everyone in the camp tensed and glanced toward the ceiling, half expecting a large cypress to come crashing through the roof.

Within seconds, the ground shook and Red glanced toward the back of the camp.

"That was a big one," he said, his voice revealing the concern he felt. "I've not felt winds this strong out here before. I'm sure I'll lose more trees."

"If one of those things falls on us," Shade said with a grunt, "it'll definitely ruin our night."

Brennan squinted in the dim glow from the lamplight. "How long you been a cop, boy?"

"Not long enough to be dry behind the ears yet," Shade said with a quick smile.

Melvin chuckled, and so did the rest of the men in the room, including young Paulie. Shade was accustomed to people dismissing him because of his age, and it didn't bother him one bit. He had once told Melvin he used it to his advantage.

"I love it when folks underestimate me," he'd said, "especially if they're violent suspects. It's always fun to see the looks on their faces when I flip them on their heads and slap the cuffs on them."

"Well, if you decided to follow Melvin into this beast of a storm, you're alright in my book," Brennan said. "You've gotta have balls the size of marsh buggy tires to come out in this weather."

There was more rumbling from outside and a violent blast of wind caused the windows to rattle.

"Dad, do you think it'll hold?" Paulie asked, suddenly looking as concerned as his father. "I can feel the floor shaking under my feet."

Red only nodded, but Melvin noticed that the motion lacked conviction. Sure, it was a well-built home, but the last time they'd had a storm like this one was when Hurricane Samson had blown through the area. Still, it did no good to worry, so he turned the conversation back to the missing boys to help distract Paulie.

"Did y'all notice anything when y'all were heading in from the restaurant?" Melvin asked. "We found the boat the boys were in, but it looks like it's missing some things, so the stuff might've been floating on the water."

Brennan looked at Sid. "Did you notice anything?"

"Shit, I couldn't see the hand in front of my face," he muttered. "I don't know how you even made it here."

"I'm like that old dog, Lassie," Brennan said. "My sixth sense can get me home no matter where you drop me." He then leaned his arms on the table and indicated Melvin. "You going back out there to find them other boys once the storm passes?"

"That's the plan," Melvin said. "I just hope we're not too late.

There aren't many shelters out there on the lake, so they're most likely out in the open."

"I hope they know enough to climb a tree, because that water's rising fast," Sid said. "I've never seen waves like that on the lake."

"It'd better be a stout tree," Red muttered, "or they'll end up in the wash."

Melvin stood from the table and walked toward one of the windows. He pulled out his SAT phone and dialed Clint's number as he watched the rain whip around in the rain. He felt a drop on his head and glanced up. A tiny leak had sprung in the roof, but that wasn't a surprise. He only hoped the roof would hold throughout the night, otherwise it would be a rough one.

Clint didn't answer his SAT phone, so Melvin called the police department.

"Melvin, are y'all okay?" Susan asked. "The storm made landfall and it's heading right for us. It's coming faster than they expected, but it did weaken a little."

"Weakened?" Melvin scoffed. "Tell that to the giant tree that just broke in half somewhere in the woods. But no, we're good. We're still holed up at Red's place. As soon as this thing blows through, we're heading out to search for the boys."

"Okay, I'll see if the sheriff can spare some people to help out once it's safe enough to do so," she said.

"Get them to help you out," Melvin said. "Brennan Boudreaux and Sid Punch decided to join the party. They're holed up with us and they said they'd help search for the boys in the morning."

"That's great," Susan said. "When the eye wall passes over us, we're gonna take a quick drive through town to see if anyone needs rescuing, but then we'll come back here to wait out the second half of the storm."

"Have you heard from Clint and Amy?" Melvin asked hesitantly. Since Susan hadn't led with that information, he figured she didn't know much.

"Not a peep," came the despondent reply.

CHAPTER 35

Old Blackbird Highway

Amy and I had gripped the edges of the cast iron bathtub for what seemed like forever, holding on for dear life. It felt like we were in a giant blender, the blades of which were tearing violently at the camp in which we huddled. With each gust of wind, it seemed like another piece of the structure either collapsed to the ground twenty feet below or went sailing into the black nothingness that surrounded us.

Finally, after surviving more than three hours of Hurricane Ursula's fury, an eerie calm fell over the camp. The wind died down to a firm whisper, and the only other sounds that could be heard were the creaking of loose boards and corrugated roofing panels as they swung back and forth against the breeze.

"We're in the eye of the storm," I said, trying to release my hold on the tub. My hands cramped up and I had to force them to open. "We need to get the hell out of here. This building won't survive another beating like that."

Although I couldn't see Amy, I knew she agreed with me, because I felt her moving around in the tub and then heard her plop to the floor of the bathroom.

"Everything's asleep," she said with a groan. "I can't move my legs. Even my ass is dead."

My limbs were also numb, and it took some work to get out of the tub without falling. With the help of a nearby wall, I steadied myself and reached for my flashlight. I flicked it on and quickly reached for Amy.

"Don't move!" I said, pointing to the hole that had formed in the floor three feet from where we had been riding out the storm. She cursed and nodded, shaking out one leg and then the other, groaning against the invisible needles that stabbed at her flesh.

There was a giant hole in the room where we had located Elton White. I walked to the edge of the hole and shined my light to the right, trying to see past the living quarters, but there was nothing but a tangled mess of twisted boards and bent metal.

"I think Ray's body's gone, too," I muttered, aiming the light beneath us. "I guess they're buried in the rubble."

"I'm ready," Amy finally said. "My legs are working again."

"I don't know how we're supposed to get down from here," I said, surveying our surroundings. I didn't know what was on the other side of the nearest wall, but my guess was that it was nothing but air.

For the umpteenth time in the past hour, I reached for my SAT phone, and for the umpteenth time, I cursed myself for leaving it with Valerie. There were a few times during the night when I'd wanted to call Grace and Susan and tell them that I loved them, because I felt like it would be the last time I'd speak to them. I had asked Amy to borrow her SAT phone, but she only had her cell phone, and the cell towers had long since gone down.

"Why didn't you bring yours?" I had asked during a particularly bad part of the storm.

"Because I thought you had yours," she'd said wearily, and I could feel her feet push against my legs in the tub.

When not wondering if the end had finally come for us, I'd spent my time puzzling over the case. I had fully expected Ray to slap Elton around a little, but I had not foreseen him murdering the man in cold blood. He had lied about his knowledge of the boys going missing, of that much I had been sure since the beginning, but I didn't believe for a second that he had hurt them in some way. Knowing someone is lying and forcing them to tell the truth are two different things. Fortunately, cops were not able to torture suspects like Ray had done to compel them to talk, because there was a good chance that Elton had merely said what he thought Ray wanted to hear, just so the angry man would stop hurting him, and it could've all been lies.

While I used my flashlight to try and find a way through the hole at our feet and down to the rubble below, I shared my thoughts with Amy.

"What if Elton did have something to do with their disappearance and he *did* confess?" Amy asked. "Now that Ray's dead, we'll never know what his involvement was."

"I know another way," I said, dropping to my hands and knees to look under the floor upon which we stood. I sighed in relief when I saw a piling about three feet away. Each of the pilings had a two-by-eight support brace that extended from the underside of the camp to the lower portion of the piling. If we could reach the two-by-eight, we could slide down to the ground.

"And what's this other way?" Amy asked when I straightened.

"He's dead and he doesn't have any family that we know of, so we get to search his house," I explained. "His phone is probably wherever his body is, but I'm sure his computer is back at his house."

Removing my belt from my pants, I looped one end around a leg of the tub. I jerked on it to test its strength, and it held solid.

"But what if his computer doesn't yield anything?" Amy asked, watching me curiously.

"Then we're screwed."

Wrapping my right fist around the loose end of my belt, I dropped to my belly and lowered my feet through the hole.

"That won't work," Amy said. "You'll fall to your death."

"It's only about twenty feet," I said with a groan, "so I'll only get hurt—I won't die."

I lowered my body through the hole until my arms were outstretched and I was holding on with the tips of my left fingers and the belt that was wrapped around my right hand. Amy had dropped to her belly and was training her flashlight on the exact spot where I wanted to be.

After taking a deep breath, I swung my feet forward and backward, trying to gain some momentum. Three feet hadn't seemed far when I had been looking through the hole, but it now seemed like a mile, and the feat seemed impossible. Once my feet made contact with the two-by-eight, I would have to let go of the floor with my left hand and try to latch onto the brace.

"If you get hurt," Amy said from above me, "I'm not carrying your broken ass to the truck, so you'd better not fall."

I laughed, but only briefly. The damp coolness from the storm was inviting in the middle of the summer, but I was sweating nonetheless. I suddenly remembered almost falling from the water tower hours earlier, and a feeling of calmness suddenly swept over me. This was nothing!

I swung my legs with gusto now. On the third try, my left boot made contact with the wooden brace. I hooked my foot around it and let go with my left hand, which allowed me to wrap more of my leg around the board. I stretched out with my left hand, but was only able to curl two of my fingers around the edge of the brace.

"Here goes nothing," I whispered, and pulled with my leg and fingers while letting go of my belt. It didn't work. The momentum of my body swinging forward ripped my fingers free of the support brace and I fell straight down. I didn't have time to think or yell—even if I had wanted to—because I landed with a thud on a flat surface and then started sliding downward.

"Shit, Clint!" Amy hollered, her flashlight darting wildly about as she tried to see what had become of me.

I was about to curse my luck as the object upon which I had fallen took a steeper dive and I began sliding faster toward the ground, but then I came to an abrupt stop against something soft. I looked up. Thanks to the glow from Amy's flashlight, I was able to see that I had fallen onto the collapsed floor of the sleeping quarters.

"Wait a minute!" I twisted around and felt for the soft object that I had bumped into and realized it was Elton's body. His feet and hands were still bound with tape. Beyond him and resting on the ground was the wall of the sleeping quarters.

I lifted my head and glanced over my shoulder to survey the damage to the camp, and my mouth opened in dismay. From my vantage point, I could see that only a small portion of the building was still intact and resting on the pilings, and that portion was almost exclusively the bathroom in which Amy and I had hunkered through the first half of the storm. There was no way it would survive another onslaught from Mother Nature.

"Get the bastard's phone!" Amy hollered from twenty feet above me. "We need that phone!"

I jumped into action and began rifling through his pockets. He wore cargo shorts, so he had at least two pockets in the front, two in the back, and one on each leg. I had just finished checking the leg pockets when I heard a crashing sound above me. I looked up in time to see Amy and her flashlight sliding toward me boots first. She was picking up speed rapidly. Instead of leaning out of the way, I braced myself and offered my shoulder to help break her fall.

She landed harder than I thought she would, and my knees dug into Elton's body and sent him sliding away from me.

"Thanks, partner," Amy said with a grunt when I helped her to her feet. "I figured if you could survive that fall, then so could I. After all, my bones are a lot younger and stronger. Oh, and here you go...I rescued your belt."

I smiled my thanks and took the belt. I quickly ran it through the loops on my pants, cinched it in place, and then continued frisking Elton for the cell phone. I could feel his blood all over my hands and wished for a pair of gloves.

"Do you see Ray's body?" I asked when I had turned Elton over to check his back pockets.

Amy began scanning the area with her light. "Shit, he's probably buried in that debris. Damn, Clint, we're lucky to be alive."

I mumbled an agreement and removed Elton's wallet from one of the back pockets. The other one was empty. I cursed and stood to my feet. I grabbed my flashlight with a bloody hand and began searching the wall on which we stood. It was odd to see a window on the ground, but there, resting on the cracked glass, was Elton's cell phone.

"Got it," I said, lifting it triumphantly in the air. "Now, I need to find some water so I can rinse my hands and we can get the hell out of here before the back end of that storm catches up to us."

"You won't have a problem finding water," Amy said, aiming her light all around us. "It found us."

I frowned when I saw that the entire yard was covered in water that was at least a foot deep. The bridge upon which my truck rested stood high and dry, but I could see that the highway beyond it was also flooded. I shook my head. It would be a long, slow drive back to town. I just hoped we could outrun the back end of the storm.

CHAPTER 36

As I crept north along Old Blackbird Highway, Amy called Baylor's SAT phone and asked him to put her on speaker so she could also talk to Susan. When he had, she told them everything that had happened out at the camp, and she said that the eye of the storm was over us.

"Are y'all okay?" Baylor asked when she was done talking. There was real concern in his voice, and I figured he probably thought he'd lost her. "Y'all aren't hurt?"

"Nah, we're fine," she said, "but we don't know what Elton told Ray, so we're heading to Elton's house to search his computers. He might not have fed Ruben to an alligator, but he contributed in some way to the kid's death, and we need to find out how. Once we figure out his angle, we should be able to find the other boys. Well, at least we might have a place to start looking. Hopefully, we're not already too late."

"The power's out all across town," Susan said. "Y'all won't be able to search anything at his house. Gather up his computers and bring them to the police department. It'll be safer here anyway. Oh, and Clint, I spoke with Gracie and my mom. They're doing fine. Gracie said she had a bad dream about you and she asked if you were okay. I...um, I didn't know what to say."

I bit back the burning in my jaw. "Well, you can call her back and tell her that I'm great. I've never been better."

There was a long moment of silence on the other end of the line. Finally, Susan said, "Y'all just be careful and get back here in one piece."

"Yeah, and Amy," Baylor chimed in, "you're not getting out of the wedding that easy."

"Oh, don't worry," Amy said, "I'm getting married even if I'm dead. I will *not* go into the ground a single woman."

They talked a bit more and then I got Susan's attention before they could end the call.

"Wendy Foret still has no idea what happened to her youngest son," I said. "We'll have to let her know that Ruben and her husband are dead. It won't be easy to break that news to her, but I've got to tell her—and I've got to do it soon. I can't let her go through the rest of the night not knowing."

"It's already morning, Clint," she said, "but don't worry about it. I'll take care of it. As soon as the eye wall is over the town, I'll pick her up and bring her to the police station to tell her. I don't want her alone in that house with her thoughts. I'll let her ride out the remainder of the storm here, where we can keep an eye on her and try to comfort her."

I liked that idea and said so, continuing to drive slowly through the water. It was impossible to see the road beneath us, so I had to use the power poles and trees as my guide. Although we were creeping along, it didn't take long for us to catch up to the front wall of the storm, and the rain and wind were soon having their way with my truck.

When the storm had been out in the Gulf, meteorologists had reported that the eye was forty miles wide. While we could use forty miles worth of reprieve, I wasn't fooled. The shape and size of the storm's eye could change from hour to hour, and that was especially true once it made landfall. Eventually, it would break up as the storm moved farther ashore and dissipated, but that would happen somewhere to the north of us. I was just hoping that the land to the south would have enough of an impact to reduce the storm's strength to a manageable Category Two or Three. I didn't know where Cory and Allen were hiding out, and they could use all the help they could get—*if* it wasn't already too late for them.

"We have to go, y'all," Amy said. "The road's a mess and we can barely hear y'all anymore."

Once Amy ended the call, she began messing with Elton's phone. In my peripheral vision, I noticed a glow coming from her lap.

"If we can get the information we need from this, we won't need his computer," she mumbled. A second later, she gave a triumphant shout. "We're in luck—he doesn't have it pass-protected!"

"That might not be such a good thing," I said. "It might mean he has nothing to hide."

She grunted. "Let's hope you're wrong."

Amy hummed as she dug through the phone. After a minute, she asked if I knew Cory's number. "I can't find a contact named Cory."

"It's in my notebook," I said, keeping my eyes on the road as I reached for my console.

"I've got it," she said. I could hear her flipping through the pages. "It's funny he doesn't have the number stored—oh, wait a minute, here it is."

She lifted the phone in front of my face so I could see the screen. The contact name displayed was *Son*.

"Damn, that's weird," I said. "It didn't seem like Valerie thought of him as a father-figure to Cory yet. She made it sound like they were in the infancy stages of their relationship."

Amy didn't say anything as her thumbs flew across the screen. "Here we go," she finally said. "Text messages between Elton and Cory. The last ones are from Sunday night."

She began reading them aloud.

Elton: *I'm starting to have second thoughts about tomorrow.*
Son: *Please no. I need this.*
Elton: *If your mom finds out she'll never trust me again.*
Son: *She'll never find out. You said you did it as a kid and never got caught. Why can you do it and I can't?*
Son: *Are you still there?*
Elton: *It's too risky.*
Son: *No, it's not. No one will ever know. I swear. We'll just say we were camping and found them and no one will know where we went. Please, you have to do this. I need this. If I had a dad, he would help me do this. I don't have a dad. I have you.*
Elton: *I'm worried something will go wrong.*
Son: *LOL What could go wrong?*
Son: *Dad...can I count on you?*
Elton: *And how do you know you can even trust Ruben and Allen? If y'all get caught, you know they'll blame it all on you, and they'll say I was involved. I could go to jail.*
Son: *They don't even know you're involved. I told them I lied to you and said we wanted to go fishing. It's cool. I can't believe you don't trust me.*
Son: *Hello...*
Elton: *Okay. I'll pick y'all up near the water tower at seven. If something goes wrong, I never had anything to do with it. I can't help you if I'm involved, and I don't want to lose what I have with*

you and your mom. That means more to me than anything in the world. I want to be in your life forever, not just for a little bit.

    Son: *Deal!!!*

CHAPTER 37

I shook my head and cursed under my breath when Amy finished reading the messages.

"That's why the little bastard didn't let me see his cell phone earlier." I glanced quickly at Amy. "Are there any earlier messages that explain any of this? You were definitely reading the back end of the conversation. It seems like some planning has already gone into this crime—or whatever it is that they were planning."

"I'm looking, but so far there aren't any," she said. "They text almost every day, but they mostly talk about random things. Here, Elton's asking if Cory's working today. Um, Cory just sent Elton a picture of a snake he killed, and Elton says he shouldn't kill snakes. A week ago, Elton sent Cory a picture of some lyrics from a country song. Cory sent Elton a profile picture of a girl and wants Elton's opinion on whether or not he should ask her out."

"What does Elton say?" I asked curiously.

"Elton asks if she's rich, Cory says no, and then Elton says to go for it," she said. "Two messages later Elton says he dated a rich girl once and she left him for a richer guy."

I was only half listening now.

"What does Cory need?" I asked.

"Who the hell knows?" Amy mumbled. "But he definitely knows how to play Elton. He's got that man wrapped."

"Can you call Susan and ask her to put Valerie on the phone?" I asked. "Maybe she knows what Cory needs so badly that he'd plot some kind of crime with Elton."

Amy glanced at the dash clock. It was almost two in the morning. "You think she's still up?"

"Her son's missing," I said wistfully. "She hasn't slept a wink since we met her. She should still have my SAT phone, so you can call that."

Amy did what I asked, and Valerie's voice was soon coming through my truck speakers. Amy explained everything that was going on and then read the text messages to her. Valerie broke out in sobs upon hearing the exchange.

I scowled. I could hear the pain in the woman's voice and my heart was breaking for her. I didn't know how we would do it, but we needed to get her son back alive.

It took a few minutes for Amy to get Valerie to calm down enough to speak coherently, and when she did, Amy asked if she knew what they were talking about.

"Cory doesn't talk to me about his relationship with Elton," she said, still fighting back the sobs. "I didn't know he called Elton dad and Elton called him son."

"Did Elton ever mention this thing he did wrong as a kid?" Amy asked.

"I mean, he's talked about his childhood and he's told me some mischievous things that he's done, but I don't know if that's what they're talking about."

"What kinds of things has he done wrong?" Amy asked.

"Well, he loved going to the movie theater as a kid. He said he and his friends would pay for one movie, watch it, and then sneak into other rooms and watch those movies for free." She took a trembling breath. "He said he spent a lot of time on the water, and he said he snuck into a camp once when it was raining, but he didn't steal anything. He was just trying to get out of the rain."

"Did you know that Elton had a boat?" Amy asked.

"I did," she said. "He showed Cory how to drive it. Cory's never driven a boat before, so that was a new experience for him. Um, why do you ask? Does the boat have something to do with this?"

I didn't have to tell Amy not to say anything about finding the boat or Ruben's body. She already knew what we could and couldn't divulge at the moment, and she played it off like a pro.

"We're still not sure what matters and what doesn't matter," she said smoothly, "so we're looking into every possibility."

After a brief pause, Amy asked if Elton had ever mentioned stealing anything.

"Oh, God no," she said. "I would never be involved with a man who stole something, and he knew that. I had my house broken into a few years ago, and I hate a thief. If you ask me for something, I'll give it to you if I can. Even if I can't afford to help you, I'll try to find a way. Just don't steal from me."

I could see Amy's head bobbing up and down in agreement, as she stared down at the phone.

"And this thing that Cory told Elton he needs," Amy began, "do you know what he was talking about?"

"I mean, I guess, but how can I be sure?" The frustration and fear were evident in Valerie's voice. "When he wants things, he always says he *needs* them, but I'm trying to teach him the difference. Let's see, he's always saying he needs a dirt bike, but I just can't afford one. He says he needs a pit bull, too, but I'm afraid of them, so I told him he could get one after he moved out of the house. I mean, is he talking about a dog? That could be it, but I'm not sure. Do you think Elton was planning on helping him steal a dog to keep at his house? Because Cory knows he can't keep a dog at my place."

"We're not real sure." Amy glanced at me to see if I had any questions. I shrugged. It didn't seem like Valerie knew enough to help us, but that wasn't unusual. As a former teenage boy myself, I knew it wasn't typical for us to confide in our mothers much. My mom never knew what was going on in my life, and I was fine with that.

Amy thanked Valerie and promised to update her as soon as we had any word on Cory.

While I drove through the water, careful not to leave the roadway, I pondered all of the information we had gathered so far. Something we'd learned earlier was nagging at me, but I didn't know how it related to what we already knew about the case. Meanwhile, Amy continued searching through Elton's cell phone.

"He doesn't have many apps on his phone," she said, "and based on his internet search history, he's really a boring fellow. I don't know why Valerie—or any woman—would be interested in him."

"What was he looking at?"

"He wanted to know how long to bake chicken breasts in the oven," she said. "He tried to find out how to *dress to impress*. He searched for someone who delivered flowers in his area, which translates roughly to, *How do I beg forgiveness for being an asshole?* He searched the tax brackets for the upcoming year. Just a bunch of boring shit."

While listening to Amy going over Elton's internet search history, I kept an eye on my surroundings. We were driving through the front half of the storm, where the wind and rain were still battering everything in its path, and I was not interested in having a tree branch or some other debris come flying through my truck window and put us down.

"Okay, now we're getting somewhere," Amy mused. "He did a search for incubators. We don't have internet connection, so I can't see the images or where he purchased it, but we should be able to find out once we get this thing connected to the internet someday. I'm guessing that won't be soon."

"Did you check his picture file yet?" I asked. "Maybe he took a screenshot of the incubator and other things from the internet. It might give us some clues about what was going on with him and Cory."

"I was going there next," she said. "Let's see…the last picture he took was of his foot. Why, I have no clue, but he took a picture of his foot. There's a picture of the chicken he apparently cooked in the oven, along with a screenshot of the instructions. Dumbass can't even bake a chicken without cheating. Let's see…here's one of him and Valerie sitting on a swing. One of Cory with a DeWalt drill in his hand. Oh, wait a minute, here we go. He's got a picture of the incubator in the shop, but it doesn't have a room built around it. He built that room later."

"When was that picture taken?" I asked, growing more excited as she talked.

"Three months ago," she said. "There are no *after* pictures, but we know what it looks like now. Before that, he's got some screenshots from the internet of a few different types of incubators. I guess he went with the cheaper one. But you know what? I didn't see any internet searches relating to emus or emu eggs, and there're no pictures of them so far. He was lying about that."

My ears perked up. "Are there any pictures of alligators?"

"Yeah, he's got a few alligator pictures, but they look like screenshots and not some he took on his own," she said.

"What about his search history—did you find anything about alligators?" I asked. "I have a feeling the boys were messing with alligators, and that's why Ruben got attacked."

Amy could sense my excitement growing, and it spurred her on. She began mumbling to herself.

"Let's see…" Her thumb slid rapidly across the screen, scrolling through Elton's search history. Finally, she stopped and pulled the phone to her face. "Here it is—a search about alligators!"

"What's it say?"

"Oh, wait, it's nothing," she said with a huff. "It just asks the difference between an alligator and a crocodile—like a nerd—but there's more. This search is about alligator attacks in the United States. This one asks what's more aggressive, a gator or a croc. This one…"

Her voice trailed off. I glanced over at her and saw her scowling. She started working the phone again and I saw some pictures come up.

"What's going on?" I asked.

"That's the end of the internet searches, but I thought I saw more alligator pictures."

A strong gust of wind rocked my truck and it swerved in the roadway. It was so unexpected that Amy jerked in her seat and the phone fell from her hands.

"Shit!" she said. "I think I had something."

She bent in her seat and scooped the phone from the ground. "He took a screenshot of information on hatching alligator eggs and—"

"Holy shit, that's it!" I said. "That's what they're up to!"

CHAPTER 38

Amy glanced over at me. "What do you mean?"

"The thing that Cory said he *needs* and that Elton did when he was a kid," I said, snapping my fingers with one hand while gripping the steering wheel with the other. "I bet he wants to harvest some alligator eggs. Remember how Elton was acting when we found the incubator? I could tell something was off with him, like we had just found him out. It's because the incubator's not for emu eggs—it's for alligator eggs."

"And you think they went into the swamps to steal eggs from some alligator mommas?" Amy asked, her expression filled with skepticism.

"Yeah, that's how the alligator farmers do it," I explained. "It's regulated by Wildlife and Fisheries. The farmers have to get permits to harvest wild eggs from an alligator nest. It's illegal for anyone else to do it, so that's why Elton was hesitant to help out and that's why he lied to us. He knew he would've gone straight to jail for contributing to the delinquency of juveniles."

"And you think some alligators objected to them stealing the eggs, so they killed Ruben?" Amy asked, her brow still puckered.

"Yep."

"We can't arrest an alligator for murder. You know that, right?"

I did, but I didn't answer. I was still trying to figure out what was going on with the case, while surveying the roadway at the same time. My bright lights were on, but they were about as effective as the flashlight feature on my cell phone, thanks to the driving rain and unrelenting darkness.

Something didn't look right up ahead, but it wasn't until we were almost on top of it that I noticed a tree blocking the north-bound lane. I did a quick check for downed power lines. I didn't see any, so I jumped out and grabbed the chainsaw from the back floorboard. I waded right into the middle of the tree, grappling with the branches and cutting them free of the larger trunk. Amy pulled them free as I cut them, and then she dragged them to the shoulder of the road. We worked fast, and made quick work of the tree. The lane was clear within minutes and we were back on our way.

"Seeing you tangled up in that tree got me thinking about Ruben," she said, rubbing water from her face. "Melvin said Red found the boat near the body."

"Yeah," I said with a nod. "So?"

"So, that's not good news for the other boys," she said with a frown. "Had only Ruben died, the other boys would've taken the boat and gone for help. Since the boat remained, then so did the boys. I'm afraid we'll find them dead, all of them eaten by a pack of alligators that were only doing what came natural—protecting their young."

I sighed. Since all of the boys were juveniles, their chances of doing jail time for illegally harvesting alligator eggs were zero, yet Ruben's punishment had been death, and it was quite possible the other boys had suffered the same fate.

"Okay," I said, "let Melvin know our theory and tell him to scour the area where Red found the boat, but only after the storm passes. And tell him to be careful, because the alligators that killed Ruben will still be around, because that's most likely where their nests are—and they'll probably still be pissed off."

Amy nodded and picked up her SAT phone to make the call. When she got Melvin on the line, she told him everything we had discussed and asked him about the weather. They talked for about five minutes and she ended the call just as I was pulling into town.

It was weird seeing Mechant Loup cloaked in utter darkness. That didn't happen often.

"How's the weather over there?" I asked as I continued north toward Elton's house.

"It's blowing over," she said. "He thinks they'll be able to start searching within the next hour or so. He said Brennan Boudreaux, Sid Punch, and Red and Paulie McKenzie all volunteered to help him and Shade search for the boys."

I nodded. There was one thing that could be said about the people in Southeast Louisiana: when there was a crisis, everyone dropped what they were doing and rushed to the aid of those who needed their help. Even people who were feuding with each other would put aside their differences and stand shoulder-to-shoulder, working together as a well-oiled machine.

As for us, the weather was starting to pick up again, so I sped down Elton's street and we hurried inside to search for any computers or other electronics he might have.

I went straight to his bedroom while Amy took the living room and kitchen. There was nothing in plain sight, so I began searching the drawers on the nightstand next to the bed. I hadn't noticed a desktop as I'd made my way through his house earlier, and I wondered if he even owned a computer. Nowadays, most people relied on their cell phones for all of their electronic needs, and they saw no need for large computers with wires running everywhere. Even if Elton didn't possess a desktop, I figured he might at least have an iPad or laptop, but I found nothing.

Once I had given up my search, I returned to the kitchen in time to see Amy heading for the garage. I followed her and waited as she opened the driver's door of Elton's truck. She leaned inside and, within a few seconds, called out that she had found his laptop.

As we headed for my truck, I said a silent prayer that it would provide some evidence that would help us make sense out of what had happened. While our working theory seemed plausible, there was still something very wrong with the case, and I couldn't quite put my finger on it. Hell, I didn't even know if a crime had been committed, other than some wildlife violation that would've merely netted them a written citation and their day in court.

As for Elton, his crime was a little more severe. Depending on what crime he had encouraged these juveniles to commit, he could be facing anywhere from six months to ten years.

That was another part of the case that had me puzzled. What on earth had he told Ray Foret? It seemed obvious that Elton hadn't known about Ruben's death, so that was definitely not what he had told Ray. It was clear that Elton had been trying to protect his relationship with Valerie, while also keeping himself out of jail, but I was certain he would've told us if he thought the boys were in serious trouble. I imagined he was holding onto the hope that they were only late and would simply return later with the boat, at which time they could just appear at their homes with some outlandish explanation about where they had been.

I drove my truck under the police department and shut off the engine, considering another oddity with the case. Why on earth had Elton sent them out to collect alligator eggs with a deadly storm approaching?

"Damn it!" Amy said from the seat beside me. She turned the laptop to face me. "It's pass-protected."

CHAPTER 39

"Let me see the computer," I said.

She handed it to me with a grunt, as though I was too old and outdated to figure it out. She was probably right, but I had an idea. I sat there for a long minute studying the screen, trying to find the button. It was then that I remembered you had to type in the wrong password first, so I quickly typed some random letters and then hit the *enter* key. I smiled.

"What'd you try?" Amy asked. "What'd you type?"

"A bunch of random letters."

"What?" She stared incredulously at me. "You know if you type the wrong password too many times it'll lock us out, right?"

"We're already locked out," I said idly, clicking on the password hint button that had appeared when I'd hit *enter*. I smiled when some words appeared in the box, but then frowned when I read them aloud. *"Three stick-figure crayon picture.* What in the hell does that even mean?"

Amy propped her elbow on the center console and leaned close so she could read the message herself.

"Huh, I've got no clue," she finally said. "Let's go inside and see if anyone else knows."

I nodded and handed her the computer before stepping down from my truck. My legs and arms were sore from being scrunched into the bathtub for hours, and I walked gingerly up the stairs. When we stepped into the radio room, Susan jumped from her chair and came to me as fast as she could move with her pregnant self. She wrapped her arms around me, and I returned the favor.

Over Susan's shoulder, I could see Baylor hugging Amy while

Amy tried not to drop the laptop that she cradled in her hands. When Baylor released her, she opened her mouth to speak, but clamped it shut when Takecia, Regan, and Lindsey ran to her and playfully threw their arms around her.

There was a brief moment of levity, and it felt good to laugh again. At this moment, we were all safe and accounted for. Melvin and Shade were hunkered down in a stout cabin south of us, and the rest of our team was right here in this building. We didn't know what the next few hours or days might have in store for us, but at this moment, we were all okay.

"I need y'all to help us figure out the password hint on this laptop," Amy said when they released her. "What does *three stick-figure crayon picture* mean?"

"It's the lyrics to a country song," Regan said immediately. "It's called My Boy by Elvie Shane. It's about a man dating a woman who already has a son. He talks about how the boy doesn't have his eyes and stuff because he's not the real dad, but it doesn't matter—"

"Cory Verdin!" Amy and I said in unison, cutting her off.

"What about Cory?" came a voice from the hallway.

We all turned to see Valerie Verdin standing there in shorts and a T-shirt. Her hair was a mess and her eyes squinted against the bright lights. The poor woman had apparently finally fallen asleep, but must've been stirred from her slumber when we showed up.

"That belongs to Elton," I explained, pointing to the laptop. "We think he was using your son's name as his password."

The corners of her mouth turned down into a frown. "Really?"

I glanced at Amy, who had placed the laptop on the desk beside Lindsey's chair. Her fingers stabbed briefly at the keys and then she straightened.

"Yeah, he used Cory's name as his password," she announced. "The boy must've been a big deal to him."

Valerie threw a hand to her mouth and her eyes moistened. I could tell she was beginning to wonder if she had been wrong about Elton, and I knew what was coming next.

"But…where's Elton?" she asked, searching my eyes. "If you have his computer, where is he? Is he here? Does he know something?"

Although I could wear a poker face during an interrogation, Valerie wasn't a suspect and I wasn't interrogating her. She was a mother who was worried to death about her missing son, and I knew my eyes betrayed me under her scrutiny.

"Oh, no," she said, stepping closer to me. "Something's happened to Elton. What happened?"

"Let's go in here," I said, motioning toward the break room, "where we can talk in private."

Her tanned features faded as I held the door for her. Once we were inside, I offered her a chair. She fell into it and closed her eyes.

"Just please tell me nothing's wrong with Cory," she said breathlessly. "Please, just tell me."

"We don't know anything about Cory," I said quickly. "We're still looking for him, but there have been some developments."

She opened her eyes and steeled herself for what was coming. "What kind of developments?"

"Elton's gone," I said softly. "Ray kidnapped him and tortured him in an attempt to extract some information from him about the boys. Ray was convinced Elton knew something about where the boys were, and he decided to take the law into his own hands."

"What?" her mouth fell open. "Are you kidding me? This is a joke, right? This kind of thing doesn't happen here. That's absurd!"

"No, ma'am, this isn't a joke." I took a breath. "Detective Cooke and I just came back from the camp where Ray was holding Elton."

"But…but how is he?" she asked. "You said he was tortured. Does he need a doctor? Where is he?"

"I'm sorry to have to tell you this, but Elton…well, he died during the torture," I said in a soothing voice. "Ray shot him in the leg and it looks like the bullet hit an artery and he bled—"

Valerie sucked in a breath. Her eyes then rolled back in her head and she fell out of the chair.

CHAPTER 40

I quickly leaned forward and caught Valerie before she could hit the floor.

"Sue," I called, "can I get some help in here?"

Susan and Amy immediately appeared in the doorway, and Amy rushed forward. Before she could reach me, Valerie's eyes were wide again and she was asking what happened.

"You fainted," I said, and moved away so Amy could tend to her. I looked over at Susan, who had a rain coat on and keys in her hand. I frowned. "Where're you going?"

"The eye's over us, so I'm heading to the Foret residence," she explained. "I'm taking Baylor with me. We'll bring Wendy back here and I'll break the news to her. Regan and Takecia are gonna make some passes through town to see if anyone's in need of immediate assistance. I was listening to the radio, and they said the storm's losing energy fast, so that's good news."

Even though the eye of the storm was upon us, I didn't want her going out there, because it was still dangerous. There could be trees and power lines down, as well as other debris in the roadways. There would definitely be roofing shingles scattered around with nails still attached to them, making flat tires a real possibility. However, it wasn't my call.

"Please be careful," was all I said.

She smiled and winked. "I'm always careful."

"If you need backup, feel free to pull out Baretta," I said, winking back at her. "Any boy of mine will come out ready to fight."

"We're not naming our son after a porn star," she whispered, and then walked away before I could say anything.

I joined Amy at the table. She had returned Valerie to her chair and the distraught woman was holding a glass of water with trembling hands.

"I...I just can't believe Elton's gone," she said. "And the thought of Ray torturing him just makes me sick. Did...did Elton know anything? Did he say where Cory was?"

"Ray said Elton knew where the boys were supposed to be, but he refused to tell us," I said slowly. "He also said that Elton had an idea about what might've happened, but he wouldn't divulge that information either."

"Well, let me talk to him," she said, standing to her feet. "I'll be damned if he denies me that information."

I shifted my feet under the table. "I'm sorry, ma'am, but Ray's no longer with us either."

She blinked, then turned from me to look at Amy. When she turned her gaze back to me, she sighed, realization setting in. "Y'all had to shoot him," she said in a weak voice. "That bastard made y'all kill him."

I nodded.

"Ray always was a hothead," she said absently, as she lowered herself back to the chair. As an afterthought, she looked up. "Does Wendy know?"

"Susan's on her way to tell Mrs. Foret right now." I took a breath and hesitated. "And look, there's something else we need to tell you, but it doesn't have any bearing on Cory's well-being."

"What is it?" There was genuine fear in her eyes. "What happened?"

"It's Ruben," I said. "A fisherman and his son found him in the water."

"Is...is he okay?"

"No, ma'am," I said somberly. "He was attacked by alligators out on the lake."

"Alligators?" Her expression of fear had turned to confusion. "What was he doing out on the lake? Is Cory out there now?"

"We've uncovered some evidence that the boys might've been hunting alligator eggs," I explained. "There's a lot of money in harvesting eggs and then hatching them. Elton purchased an incubator and set it up in his shop. It looks like he was preparing to bring in some eggs and hatch them—"

"Oh, no," Valerie said, shaking her head slowly. "The message y'all read to me earlier—the one between Elton and Cory—I understand it now. It was Cory who pushed him to do this. It was all

Cory's idea. It makes sense now. What they were saying in the messages, and how it looked like Cory was the one pushing everything, that's the way it was. Cory was doing it, and he was doing it for us."

Amy and I traded curious glances. I'd already had the idea that Cory was doing this for money, but there was nothing odd about that. Money was as strong a motivator as there was. People made decisions every day based on money—or the lack thereof—and that was a common thing. However, I was positive Valerie knew something we didn't.

"What makes sense?" I asked. "What do you know?"

"It's all my fault," Valerie said. She lowered her head and began to cry. When she spoke again, her voice was so muffled that I couldn't understand what she was saying, and I had to ask her to repeat it.

"I said I should've never told Cory we were in trouble," she wailed. "I knew it would be too much for him. I should've kept it to myself until the last minute."

"Trouble?" I leaned forward and put a hand on her shoulder. "What kind of trouble are you talking about?"

"We're being evicted," she said. "I'm six months behind on the note and the bank is repossessing the house. They've given us until the end of the summer to be out of here. I only told Cory because I didn't want him to be shocked to find out at the last minute. I mean, I knew I would have to eventually tell him because I'd have to take him to register at his new school, but I didn't think it was fair for him to find out so late. I told him around the same time I found out. I wanted him to make good use of the last few months he'd have with his friends. Plus, I didn't want him to leave for the summer without having a chance to say goodbye to the kids he only sees at school."

"Where were y'all moving to?" I asked. "And how did Cory take the news?"

"Not good," she said with a shake of her head. "Not good at all. My dad said we could move in with them, and they live in Alexandria. Cory...he was *really* upset. Ruben and Allen are the only friends he's ever had and the idea of being separated from them was killing him. I was really worried about him. He threw a fit and punched a hole in the wall when I told him. He had school that day and then had to go to work afterward, so I didn't see him until late that evening. I was so scared he would never come back home, but then he did. He was later than usual, but he came home that night and he seemed fine."

"What do you mean when you say he seemed fine?" I asked.

"He wasn't angry anymore," she said. "It seemed strange to me at the time. I mean, he was ready to break stuff earlier that morning, but when he got home from work, he was normal. He had a positive attitude about all of it, and he told me everything would be okay. He said that he knew things would work out. I didn't know what he meant by that, but at the time I figured he had embraced the upcoming change. When school ended and summer came, he went about enjoying it like he always did. He's been as happy as ever."

I nodded thoughtfully. "Has he brought up moving at all since that first time you told him?"

"Not once. He's just been enjoying life and acting normal. I didn't even think to tell y'all"—she indicated Amy and me with a nod of her head—"about the move yesterday when y'all asked about any potential problems. I had no idea it was still an issue, and I certainly didn't know he was planning something like this. I would never allow it. But it all makes sense now. I finally understand why he was acting normal. It was all just a show—an act. He hadn't accepted the move at all. He just wanted me to think he had while he figured out a plan to save the house before the end of summer."

I sighed. Not only did it make sense to her, but it made sense to me now. She was right. The kid hadn't accepted what his mom had told him. Instead, he'd gone to the three most important people in his life—Ruben, Allen, and Elton—and they had devised a plan to keep him in Mechant Loup.

While Elton seemed to love Cory, I had to guess he was mostly motivated by his desire to be with Valerie. Regardless, neither his love for Cory nor his desire for Valerie was as strong as his will to survive, because he had not been willing to get in trouble for Cory. Had he been honest with us from the beginning, we might've been able to reach the boys before it had been too late for at least two of them. As it stood right now, we had no idea exactly where to search, and it might already be too late for Cory and Allen.

"Did Cory ever mention anything about alligator eggs?" I asked, leaning close to Valerie. "Anything at all?"

She shook her head, still seemingly shocked by this new revelation. "This is the first I'm hearing of it."

"Do you have any idea where they might go to find eggs?" I knew she probably had no clue where to look for alligator eggs, but I had to ask. "Did he ever mention in passing where there might be alligator eggs? Like, maybe they had gone camping and he said that he'd seen some eggs out in the marsh somewhere?"

"No," she said. "I didn't even realize that alligators laid eggs. I thought they gave birth like dogs and cats."

"Did he ever mention any place in the marsh that he might like to visit some day?" I pressed.

"None. As far as I knew, they only went to the woods on the east side of town. I never really heard him talk about the marsh or the swamps or alligators." She frowned. "He did go in the boat with Elton, but I don't really know where they would go. Like I told you earlier, Elton taught him to drive the boat, and I know he really enjoyed their time on the water. Maybe that's when they went looking for a place to get the eggs? But if they did, Cory never mentioned it, and neither did Elton."

Valerie sucked in a trembling breath at her own mention of his name. "Elton knew better than to tell me something like that," she continued. "He knew I would never approve."

I sighed and turned to Amy. "You got anything?"

She nodded and asked Valerie a few follow-up questions, but it seemed that Valerie could offer no more than she already had. While there was still Wendy to question, my guess would be that she knew even less than Valerie, and I also figured she would not be in the condition to answer questions after learning that her husband and son had been killed. She would be especially averse to answering questions from Amy and me, considering we were the ones responsible for her husband's demise, so any questioning would have to be done by Susan.

When Amy had finished her inquiry, I asked Valerie if she would like to return to her sleeping quarters while Amy and I got back to work. I told her we wouldn't sleep until we found Cory, and I was careful not to make any promises about the condition in which we would find him.

"I won't be able to sleep," she said weakly, "but it would be nice to lie down."

CHAPTER 41

Amy and I stopped in the radio room to retrieve the laptop, and I asked Lindsey if she'd heard from Susan.

"Yeah, she and Baylor just left the Foret home with Mrs. Foret," she said. "They should be here any second."

"What about Melvin and Shade?" I asked. "Have you heard from them?"

"Yeah, I actually just got off the phone with Melvin," she said with a nod. "They're gonna start searching for the boys at sunrise. He said the back end of the storm isn't as bad as the front half, so everything should be fine."

I wanted to be grateful that it hadn't spawned any more tornados, but I had to be cautious. Although we hadn't received any reports of additional tornados, it didn't necessary mean that there hadn't been any. The town had been out of power and cell service for hours, and a lot of our townspeople didn't own landlines. Most of the old timers still had them, but the majority of the younger families had done away with what they referred to as *prehistoric technology*, so we might have some surprises once it was safe enough to start driving around and assessing the damage.

I thanked Lindsey and headed for my office. Amy pulled a chair around to my side of the desk and sat beside me as I shook the laptop to life. I had to reenter the password. Once the screen was up, I began going through the files on his desktop one at a time, looking for anything that might be even remotely connected to our case.

It was apparent that Elton spent a lot of time on his computer, because he had dozens upon dozens of files. He had thousands of pictures of his handiwork—mostly kitchen cabinets—and since they were mixed in with other pictures, we couldn't just ignore them and move on. We had to make sure the pictures that were interspersed within the files of his work product weren't of evidentiary value.

I found myself closing folder after folder, stopping only twice during the next few hours—once to use the bathroom, and a second time to meet with Susan and Wendy Foret.

As I had expected, Wendy was a total wreck and she was angry at me and Amy for killing her husband. Susan hadn't given her the details about which one of us had pulled the trigger, and I was perfectly fine with the distraught woman blaming me for her husband's death.

"Why did you have to kill him?" Wendy had demanded through her tears, pounding my chest with her fists. I hadn't even tried to stop her, and I didn't defend our actions. I just stood there allowing her to get it out of her system. When Susan and Amy had started to move in to grab her, I had waved them back.

When Wendy had dropped to her knees on the floor, exhausted and drained of energy, I had knelt with her and told her how sorry I was, and that I wished things hadn't gone down the way they had. I also promised that I would do everything in my power to find Allen and bring him back home to her.

The mention of her remaining son had been enough to snap her out of her trance-like state. She immediately scurried to a kneeling position and grabbed my arms.

"Please, you've got to find him and bring him back to me!" she begged. "You just have to! You owe me! He's all I have left now that you've taken Ray from me!"

Out of the corner of my eye, I could see that Amy was not happy about Wendy blaming me for Ray's death, but now was not the time to correct the record, and I certainly didn't want her anger directed at Amy.

Once we had picked Wendy off the floor and sat her in one of the interview rooms, she asked for the details surrounding Ray's death. It was then that we told her exactly what had happened out at the camp, and Amy spoke up to let her know that she had killed Ray.

"He had murdered Elton White and he was about to kill Clint," Amy said pointedly, "and I was *not* gonna let that happen."

Wendy had leaned back in horror and stared from me to Amy, seemingly realizing for the first time that her husband had brought this on himself.

By the time Amy and I were done speaking with her and had left her with Susan, the windows in my office had started to lighten ever so slightly as the day began to break. We returned to searching files, but couldn't find anything even remotely related to alligators.

CHAPTER 42

I had just closed the last file on Elton's computer and the rain had stopped falling outside when Amy reached over and pulled the laptop in front of her.

"I wonder if he's got any hidden folders," she muttered, mostly to herself.

"Hidden folders?" I asked, suddenly not feeling as computer-savvy as I had earlier when I'd found the password hint. "How do you do that?"

"Watch the master and learn," she said idly.

I did watch, but her fingers and the cursor were moving too fast for me to learn. Before I knew it, she had the *Folder Options* menu up and was clicking a box that read, *Don't show hidden files, folders, or drives*. After clicking it, she closed the box and stabbed at the screen.

"Read it and weep!" she said.

I stared in awe as three folders appeared on the desktop. They were faded and harder to see than the others, but they were there nonetheless.

Amy clicked the first folder and opened it. There was only one Word document inside, and she accessed it. We quickly glanced over it, but it contained nothing but passwords for his bank accounts, social media accounts, and retirement savings account.

"Good thing we're not thieves," Amy said. "He shouldn't leave his passwords on a Word document like that."

She closed the folder and opened the next one. In this one, there were several Word and Excel documents, but they were all related to his business. With a frustrated sigh, Amy closed out that folder and double-clicked on the last one.

"Well, here goes nothing," she said when the folder opened.

We both stared for a second, as it mostly contained media files and it was in the *Details* view. The dates were displayed, so we could see that all of the files had been created within the last few months. Instead of opening each file individually, she switched to the *Extra Large Icon* view and a thumbnail of all of the images appeared at once.

I leaned close and squinted. "What have we here?"

"Here's a picture of alligator eggs." She pointed the cursor at one file and clicked on it. When it opened, we could better see a plastic basket containing several alligator eggs resting on a metal shelf.

"The fact that he kept it in a hidden folder," I said, throwing the phrase around like I was an old computer pro, "tells us he was involved in some shady shit."

She nodded and advanced to the next slide. This one was a screenshot of the exact brand name and model number of the incubator that we'd found in his shop. The next slide was a screenshot of an article that talked about several men from Florida being arrested for poaching alligator eggs.

"Even if ignorance of the law was a defense, he couldn't claim it," I said. "He knew damned good and well that what they were doing was illegal."

"Yep," Amy said, advancing through the next few slides, which were pictures of an existing alligator farm.

"I guess this was their ultimate goal," I said, "to have an alligator farm of their own, but that would take a lot of land and access to fenced pools and such so they wouldn't wander off."

"Yeah, it would be hard to raise alligators in his shop," Amy said, pointing to the next article that we came to. "According to this, the sale of baby alligators is lucrative business."

I nodded thoughtfully as she continued to flip through the images in Elton's hidden folder. A nagging thought kept coming back to mind, and it was related to something Cory had mentioned in his text message to Elton.

We'll just say we were camping and found them and no one will know where we went.

I scratched my head. It was illegal to poach alligator eggs without a permit, regardless of where they were located, so it didn't make sense that Cory would say that to Elton. And what did he mean by *where we went*? Was that what Ray had learned from Elton? Was there something significant about the location of the eggs? But what if the text message had nothing to do with the eggs?

I shook my head. Surely, they were referring to the alligator eggs. It could be nothing else.

"Wait, stop right there," I said to Amy when she had advanced to the next slide and some maps appeared. "That's a map of Lake Berg."

I leaned close and studied it. There were no markings on the map, so I told her to go to the next slide, which was another image of Lake Berg, but this one was from the satellite view.

"Where was Ruben found?" Amy asked.

"I'm not sure," I said, "but according to what Red described, I would say it was somewhere in this area. Melvin can tell us more once they start searching."

I glanced at the window in my office. While it was still overcast and windy outside, it was getting brighter. Official sunrise was still about an hour away, but it was light enough to start searching, and I knew Melvin and Shade would already be on the move.

I was thinking about calling them as Amy continued clicking through the slides. More maps appeared, and some of them had markings on them. Mostly, the markings depicted routes to and from different parts of Lake Berg, along with the travel times associated with each route.

"What in the hell were you doing?" I asked in a low voice, as though hoping Elton would speak to me through his computer. I grabbed Amy's arm when she advanced to the next slide. "You see that route?"

She nodded.

"It begins in Bayou Tail behind Elton's shop," I said, tracing my finger north along the bayou to where it curved around town and then headed to the west. The map had been magnified and there wasn't enough room to fit the entire route, so I waited while she advanced to the next screen. This portion of the map showed the route into the middle of Lake Berg, but it was also cut off.

"Go to the next one," I said slowly, my curiosity growing along with my suspicions. When the next part of the map appeared, I sucked in my breath. A red star had been placed over several alligator farms, and the route led from one to the other. The boys weren't swiping eggs from wild nests—they were stealing them from alligator farms! "I bet Elton's plan was to have the boys go to these locations and swipe a few eggs from each farm. If you steal a bunch of eggs from one farm, the owner might notice and report it, but if you grab a few eggs from each, it would be easier for the theft to go unnoticed."

"So," Amy began slowly, "you think Ruben got eaten at one of these farms?"

"His wounds make perfect sense now. A lot of those farmers keep any number of alligators together in a pit, where they feed them regularly, and if Ruben fell into one of them, the gators would've figured him for dinner." I stabbed at each of the stars on the map. "We'll find Allen and Cory at one of these farms. I just hope they're still alive."

Amy scowled. "But if that's where they were heading and that's where you think Cory and Allen will be, then how'd the boat and Ruben get to the opposite side of the lake?"

I shook my head slowly, studying the map. Everything was starting to make sense except for that one important question. If the boys had rescued Ruben from the pit and driven his body to the opposite side of the lake, then they would no longer be at any of the farms. Eaten the way Melvin had described, there was no way Ruben had freed himself from the pit and then driven the boat out of there.

"It's possible one of the boys took Ruben away and the other was left behind," I said, holding out my hand for her SAT phone. "Regardless, we need to call Melvin and have him check the farms as soon as possible."

CHAPTER 43

Red McKenzie's Camp
Earlier

Melvin opened his eyes but didn't move. He had taken a seat on the floor in the living room after speaking with Lindsey on the phone earlier, and had decided to get some rest. No one knew when they would have a chance to sleep again, so the men had ignored the storm outside and taken advantage of the down time. Shade was stretched out on the floor against the opposite wall, and he heard the younger man stir.

The violent rocking of the camp from earlier had been reduced to an occasional tremble, and the beating of the rain on the metal roof had ceased. Although the wind still howled outside, it was nothing compared to the screaming that had taken place throughout the night.

Something had awakened Melvin, and it took him a second to realize that it was the gradual brightness enveloping the room. While the sun hadn't risen yet, it was light enough in the cabin to distinguish shadows, and he could see Brennan Boudreaux on the sofa and Sid Punch in the recliner. Both men were snoring softly.

Melvin pulled himself quietly to a seated position and noticed an instant reaction from Brennan, Sid, and Shade. All three sat up and rubbed their eyes.

"Is it that time already?" Brennan asked. "It seems like I just closed my eyes."

"It's light enough to see where we're going," Melvin said, "so I'm heading out now. If those boys survived the night, they'll need us to find them quickly."

There was stirring from one of the two bedrooms in the camp, and Red emerged fully dressed, and also wearing a slicker suit.

"I'm ready," he said. "I know what it's like to have a boy missing out in the swamps, and we can't waste a minute."

Melvin and Shade beat Brennan and Sid to their feet, but not by much. Paulie came from the back carrying a duffel bag and a large spotlight, and all six men had soon made their way out from the protection of the camp.

There was a heavy dampness to the air and, although everything was cloaked in dark shadows, it was easy to see that the roots of at least a dozen trees had lost their grips on the earth, thanks to the strength of Hurricane Ursula's winds, and they lay in various positions of rest. One giant cypress had fallen on Red's boat shed, while another was suspended precariously over the center of the camp, held in place only by a single arm of a nearby oak tree.

"Hey, Dad," Paulie called, pointing to the cypress tree over the camp. "If that thing falls, we won't have a house anymore."

Red nodded grimly, but didn't say anything.

Melvin grabbed his flashlight and walked over to where Shade had parked his truck. Although it was covered in cypress needles, Spanish moss, and oak leaves, it appeared unscathed. Next, he checked on Elton White's boat. It was still operable, and so was the boat in which Brennan and Sid had arrived. Red's boat, though, was demolished.

Melvin went to Shade's truck, retrieved his AR-15, his rucksack, and a chainsaw, and then headed for the boat. Shade grabbed his own rifle and a backpack, and followed Melvin, stopping beside him when they reached the wharf.

"Why do we need our ARs?" Shade asked.

"Have you ever tried to shoot a moving gator with a pistol?"

Shade shook his head slowly. "But I heard about Clint shooting Godzator with his pistol."

"Right, and it didn't work out so well for him." Melvin lowered his gear into Elton White's boat. Paulie was already sitting on the bench at the stern, and he was holding a .22 rifle in his hands.

"There're a lot of gators where we're going," he continued, "and—judging by the damage to Ruben's body—they like to gang up on humans. If we find the boys, there's a good chance it'll be around one of those nests. It'll be surrounded by gators, so we might have to start shooting lizards. If we do, we won't have time to plink at them with our pistols—we'll need to blow their asses out of the water."

Shade nodded his understanding.

Melvin indicated Sid with a nod of his head. "Do you want to get in with Paulie and me? That way, Shade can get in with Brennan and we'll have a law enforcement officer on each boat."

Sid—who had already boarded Brennan's large flat boat that had three rows of split-bench seats for giving swamp tours—nodded and grabbed his gear. He made his way onto Elton's boat and took the seat beside Melvin.

Once Shade had joined Brennan and Red, Melvin waved for Brennan's boat to lead the way so Red could show them where he had located Ruben's body. The travelling was rough at first. They had to stop several times to pull out the chainsaws and cut a path through the fallen trees, and it was considerably brighter by the time Red pointed to the area where he'd found the boat. It was still gloomy and the wind continued to howl, but it was nothing compared to what they had just been through.

Melvin slowed the boat he was driving and pulled up beside Brennan's aluminum hull.

"How far away from here did you find the body?" Melvin asked Red.

Red scowled and scanned the area. He finally turned and pointed to an area about two hundred yards away where a tree had fallen across the water, but he glanced at Paulie for confirmation before identifying it as the right tree.

Paulie nodded. "That's the one."

"Yeah, it is," Red said. "He was tangled up in that mess. It was hard to get him out because the wind was blowing hard and we had to climb out onto the trunk with the branches sticking up all around us, but I felt like we had to do it. It just seemed wrong to take his boat and leave him here. Besides, I knew his body would never be here after the storm, and that…that would've been the worst for his family."

Melvin frowned, knowing the man was thinking back to when they had been searching for Zeke. He wondered if this task would be too difficult for Red and Paulie, but he decided Red was a grown man—much older than him—and he could decide what was best for himself and his son.

Melvin knew it would be impossible to find tracks or any sign at all that the boys had been here, so he was going to suggest riding their boats along the shoreline in hopes of spotting the boys inland, but before he could do so, his SAT phone rang. He glanced at the screen and saw that it was Amy. However, when he answered, it was Clint's voice.

"Hey, man, it's good to hear your voice again," he told Clint. "Amy said y'all had one hell of a night."

"Yeah, it's not one I'd like to repeat anytime soon," Clint said, and then quickly got to the point.

Melvin nodded as he listened. When Clint finished talking, he ended the call and turned to Brennan and Sid.

"These boys weren't out here poaching eggs from nests," he explained. "They were trying to steal from your farms."

"What?" the men echoed in unison.

"Clint found a map on the suspect's computer that detailed nearly every alligator farm out here," Melvin explained. "He thinks they had planned to steal a couple of eggs from each of y'all so none of y'all would notice anything missing."

"Ain't nobody stole none of my eggs," Brennan said, shaking his head. "I was at my place all day until late last night when we left to head back inland, and I didn't have no visitors. I didn't see nobody on the lake. Everybody was gone. What about you, Sid?"

"I didn't see a single person out on the water yesterday, and I was at my camp all day. I can tell you for sure that nobody robbed me, unless they did it after we left." He paused for a moment and then scowled. He indicated Red. "But that can't be, because you had already found that boy by then, right?"

Red nodded.

"When Brennan picked me up," Sid continued, "we left from my farm and headed straight to your place. We didn't see a soul, and there was nothing wrong when I left, so nobody robbed me."

Melvin nodded thoughtfully, not bothering to explain the difference between robbery and theft. Instead, he named the alligator farms that were listed on the map that Clint had found on Elton's computer, and he suggested they split up.

"Brennan, we can head across the lake and check on the farms," Melvin said, "while you, Shade and Red search this area, if that's okay. There's still a good chance the other two boys made it out this way and got into trouble here."

Brennan nodded his head.

"If those other two boys made it this far, why'd they abandon the boat?" Paulie asked. "The storm wasn't that bad before we found it, so why'd they stop here when they did? They weren't out of gas, so they could've kept going."

"That's a good question," Melvin said. "I just hope we can find them and get some answers."

Sid spat a stream of tobacco into the water. "If those boys spent the night outside in that storm, they're goners. Grown men couldn't have survived that demon, so there's no way two tenderfoot boys did."

Melvin figured he was probably right, but he also knew they had to try and find Allen and Cory. He was afraid this was a recovery mission, rather than a rescue mission, but he was still hoping for some good news.

CHAPTER 44

The water on Lake Berg was extremely choppy, and Melvin had glanced at Paulie a few times, wondering if he should turn back for the kid's safety. Although they were all wearing personal flotation devices, if Paulie got tossed into the water, he could be hit by any number of logs or other debris that were being tossed around by the rough water. One blow to the head from any of those objects could spell the end for the boy, and he was all Red had left.

"How're you doing, Paulie?" Melvin asked once they'd reached the opposite side of the lake and were coming upon the first alligator farm.

"I'm fine," he said, his voice not betraying an ounce of fear. "This is nothing."

Melvin grinned. The little swamp rat was certainly tough. He had proven that on more than one occasion, but Melvin was hoping he didn't have anything left to prove in his young life. He had already been through enough shit to last a lifetime, and he wasn't even old enough to get married yet.

Once Melvin had pulled the boat up to the wharf, Paulie jumped out first and tied the line to the cleat. There were signs along the wharf welcoming guests to get down and tour the place, but there wasn't much to see. They ran into a locked gate on the boardwalk that led to the office, but it didn't deter them. They scaled it with ease and continued along the boardwalk toward the office.

Melvin placed his flashlight against the glass of the door and peered inside, but it was secure. They continued toward the alligator pits and toward where the incubation chambers were stored. They yelled loudly over the noise of the slapping waves and bending trees as they called out the names of the missing boys, but their voices died on the wind and they received no response.

The alligators were crammed into the pits like sardines in a can, and Melvin felt sorry for them. He made a mental note to have wildlife and fisheries come out to visit this farm to see if they were overcrowded. When they reached the incubators, they found them all locked.

"Ain't nobody been here," Sid said, resting his rifle on his shoulder and surveying their surroundings. "Look, why don't we head to my farm next? It's about three miles that way. I left my boat tied with enough rope to ride a twenty-foot tidal wave, so it should be okay. If it's still floating, I can take it and check the farms north of my place while y'all hit the ones to the south. We can meet back up where Brennan and your guy are searching when we're done."

Melvin was thoughtful. He liked the idea of dividing their forces and adding another boat to the search, but there was the matter of communication.

"Do you have a SAT phone?" he asked Sid.

The old timer shook his head. "I never seen no use for one of them things. If I want to talk to somebody, I take my boat to their camp."

"How will you let me know if you find one of the boys?"

Sid's brow furrowed as he pondered the question. Finally, his eyes lit up. "I can fire a shot in the air."

"No," Melvin said quickly. "Never fire a shot in the air—it's not safe—but you can fire a shot in the ground. If you find one of the boys, fire one shot, wait five seconds, and then fire another shot. If both boys are together, fire three shots total in five-second intervals."

Sid nodded, and the three of them headed back toward where they'd left the boat. Paulie was the first to reach it, and he returned to the bench at the stern before Melvin and Sid had gotten to within fifty feet. Melvin noticed that his eyes were constantly roving. First, he scanned the surface of the water, stopping to visually inspect every object within view. Next, he scoured the tree line, trying to penetrate the depths of the woods that lined the lakeshore. And then, he would repeat the process all over again.

The clouds were thick and dark overhead, which made the shadows in the swamps almost impenetrable. The heavy wind caused the leaves and underbrush to rustle something fierce in the woods, which would make detecting movement almost impossible. The same was true for the surface of the water. The lake was choppy and the waves made it hard to differentiate between the various objects that were being tossed around—many of which could have easily been mistaken for a floating human body—but Paulie was not dissuaded by the difficulties of the job, and he was not fooled by his surroundings.

Melvin nodded his approval. He loved the kid's intensity and admired his knowledge of the outdoors, and he said so to Sid.

"Yeah, that's a good boy," Sid mumbled. "It's a shame about his brother. Those two were inseparable until…well, until what happened to Zeke. I know it just about killed Red. I remember driving over to his camp right after it happened one night and found him on the wharf with his shotgun. I don't know what he planned on doing with it, but I had an idea. So, I tied up and sat next to him. I started talking about everything I could think of under the sun, including Paulie, and before long, he was laughing. I don't know what you're supposed to say to a man in a situation like that, but I thought he needed to be reminded of his other boy. After he started laughing and telling stories about when they were young, I figured he would be okay."

"You did a great job," Melvin said in a low voice, slapping Sid's back in the process. "You probably saved his life."

Sid dismissed the comment with a wave of his rough hand, and the two men boarded the rocking vessel.

Melvin didn't mind the rough seas. He always found the rocking motion of a boat soothing and relaxing, even under the pressures of their current situation. He leaned forward to release the line from the cleat that was attached to the side of the dock, and then gave a push to send the boat gliding toward the open water. After taking his seat, he pushed the throttle and headed in the direction of Sid's camp. As a precautionary measure, he glanced over his shoulder every now and then to make sure Paulie hadn't been bounced from the boat, and it was during one of these backward glances that he noticed the boy stand wobbly to his feet.

"There!" Paulie shouted. "Over in the woods—there's something moving!"

CHAPTER 45

Melvin turned his attention to where the boy pointed, but didn't see anything along the edge of the shoreline. He shifted his focus farther inland and that's when he noticed a flash of movement that seemed out of place in the rustling leaves. It was located about several dozen yards from the water's edge, where the ground was significantly higher, and it was moving in an upward and downward motion. With each upward thrust, he could see flashes of white.

Imploring Paulie and Sid to hang on tight, Melvin turned the boat in the direction of the movement, but realized in a flash that he would not be able to make it to the bank of the lake. A long line of trees had been blown over by the wind, and they blocked direct access to the land. There was a narrow opening between two of the nearest trees, and it was through this thin alleyway of greenery that Melvin headed, but there was no way the boat would get any closer to the land.

Melvin slowed and shut off the engine when they were close enough to grab onto one of the trees. When the noise from the motor had faded to nothing, they could hear the muffled cries of what sounded like a young boy, and those sounds were coming from the spot Paulie had pointed out in the trees. Now that they were close enough to hear the human cries for help, the white flashes of color made sense—they were a pair of boy's sneakers, and the legs attached to those shoes were kicking up and down wildly. It seemed the boy was consciously trying to get their attention.

It was obvious to Melvin that the reason the boy hadn't risen to his feet when he'd heard their boat approaching was because he was pinned beneath one of the fallen trees. It was also possible he was trapped under multiple trees, because it seemed half the forest had come down in this area.

"This is where me and my dad saw the tornado," Paulie explained, extending an index finger and running it from left to right across the horizon. "It went right across there."

Melvin sighed heavily. It would take a chainsaw and a dozen strong men to free the kid, but they didn't have a dozen strong men.

"Hey, there," he hollered at the kicking feet. "Are you okay?"

"No!" a boy screamed in a weak and muffled voice. "I'm not okay! I've been stuck here all night. I can't move my left arm. It's stuck under a tree and I can't get out. Please help me!"

Melvin winced inwardly. If the tree had been resting on his arm all night, then there was a good chance the weight of it had significantly reduced the blood flow to his limb, and that could mean he would lose that arm.

"What's your name, buddy?" Melvin hollered as he removed his gun belt, hung it over the steering wheel of the boat, and then sat down to remove his boots.

"Allen," said the terrified boy. He then mumbled something that was unintelligible. Melvin could barely see him from his vantage point, because the trees were thick and they were too far away, so he told the boy to conserve his energy.

"I'll have you out in no time," Melvin said assuredly, although he wasn't sure. There were at least ten to twelve broken trees strewn about like matchsticks, and it would be a job just to reach the kid. However, he needed to exude confidence for the kid's sake, so he told him he could rest easy because the cavalry was here. "All you have to do is lie still and rest. We don't know what other injuries you might have, and I don't want you making anything worse by moving the wrong way. Just let me do all the work."

Melvin saw Sid grab onto a nearby branch and secure the bow line to it. He nodded his thanks and stood in his bare feet. The puddle of water that sloshed around the hull of the boat felt surprisingly warm, and he was grateful for that one miracle. He didn't relish being wet again, but there was no other way around it. He would have to wade through the water and start cutting a path through the trees in order to reach Allen. At least he wouldn't also be cold.

After making his way to the bow of the boat carrying his chainsaw, Melvin lowered himself into the lake and paused for a second to allow the water to completely saturate his clothes. He felt the sloppy mud of the lake bed seeping between his toes as he sank to his ankles, and he grimaced as he reached for his boots. He would want them once he reached the land.

The water was only chest-deep in this area, but an occasional wave would reach his face and one even went over his head. He held the chainsaw and his boots high above him to keep them from drowning, and he was grateful when he finally reached the original shoreline, which was still three feet under water, thanks to the surge that the storm had pushed into the lake.

Although the low-lying area of the shoreline was inundated, the ground wasn't as sloppy as earlier, and Melvin's feet were able to get better traction. The spot where Allen was located was on higher ground and well beyond the dangers of flood waters, and that was a very fortunate thing. Had the tree fallen on him just twenty yards earlier, he would've drowned on his face.

"I'm almost there, buddy," Melvin called as he stopped to put on his boots. "I just need to find a pathway through this mess."

Allen strained and twisted his head around in an attempt to see Melvin, but Melvin told him to relax.

"Are…are you gonna hurt me?" Allen asked.

"Of course not," Melvin said. "I'm here to help you. I'm with the police department. We've been out here all morning looking for you. Your mom and dad reported you missing."

"You're a cop?" The boy's voice was weak and he sounded exhausted.

"Yeah, I'm with the Mechant Loup Police Department." As Melvin talked, he climbed over one trunk and then another, careful not to slip on the rounded and slick surfaces. Wet branches whipped at his face and arms, and sent droplets of water cascading over him. He was still about twenty feet from the boy when he slipped and his leg shot out from under him. Luckily, he was holding onto a stout branch with his right hand, and the most that happened was he swung backward and slammed into a nearby trunk. Somehow, he was able to maintain his grip on the chainsaw.

After letting out a few curse words, he righted himself and continued the dangerous trek across the twisted wreckage left behind by the tornado. When he finally reached Allen, he paused for a breath and to study the branches that extended in every direction from the tree that rested on top of the boy. A large limb had stabbed the ground violently a mere foot from the back of Allen's neck, and Melvin shuddered when he noticed it. Just a few inches in the opposite direction and Allen would not have been alive to kick his feet and alert them to his presence. Had he died, they might never have found him. It was rare for anyone to come this far out into the swamps to clear trees that had been dropped by a storm. And if they did, it was usually only to clear out the shoreline. The rest were left as they had fallen, to provide shelter and other resources for the abundance of wildlife out there in the swamps.

Melvin quickly devised a plan that would allow him to cut Allen free from his trap without causing more injuries. He could see the limb that was resting on the boy's arm, and if he cut the wrong branch first, more weight could come to bear on the arm and might make things worse. Of course, judging by the deep purple color of the exposed hand, Melvin didn't think it could get any worse.

Allen began mumbling something when Melvin was upon him. His words were coming in rapid succession and his voice was fading, so Melvin couldn't make sense out of the message he was trying to relay.

"Just relax and slow down," Melvin said. "I can't understand anything you're saying."

When the boy didn't respond, Melvin leaned close to his head and listened to see if he was breathing. He was, but it was shallow. This boy was in trouble.

CHAPTER 46

Melvin quickly went about the task at hand, first cutting away the branches that prevented him from reaching the part of the tree that was crushing Allen's left arm, and then cutting the trunk just above that location to lighten the load that was bearing down on it. Once he was ready to make the final cut to free the boy, he gently tapped Allen on the back. The boy stirred.

"Allen," Melvin said, knowing the boy was in extreme pain, "I need you to slide over to your right when I tell you to, okay?"

Allen's head shifted a little to indicate that he understood, but instead of moving, he screamed and began to flail about when Melvin made that final cut. The arm was free now, but it flopped when the boy lifted his left shoulder from the ground.

Melvin dropped the chainsaw and put pressure on Allen's back, pinning him to the ground.

"It's okay to scream," he said, "let it all out."

And Allen did. Once the boy had calmed down, Melvin helped him to a seated position and propped his back up against one of the nearby branches so he could look at the arm. It was mangled above the elbow, where the flesh was torn and the humerus bone was exposed, while everything below the elbow was a deep purplish color.

Upon touching the back of Allen's hand, Melvin found that it was ice cold. He frowned. He was no doctor, but he knew there was no way of saving the arm.

"It hurts so much!" Allen said weakly, the tears streaming down his pale face. "I'm scared to look at it. Is…is it bad? Is it broken?"

"Did you feel any pain when it happened?" Melvin asked,

ignoring his question.

"A lot," he said with a nod, "but then it stopped hurting and I couldn't feel it anymore. It was numb for most of the night. I tried to pull it out from under the tree a few times and it started hurting again, so I stopped. When I heard your boat coming, I tried to pull myself free, but it hurt too much, so I started screaming and kicking my legs. I didn't think you would see me. I thought I was gonna die out here."

"Well, you're safe now." Melvin removed his life vest and then his BDU shirt, wearing only his BDU pants and a white T-shirt now. "I'm gonna make a sling with my shirt and then I'll strap your arm real tightly to your chest. It's gonna hurt a bit when I move it, but we need to immobilize your arm without doing more damage. In order to do that, I'll need you to stay still and not fight me. Can you handle that?"

Allen nodded his head and gritted his teeth. "I think I can, but if it starts to hurt too much, can you stop?"

"Sure." Melvin tore off a piece of the shirt, fashioned a sling out of it, and looped it around the back of Allen's neck. Moving as slowly as he could, he then lifted the damaged arm and eased it into the sling. He heard Allen gasp when he first touched the arm, but then the boy gritted his teeth and grunted silently, truly putting up a courageous front.

Once the arm was resting in the sling, Melvin tore more strips from his shirt and used them to secure the arm against Allen's chest. When he tightened down the knot, a guttural grunt escaped from Allen's throat and the boy cursed.

"I'm done," Melvin said. "All we have to do now is get you on your feet, over these trees, through the water, and into the boat. Can you move your legs, or did they fall asleep?"

Allen wriggled his legs to show that they were mobile, and Melvin took his right wrist and elbow in both of his hands and slowly helped the boy to a standing position.

"Whoa!" Allen said, swaying and reaching for something to grab onto with his good hand. "I'm dizzy."

He was about Melvin's height but much thinner, and Melvin knew he could carry the kid if need be, but he didn't want to. If he slipped like he had earlier, Allen could fall and rip what was left of his arm completely off. Melvin moved around him and lowered his left shoulder.

"Put your arm around me," he told the boy. "I'll support your weight all the way to the boat."

Allen hesitated, staring at the mangled trees that stretched before them. "Do we have to go through that? What if we go around to someplace where the boat can get closer to the land and where there aren't as many broken trees? I...I don't know if I can make it."

"There's no other way," Melvin explained, pointing in the direction from which he had come. "That's the shortest distance to the boat. We're surrounded by fallen trees, so if we go in any other direction we'll have to crawl through more of this stuff. Unless..."

Melvin paused and peered through the leaves in an attempt to put eyes on the boat, but it had drifted away from the narrow lane between the trees. It was out of view. He could still hear the water lapping against the hull, and he could tell it was still nearby.

"Hey, Sid," he called, "do you think you can get the boat closer?"

He turned and watched the beads of sweat form on Allen's forehead as he waited for Sid's response.

"No!" came his reply. "Even if we all had chainsaws and worked for an hour, we wouldn't be able to reach the bank. The trees are just too thick."

Melvin apologized to Allen and, gathering up his chainsaw, began picking their way through the timber that he had cut away from the offending tree.

"Is there an ambulance coming?" Allen asked. "I feel like I'm dying. It hurts so much and I feel so weak."

"You've lost a bit of blood, so it's normal to feel weak," Melvin said, trying to keep him calm. "As soon as we get to the boat, I'll use my satellite phone to call ahead for an ambulance. The storm's already blown through, so they should be able to meet y'all at the boat launch."

"You...you're not coming to the boat launch?" Allen asked, pushing his way gingerly through a patch of leaves.

"No, I have to stay behind to look for Cory."

Allen swallowed hard and nodded his head, and Melvin got the sense that he already knew what had happened to Ruben. He had a lot of questions for the boy.

"Do you know where I can find Cory?" he began as he helped Allen over some tangled branches that they came to. The boy leaned heavily on him as he stepped over them, and Melvin knew the dizziness wasn't going away. He had hoped that the feeling would pass once the boy had been standing for a while, but it seemed like the problem was persisting.

"The last I saw of Cory, he was running that way," Allen said, indicating the south with a nod of his head. "We got separated when the trees started falling. I don't know if he got hit like I did, or what, but I never saw him again."

Melvin paused and looked toward the entanglement to his right. If Cory was somewhere under that mess of trees, they might never know it until every tree had been removed—and that would take days or weeks to get done.

Allen had no choice but to stop walking, and he stared off in the direction that he had pointed out to Melvin.

"Do you think you'll find Cory?" he asked softly. "It doesn't even look like you can walk through there."

"We'll find him," Melvin said with a nod. "One way or the other, we always do."

He didn't want to explain what he meant by *one way or the other*, so he gave a nod for Allen to continue walking. The boy didn't. Instead, he just stood there searching Melvin's eyes.

"Will…" His voice trailed off and he licked his chapped lips. "Are you gonna also find the man who killed my brother?"

CHAPTER 47

Melvin opened his mouth to speak, but nothing came out on the first try. Finally, he asked Allen what he was talking about.

"I'm talking about my brother, Ruben," Allen said, resting his weight on Melvin. "He was with us last night. You asked about Cory, but you didn't ask about Ruben, so I thought y'all didn't know about him."

"We knew he was out here with y'all," Melvin said slowly, "and we did find him, but he wasn't killed by some man. It was some alligators that got him."

"Oh, I know it was the alligators that got him," Allen explained, "but it was a man who pushed him in the tanks."

"What?" Melvin's heart turned cold. "What man? What tanks?"

Allen lowered his eyes and hesitated.

"Look, we know all about the plan to sneak into the alligator farms and steal some of the eggs," Melvin said. "I'm not the one investigating the case, but I can assure you that everyone will agree y'all have been through enough. And I don't need every detail, just enough to help me search for who did this."

"We…um, you're right. We were going to different alligator farms to gather some eggs—just like you said—and we were taking turns getting them. Cory got an egg from the first place, I got two from the second place, and then, when it was Ruben's turn, he left and was gone a long time. We started to worry about him."

Allen took a deep breath and exhaled shakily. "Cory and I were waiting by the dock and the wind was blowing really hard and we couldn't hear anything, so we started walking toward the farm. We didn't get far when we heard a loud scream. It sounded like Ruben, so we ran to see what was wrong. Before we could reach the incubation tanks—I think that's what Cory called them—we heard Ruben scream again and then...then that's when we saw a flashlight from over by the alligator tanks."

Melvin scowled, trying to wrap his mind around what he was hearing.

"The man was holding the flashlight and a rifle," Allen continued, "and he had both of them pointing at Ruben. We...we thought he was gonna shoot Ruben, but he pushed him instead. He pushed my brother right into one of them big tanks full of alligators. And he pushed him hard, too. Ruben went flying backwards and he disappeared in the tank. It...it scared the shit out of us."

"Are you sure?" Melvin asked. "Are you sure someone pushed your brother?"

"Yes, sir." Allen nodded vigorously for emphasis. "We saw him clear as day. He didn't see us, though, and we hurried and jumped in the trees next to the wharf, because he started walking toward our boat."

"When you say *your* boat..."

"I mean Mr. Elton's boat," Allen corrected. "He was always loaning it to Cory, and he let us use it last night."

"You do realize you've been out here for two nights, right?" Melvin asked.

Allen was thoughtful. "I've been trapped under that tree for two nights?"

Melvin nodded.

"Huh." Allen seemed surprised.

"What happened next?" Melvin asked.

"We, um...we hid for a while, and then we saw that man dragging Ruben to the boat. I don't know where he went with him, but he left in Mr. Elton's boat and we never saw him again. It...it was the last time I saw my little brother. I...I'll never forget..."

Allen's voice trailed off and he began to silently cry.

"It's okay," Melvin said, squeezing his shoulder. "Let it all out, buddy."

As he waited for Allen to continue, Melvin looked up and scanned his surroundings. His jaw was set. So that's how the boat and the boy had gotten to the other side of the lake. It suddenly made sense. He reached for his pocket to retrieve his SAT phone to call Shade, but remembered he had taken it out of his pocket before entering the water.

"Did you get a good look at the man?" Melvin asked when Allen had stopped crying enough to answer his questions.

"A little," he said with a nod. "I mean, it was dark most of the time, but he had a light when he pushed Ruben and he used it when he was dragging Ruben to the boat, so I saw him a little bit then."

"Let's go," Melvin said quickly, squatting under Allen's arm. "Let's get you out of here so I can call some people to start looking for that man while I search for Cory."

As they continued picking their way through the fallen trees, Melvin asked if Allen remembered where the camp was located.

"I think it was over there somewhere." Allen nodded his head toward their left. "We hid out until daylight because we heard alligators splashing not far away, but I couldn't sleep. Every time I closed my eyes, I saw Ruben. I don't think Cory could sleep either. He kept saying it was all his fault, but I told him it wasn't."

"Did he say it was his fault because it was his idea to steal the alligator eggs?" Melvin asked, casting a sideways glance at Allen.

Allen hesitated. "Is he gonna get in trouble?"

"I doubt it. Like I told you a minute ago, I believe everyone will agree that y'all have been through enough."

"Yeah, well, I guess that's why he was saying it was his fault. He needed the money to save his house, and me and Ruben were gonna help him get it. I mean, he would've done the same thing for us."

Melvin nodded. "What happened with the tree?"

"That was later during the day yesterday—" Allen suddenly stopped. "Wow, I guess we really were here for two nights. It seemed like only one very long night."

"Did Elton pick y'all up after baseball practice on Monday?" Melvin asked.

"Yes, sir."

"Today's Wednesday."

"Oh, man, I feel like one of those people that got abducted by aliens and lost time."

Melvin nodded, and asked again what had happened with the tree.

"We got lost at some point after the sun came up, because we ended up walking away from the water instead of toward it, and it took us most of the day to find the shore again. Once we did, we started following the lake again, but by then the weather was getting bad. That's when we saw that water spout. We could see it for a while, but then it disappeared. All of a sudden, we heard some noise through the trees, and it sounded like a train was coming. That's when we started running. Cory was faster and he was well ahead of me when the trees started crashing all around us. I couldn't even see him anymore when the tree fell on me. I think…I'm afraid one of them might've gotten him, too. I yelled out for him a bunch of times, but he never yelled back."

"So, you think he's in this area?"

Allen nodded, but didn't say anything more as they carefully made their way through another stand of fallen branches. Melvin found himself almost carrying the boy over some of the larger branches, because he was too weak to lift his legs that high.

Melvin had grounded his chainsaw about ten yards behind them—since he was staying behind to search for Cory anyway—and it was making it easier for him to guide Allen through the maze of trees. They made better time and were soon at the edge of the water.

"Here," Melvin said, offering his life vest to Allen, "put your right arm through the hole and I'll snap it in place."

Allen didn't object. Once the vest was secured around the boy, Melvin removed his boots and asked Allen if he wanted his shoes removed.

"They're already wet," he said, "so it doesn't matter."

Melvin then steadied Allen as they descended the gradual slope of the shore. As he walked, his mind was leaping ahead. He would help Allen get onboard the vessel and then ask Sid to take the boy to the boat landing, where he would arrange to have an ambulance waiting. As for Paulie, if he wanted to stay behind and help him search for Cory, Melvin would welcome the assistance.

When they pushed through the heavy leaves of a tree that had fallen lengthways along the shore, Melvin noticed that Elton's boat had drifted away from the tree to which it was secured, and it was rocking gently on the open water. Although the wind had died down a little and the clouds weren't as angry as they had been earlier, the line attaching the boat to the tree was taut, and Melvin knew if it broke free, the boat would be pushed all the way to the other side of the lake, unless there was some intervention on the part of those onboard.

Melvin snarled as he thought about the killer transporting Ruben's body across those same waters, only to toss the boy out like last week's trash. The bastard was probably still out here somewhere, just lurking in the shadows. Melvin needed his SAT phone. Not only did he have to call for an ambulance, but he had to call Clint and give him the latest information. They would have to try and identify the farm at which the attack had happened, and that should lead them to the killer. This might be easier said than done without Cory, since he had been the one orchestrating the egg thefts with Elton, and he would be more familiar with the layout of the area.

"Watch your step," Melvin said to Allen as they reached the edge of the original embankment. "The bank drops off sharply in a few feet, but it's impossible to see because of the flood."

Allen just nodded and watched his every step. He still seemed a bit woozy, and Melvin was starting to worry about him. He was lowering his left leg into the deeper water off of the bank and holding Allen steady when he felt the boy stiffen.

Suddenly, and before Melvin could look up, he felt a burning sensation along the back of the arm that was steadying Allen, and it was followed almost instantly by the explosion of a rifle shot. A small hole about the size of a pencil eraser suddenly appeared in Allen's chest, and the boy sank to his knees.

Melvin's right hand instinctively moved to his hip, but his brain knew it was a waste of time, because his gun wasn't there—it was in his gun belt on the boat. He looked up in time to see Sid standing on the bow of the boat working the lever action on his 30-30 rifle. The man then coolly lifted the rifle, pointed it directly at him, and pulled the trigger again.

CHAPTER 48

One mile from Melvin's location

Amy and I were making our way as fast as we safely could across the lake to find Melvin.

Once the back end of the storm had blown through town, which had been a few hours after daybreak, she and I had launched the cabin cruiser and set out for Red McKenzie's place. The water had been rough and—as was the case with all storms—had turned into a minefield of visible and invisible obstacles that could destroy one's boat in an instance. The last thing we had wanted was to get tossed into the drink, so we had been forced to take things extremely slow. Even though we were equipped with Coast Guard approved personal flotation devices, we knew better than to take anything for granted. We had worked numerous cases where some well-equipped and highly skilled individuals had died from being crushed between floating logs or snagged in underwater debris and drowned just beneath the surface of the water, and we weren't ready to be discussed in the past tense.

Once we'd made it to Red's place, we'd found that the boats were still somewhere out on the water. Amy had tried calling Melvin on his SAT phone, but he hadn't answered. She'd called Shade next, and he told her about where we could find him.

"Did y'all find anything?" I'd asked Red McKenzie when we'd located them. Red and Brennan Boudreaux were in the boat, and Shade was searching a patch of swamp grass where an alligator nest was located. I noticed he kept his AR-15 held in a ready position, just in case he was attacked.

"No," Red had responded. "Melvin, Sid, and Paulie are checking the alligator farms across the lake, but we haven't heard from them in a while."

I'd glanced at Amy, and she had tried calling Melvin again, but he still hadn't answered his SAT phone. That had me worried, and I'd said so to Shade when he'd returned to Brennan's boat. I asked if they had more area to cover on this side of the lake.

Shade had glanced at Brennan, and the old alligator farmer had shrugged.

"We've got one more nest to check on this side," Red had said, but there was a scowl on his face. "I don't understand how we didn't find them yet. The boat was tied to a tree when me and Paulie found it, so that means the boys definitely drove it here. It didn't just drift across the lake on its own, you know? They have to be here somewhere. I don't know where they could've gone."

A dozen different scenarios had played through my mind, but I hadn't taken the time to discuss them. I'd just nodded and reached in my pocket to pull out the maps we'd found on Elton White's computer. I'd handed a copy to Shade.

"We're gonna head this way"—I'd dragged my finger across the map—"backtracking the route that Elton had planned out for the boys. Hopefully, we'll run into Melvin soon. In the meantime, I want y'all to check that last alligator nest and then circle the lake in the opposite direction. Y'all can stop and check the alligator farms to see if the boys are there, but be quick. We need to find Melvin."

"You think something's wrong with Melvin?" Red had asked, his voice laced with concern. "Paulie's on that boat with him."

I had hesitated, wondering if the phone meant anything. It was possible Melvin couldn't hear it over the boat motor, and it was also possible he'd lost it. However, I didn't get to voice any of my concerns—or lack thereof—because my hesitation was enough for Red.

"To hell with that last nest," Red had said. "We're leaving now! I'm going find my boy!"

And so they had. As Amy and I had headed for the opposite side of the lake, Shade, Brennan, and Red had headed to the north to begin searching that shoreline.

Now, as we were nearing the opposite shore and approaching the first alligator farm at the end of Elton's list, I saw movement from a thick stand of cattails. The perennials extended from as far to the south as I could see toward the north, where they ended at the tree line. A lot of the tall plants had been pushed over by the strong winds that had swept across the area overnight and into this morning, so it made it easier to see the figure that was jumping up and down waving his arms.

"Clint!" Amy clawed at my arms, her nails digging into my flesh. "I think that's Cory Verdin!"

We were still some distance away, but I was inclined to agree with her. Even under the gloomy conditions in which we found ourselves, I could clearly see a head of bushy brown hair bouncing up and down.

I was tempted to gun the engine and race to the water's edge, but there were too many obstacles littering the waterway. I did speed up a little, and I was pushing the hull of the boat against the banks of the lake just as the kid was breaking through the cattails.

"Help!" he cried out, waving his hands hysterically. "We need help!"

Before I could shut off the engine and head to the foredeck, he had leapt up, grabbed onto the railing that was attached to the gunwale, and came aboard.

The front door to the cabin was open and he rushed inside. He took one look at my gun and dropped to his knees, seemingly exhausted and relieved, but still terrified. I recognized him from the picture that Valerie had given me of her son. The joy I felt was overshadowed by what he said next.

"My friend," he said through gasps, "someone killed my friend."

I shot a confused glance at Amy and then squatted in front of him. "Allen?" I asked. "Someone killed Allen Foret?"

"No." He shook his head, still trying to catch his breath. "Ruben—Allen's brother. A man pushed him into an alligator pit. The...the alligators tore him apart. It was horrible. We could hear him screaming the whole while, and then the man stole Mr. Elton's boat and took Ruben away. I guess he wanted to hide the evidence, but we saw him. We saw him and we got away without him knowing we were there."

"Who was this man?" I could feel my mouth hanging open. "Where'd this happen?"

Cory brought himself higher on his knees and pointed toward the north. "Somewhere over there," he said. "It was the third alligator farm on the list."

I pulled out my copy of Elton's map, unfolded it, and held it so Cory could see.

"Show me where," I said.

He pointed to Sid Punch's farm, and my heart suddenly ran cold.

I knew instantly that Melvin had run into trouble with the man, and that's why he wasn't answering his phone.

"It was right over here near the incubators," Cory was saying, but I was barely listening anymore. "The man caught him trying to steal the eggs and pushed him into a pit filled with alligators…"

Cory's voice continued to drone on as he stared blankly at the map, but I was barely listening. I jumped behind the wheel and pulled on the throttle to back us away from the shore. I didn't have to say anything to Amy, as she was already trying to call Melvin's SAT phone again.

"He still doesn't answer," she said, her expression a mix of concern and anger. "If Sid did anything to him, I swear I'll murder that son of a bitch!"

I only nodded as I tried to navigate the precarious waters of Lake Berg. Amy called Shade next and told him what we had just found out from Cory, and she asked him to head directly for Sid's farm with Brennan and Red.

I had never been to Sid's farm, but according to the map, we were still about a mile away when I rounded a bend in the lake and heard something that made my heart leap in my throat. Although the boat motor was roaring and the wind was whipping against the cabin, there was no mistaking the sharp crack of a rifle echoing across the water.

"Clint!" Amy shouted, pointing off in the distance. "Over there! That's them!"

I revved the engine and the cabin cruiser shot forward, rocking roughly every time we hit some form of underwater debris. The gray sky reflecting off the water made it difficult to discern objects in the distance, but I was sure I saw a boat rocking on the rough seas near a stand of fallen trees. The boat appeared to be that of Elton White, and there was a large figure standing on the foredeck with a long gun. It didn't look like Melvin and it was too large to be Paulie, so it had to be Sid.

As we closed the distance to about five hundred yards, I noticed the large figure jerk a little, and the movement was consistent with him having fired the gun he was holding. A moment later, the sound reached us, but what we actually heard sounded like two shots being fired almost simultaneously. The first was a *popping* sound, while the second was the sharp crack of a high-powered rifle round.

I was confused. Was there a gun battle raging down there? Had Melvin somehow discovered that Sid was involved and they were shooting it out? If so, how had Sid gotten Melvin off the boat? And where was Paulie?

We were within four hundred yards now. Out of the corner of my eye, I caught sight of Amy pushing Cory to the floor. She hollered at him to keep his head down and not move, and then she grabbed her AR-15 and pushed open the door to the cabin. Although she rested her rifle against the frame, I knew it would be impossible for her to hit anything at that distance from a rocking boat. She knew it, too, and I was confident she wouldn't attempt a shot under such conditions, but she was definitely getting ready for battle.

Before the echoes of the most recent shots had faded, I saw a large limb from a floating tree appear just under the surface of the water. I swerved sharply to the right to miss it, and then quickly corrected my steering. As the bow shot back to the left, I caught a quick glimpse of the shoreline toward which Sid had been firing, and that was when I realized who was in his crosshairs—it was Melvin and a boy with blazing red hair, and there was no way we would reach them in time to save them.

CHAPTER 49

The stern of Elton White's boat
Earlier…

Paulie McKenzie had been sitting patiently on the bench waiting for Officer Saltzman to return with Allen Foret. He and Sid could hear the chainsaw whining as Melvin went to work, but they couldn't see him anymore because Melvin had disappeared through the thick trees that were scattered all over the banks and at the edge of the water. He had wanted to move the boat back to a place from which they could see what was happening, but Sid had overruled him.

"It'll just keep drifting back over here," the rough man had said. "We'll be fighting it all day."

Paulie had never seen things this bad in the swamps. On the ride to this location, he had marveled at all of the downed trees, and wondered about their ages. His dad had once pointed out some cypress trees that he'd said were 100 years old, and Paulie had seen at least one of them down near their camp. It made him kind of sad to think that he would grow old and die before another tree could replace that one and all the other ones that had been destroyed by the storm.

Suddenly, a loud scream was heard from the area where Melvin was rescuing Allen, and then the chainsaw stopped. Sid had jumped to his feet and was holding his rifle in his hands. That move scared Paulie.

"What's the matter?" he asked. "Why do you have your gun? Is something wrong?"

Paulie saw Sid's shoulders relax after a second and the man

waved him off.

"It's nothing," Sid said. "It was just the boy. He must be hurt."

"Do you think the chainsaw got him?"

"No."

Paulie scowled and wondered how Sid could be so sure that the chainsaw hadn't gotten Allen. Accidents with chainsaws happened all the time and Allen had screamed like he was hurt really bad, but Paulie just shrugged and waited. He scanned the trees and water that surrounded them. He had found the first missing boy, and he wanted to find the other one. He was certain Cory was around here somewhere, because friends don't just separate in the swamps. He was confused about why Ruben was on the other side of the lake with the boat, and Allen was over here, but he knew Officer Saltzman would figure it out. His dad had told him Melvin was better than a bloodhound at tracking things down.

Paulie wasn't sure how long they sat there waiting, but Officer Saltzman's phone rang at least a dozen times. The first time it did, he reached for it, but Sid told him not to touch it. Sid said it was government property and he could get in trouble for touching it.

"But what if something's wrong?" Paulie had asked.

"Nothing's wrong." Sid had waved a dismissive hand in his direction. "You just sit there and don't worry about anything. I've got everything under control."

Finally, after what seemed like hours, a voice called from somewhere beyond the trees along the shore.

"Hey, Sid." It was Officer Saltzman. "Do you think you can get the boat closer?"

"No!" Sid hollered back, staring intently toward where Melvin's voice had originated. "Even if we all had chainsaws and worked for an hour, we wouldn't be able to reach the bank. The trees are just too thick."

"I think we can do it," Paulie said. "I'm good with a chainsaw."

"I've already made my decision, boy," Sid said, never taking his eyes off the trees.

Paulie was watching the trees, too, and he could hear Officer Saltzman and Allen making their way through the mess that the tornado had left behind. Every now and then Allen would cry out in pain or Melvin would curse, and each time it sounded like they were getting closer and closer.

Finally, there was movement near the edge of the water, and Paulie bent low to see through the bushes.

"There they are," he said. "I see them."

Sid moved to the bow of the boat and was leaning forward, shading his hand over his forehead.

"Hey, kid," he called over his shoulder, "grab the bow line and pull the boat toward those trees to our right."

Paulie moved forward and reached around Sid to get the line. He noticed the man was holding his rifle and his knuckles were white as he gripped them.

"What's the matter?" he asked.

"Just pull us to the right," Sid said gruffly.

Shrugging, Paulie did as he was told. He pulled gently on the line and the boat glided toward the trees. He reached for an overhanging branch to slow them down, and that's when he saw a flash of movement from the bow. When he looked, he saw Sid bringing the rifle to his shoulder. Almost as soon as the rifle came up, it bucked in Sid's hands and let out a deafening roar.

"What the hell?" Paulie said in horror, as he saw Allen flinch and reach for his chest. He shot his eyes upward and saw Sid working the action on his rifle, and it looked like he was going to fire another shot…but at whom? And why?

Paulie had done a lot of squirrel hunting during his time in the swamps to help feed him and his dad. Squirrels were a fleeting animal and you had to be quick to shoulder your rifle and shoot if you wanted to put food on the table. All the years of practice had developed within Paulie what his dad had once called *muscle memory*. Paulie didn't fully understand what it meant, but he did know that his rifle suddenly seemed to appear in his hands from nowhere, and he took quick aim and fired one shot to the back of Sid's head.

The low echo of his rifle was drowned out by the booming of Sid's 30-30, and Paulie nearly screamed. He couldn't see around the larger man and he dared not move, because Sid Punch was still on his feet and he was still holding onto his rifle.

Paulie sat there in shock and disbelief as he watched Sid sway on his feet. The man slowly began to turn toward him, blood dripping from a tiny hole in the back of his head. Sid's rifle was pressed up against his hip and leveled straight ahead—the way many a cowboy did in the Western movies that Paulie had watched over the years— and the barrel was swinging slowly around as though searching for him.

Scared to death, Paulie shouldered his rifle and prepared to fire another shot. He swallowed hard and it felt like tiny shards of glass were scratching their way down his throat. His stomach churned. The first shot he'd fired had been purely instinctual. He hadn't thought about it. Like when he was squirrel hunting, he had simply reacted to a situation. Now, though, as he thought about having to shoot this man again—to possibly *kill* him—he didn't know if he could do it.

"I'm sorry, Mr. Punch," he said as the man continued to turn toward him. "I don't want to have to shoot you again, but I will if you make me."

Paulie could feel his mouth moving and he recognized the voice as his own, but the words sounded foreign to him. And the voice was much more confident than he felt.

Still unsure of what he should do, he aimed down the barrel and put his finger on the trigger. His dad always taught him to never put his finger on the trigger until he was ready to shoot, and he realized at that moment that he was ready to shoot.

He was about to start applying slow, rearward pressure on the trigger when he noticed the muzzle of Sid's rifle dip a little. The man's right shoulder seemed to sag in unison with the movement of the muzzle, and then both of his hands seemed to go limp. The 30-30 slid from his grasp and clanked loudly to the hull of the boat.

Paulie quickly removed his finger from the trigger and continued to watch as the man turned.

When Sid was facing him, Paulie noticed that a large knot had formed on the man's forehead just above his left eye, and there was a confused expression on his face. As his left eye slowly puffed up and closed right there in front of Paulie, the large man plopped to a seated position on the gangway, teetered there for a moment, and then fell into the black water. He rolled once and then sank into the darkness.

Paulie made no attempts to retrieve him.

CHAPTER 50

100 yards from Melvin's location

Throwing caution to the strong wind that blew around us, I raced toward Elton's boat, intent on driving the cabin cruiser directly through Sid Punch. We were closing fast when I noticed him turn to face the stern of the boat, the rifle falling from his hands. That's when I saw Paulie standing there holding a rifle of his own. It was a small rifle, but it was pointing at Sid. I suddenly remembered the other shot that had been fired—the *popping* sound—and realized that the boy had shot Sid in the back.

I quickly pulled back on the throttle and the boat sat down hard in the lake. Our back waves caught up with us and rocked us roughly as I turned my attention toward the shore. I sucked in a mouthful of air and exhaled in relief when I saw Melvin moving through the water, carrying Allen Foret on his shoulders.

That moment of relief was immediately replaced by concern for the boy, whose lifeless head rocked roughly up and down with each giant step that Melvin took. I turned toward Elton's boat and noticed that Sid had fallen into the lake and was no longer a threat.

I worked the throttle and sidled up beside Elton's boat. Paulie looked over at us, but his eyes were still wide with shock and he was holding his rifle loosely in his hands, as though it were a grenade about to go off.

Amy hurried to the deck and reached out for Melvin, who had changed direction and was walking toward our boat. Once he was close enough, Amy grabbed Allen from his shoulders and pulled the boy up onto the deck. I had already grabbed the emergency first aid kit and rushed past Cory to help Amy, and it was then that I noticed a dime-sized wound in the boy's chest.

"He's hit bad," Melvin said from the water, "but he's still breathing. I don't think it got his heart, otherwise he'd already be dead."

I knelt beside Amy and went to work helping her stop the bleeding. I didn't need to flip Allen over to know the bullet had gone clean through, and that it had caused considerable damage on the back end. Sid had been armed with a 30-30 rifle and the distance had been short, so Allen was in trouble.

I handed Amy the bandages for which she asked and then helped to slowly turn Allen over so she could work to stop the bleeding to his back. I glanced over at Melvin while I held pressure on the wound for Amy. He was heading toward Elton's boat, but instead of pulling himself onboard right away, he circled to the opposite side. I knew he was going to retrieve Sid's body, and I agreed with that move. Neither of us wanted trash like that polluting our waterways.

Paulie put down his rifle and scrambled to the starboard side to assist Melvin. It didn't take long for Melvin to find the dead man. Once he had, he hoisted the body over the gunwale and Paulie helped drag the limp man onboard. Melvin then pulled himself into the boat and I saw him wipe rivulets of water from his face. He looked up and our eyes locked.

"Is Allen gonna make it?" he asked.

I glanced down at Amy. She frowned and shook her head slowly. "He's gone," she said, wiping a bloody hand across her pant leg. "He must've lost a lot of blood from that arm wound, and this just finished him off."

Melvin cursed the body of Sid Punch as it lay on the hull of the boat.

It was then that I noticed someone standing over me. I turned to see Cory looking down at his friend's pale and mangled body. There were tears streaming down his face.

"First Ruben and now Allen," he said bitterly. "And it's all my fault!"

I quickly stood and put a hand on his shoulder. "I'm so sorry about your friends," I said softly, "but it's not your fault. In fact, had Elton told us what was really going on when we first asked him, we could've gotten here a lot sooner, and Allen might still be with us."

"Elton would never tell on me." Cory's jaw was set as the tears fell. "He would never betray me—that I know for sure."

I scowled. He had no clue that Elton was dead, and I didn't think it was the right time to tell him, so I didn't.

Cory wiped his face and turned to look in the direction of Elton's boat. "Is Ruben in there?"

"No."

"The man who killed him put him in Mr. Elton's boat and left with him," Cory said. "He should still be in there."

I explained how Red and Paulie had located Ruben's body on the opposite side of the lake, along with the abandoned boat, and how they had recovered Ruben's body and brought him to their house.

"That should be me," Cory said, pointing down at Allen. "It's all my fault they're here. They only came because I was trying to save my house from being stolen by the bank. They came here because of me, and they're dead because of me. It…it's all my fault."

Amy was beside us now and she reached for his opposite shoulder. "If Allen and Ruben were about to lose their house and they asked you to help them save it, would you have done so?"

"Absolutely!" He nodded vigorously through the tears.

"And would you have blamed them if something bad happened to you?" she asked.

He hesitated, realizing where she was going with this logic, and then shook his head.

"Right, and they don't blame you," she said. "So, you shouldn't blame yourself. The only person you should blame is the asshole who killed them."

"I want to see him," Cory said, gritting his teeth. "I want to see the man who killed them."

Amy glanced at me, and I shrugged. I didn't see the harm in it, so I waved for Cory to follow me across the deck and to the starboard side of the cabin cruiser. We were elevated above Elton's boat and could see right down into it, so there was a clear view of Sid's lifeless body lying on the floor of the hull.

When Cory stopped beside me and glanced down, he gasped.

"That's not him!" he said. "That's not the man who killed Ruben!"

Melvin and I traded glances just as the sounds of another boat could be heard over the rustling of the leaves overhead. We knew it had to be Shade, Brennan, and Red, because they would be in the only other boat out here on the water.

"What do you think?" I asked Melvin, knowing he was considering the same thing that I was.

"It can't be." He shook his head. "It's impossible. He would never do anything like that."

"Well, we're about to find out," I said, indicating Cory with a nod of my head, "because he can identify him."

CHAPTER 51

When Brennan approached us in his boat, I noticed an immediate shift of his eyes from left to right. He read the scene in an instant, but there was one thing he couldn't see—and that was Cory Verdin.

After a quick consultation between Melvin, Amy, and me, we had decided that Cory should take refuge in the cabin of the boat with instructions not to show his face until we called upon him to do so. If we were to avoid any more bloodshed, we needed to be very careful about how we made our next move.

"What's going on out here?" Brennan demanded heatedly when he saw his friend's body sprawled out on the hull of Elton's boat. "And what in God's name happened to Sid?"

Since he had been shot once to the back of the head with a .22 caliber bullet, the only visible damage to his face was some swelling and bruising.

"It turns out that Sid's the one who killed Ruben Foret," I said calmly from the deck of the cabin cruiser. I stood relaxed, not wanting to make Brennan suspicious. While he might not be able to grab his rifle in time to do much damage, he wore a pistol and a Bowie knife on his belt and—from what I'd heard—he was supposed to be real handy with both of them.

"That's nonsense!" Brennan spat the words. "An alligator attack killed that boy. I saw the wounds myself. Ain't nobody killed him."

"This is Allen Foret," I said, indicating the body bag that now held Allen's body. "He personally witnessed Sid push his brother into an alligator pit on his farm, after his brother tried to steal some of the alligator eggs that Sid had gathered beforehand."

"Sid would never do that," Brennan said, his eyes still roving over Sid's body, trying to figure out what was wrong with him.

"Well, he definitely shot Allen, and then he tried to shoot Melvin," I said, hooking my right thumb into the front of my waistband. "And I don't appreciate someone trying to kill a law enforcement officer, especially one who happens to be my best friend."

Brennan took a breath. "So, this Allen kid, he identified Sid as the murderer?"

I nodded. "And Sid killed him for it."

"I see." Brennan looked toward the shore, which was a tangled mess of twisted branches and snapped trunks. "What about the other boy? Didn't y'all say there were three boys out here? Shouldn't we be looking for the third one?"

"He's gone," Melvin said, shooting a thumb over his shoulder. "A tree got him when they were trying to escape the tornado."

Brennan's tanned face had turned a few shades lighter when he'd first driven up, but the color was starting to return to his cheeks as he began to realize he was in the clear. In that moment, I had no doubt he was the one who had pushed Ruben into the alligator pit, and I would soon be calling on Shade to make his move.

Prior to their arrival, Amy had texted Shade on his SAT phone to say that Brennan was our suspect. She had explained that if Cory identified Brennan, I would ask if any of the camps had significant damage to them, and that would be the signal for Shade to take Brennan to the deck. We were hoping he could control Brennan long enough for the rest of us to board the vessel and assist in cuffing him.

I made small talk with Brennan for a few seconds and then casually glanced toward the interior of the cabin, where Cory was huddled in the corner. I gave a slight nod and the boy slowly raised his head above the starboard-side window. When his eyes fell on Brennan, they widened. It was all the confirmation I needed.

"Brennan, did y'all notice if any of the camps had significant damage to them?" I asked.

As soon as the man opened his mouth to speak, Shade was on him. Like a snake striking its quarry, Shade had leapt from his side of the boat and swept Brennan's feet out from under him. A tough and wiry man who was accustomed to fighting alligators, Brennan was no slouch. Although he had been taken by surprise, he played catch-up in a hurry, and his hand was reaching for his Bowie knife before they went down. Both men fell onto the hull between the split-bench seats, with Shade landing on top of Brennan.

Melvin, Amy, and I all sprang into action immediately and were heading for the fight, but it was painfully obvious that we would never make it in time to do much good. Before I could even issue a warning, Brennan's left hand was driving the large blade of his Bowie knife toward Shade's ribcage. A blade like that would plunge right through a set of ribs and destroy everything it encountered along the way.

As I leapt from the deck of the cabin cruiser and watched in horror, Shade swiftly batted Brennan's arm and the blade swept harmlessly over his back. He then hooked his right arm over Brennan's left, pinning it under his armpit. Grabbing his right wrist with his left hand, Shade gave a violent upward thrust and snapped Brennan's elbow. Brennan never made a sound—not even a grunt—but there was a glint in his eye as his right hand flashed upward from his hip, holding a handful of pistol.

I landed on the deck of Brennan's boat a step behind Melvin, but we were both too late to do anything. The space was too confined and the boat was rocking too much to get off a shot without a serious risk to Shade, and the muzzle of Brennan's pistol was rising fast toward Shade's head.

"Shade!" I hollered. "Look out!"

Shade saw the pistol and started to lean his head away, but he was too late. He would've never gotten out of the way in time, and the only thing that saved him was a heavy boot from Red McKenzie. The scrappy Cajun had taken two lunging steps and kicked Brennan in the wrist, sending the pistol flying through the air and into the lake. Not only did he lose his grip on the pistol, but his wrist made an audible snapping sound and then flopped helplessly as his arm fell to the floor of the hull.

Red wasn't satisfied with disarming Brennan. Letting out a rebel cry, he reared his leg back and kicked Brennan again, but this time the steel toe of his boot connected with Brennan's head, knocking the man unconscious.

I had reached the fracas and wrapped my arms around Red.

"You got him," I said in a loud voice, trying to break through to the enraged Cajun. "You got him, Red."

The large man's shoulders were bunched and his neck was curved, giving off the appearance of a bull about to charge again. I leaned back and looked him in the eyes.

"You got him," I repeated.

It was the third time I said it, but I think it was the first time he heard me. He took a breath and exhaled. His shoulders relaxed and he looked to the other boat, searching for his son.

When I turned my attention toward Shade, I saw that he and Melvin had flipped Brennan onto his face and handcuffed him. He was moaning and stirring a little, which relieved me. I wanted him alive. Dying would've been too easy for this piece of shit.

"You okay?" I asked Shade.

"That old man's fast," he said, rising slowly to his feet. He turned to Red and extended his hand. "I owe you my life."

Red shook his hand, but waved him off. "Anyone would've done the same."

I looked toward Elton's boat and saw Paulie standing there watching us with a blank expression on his face. As Melvin and Shade dragged Brennan to his feet and led him toward my boat, I leaned over the side of Brennan's boat and waved for Paulie to give me his hand. He did and I pulled the two boats closer.

"Are you okay?" I asked.

He only nodded.

"You know you did what you had to do, right?"

"Yes, sir."

I pointed to Melvin. "That man's alive right now because of you."

He nodded again.

"It might feel a little weird for a while," I explained. "Taking a life isn't easy. You might have nightmares and you might have this sick feeling in your stomach for a while, but it's normal. Don't try to fight it. Just let the feelings pass through you. You're a strong kid. You'll be fine."

"Yes, sir."

"And if you ever need to talk, you can call me at anytime—day or night." I tousled his hair. "You did a good job today. We're all proud of you, especially your dad."

Paulie McKenzie smiled for the first time since he'd pulled the trigger on Sid Punch.

CHAPTER 52

Four hours later

After transporting Brennan to the hospital to have his broken arm treated, Melvin and I had brought him to the Chateau Parish Detention Center to be interviewed and booked into jail. The drive to the hospital and detention center had taken much longer than usual, thanks to the storm debris and downed power lines we encountered along the way, but when we were finally seated in a meeting room at the detention center, I advised Brennan of his Miranda Rights and asked if he was willing to give us a statement.

"It was an accident," he said. "Of course I'll give a statement. I did nothing wrong."

I refrained from grunting and listened as he complained about criminals taking advantage of storm evacuations to loot and *rob* people's places.

"Those cowardly bastards would never have the balls to try that shit when they know we're home," he said with a snarl. "They only come around when there's an evacuation for a storm."

"Were you expecting trouble?" I asked.

"We always expect trouble."

"But more so since there was an evacuation recommendation?"

He nodded. "Sid and me, we decided to hole up at my camp for the storm. That camp survived Betsy in 1965 and Katrina in 2005, so I wasn't worried. We decided we would take turns making the rounds of the other camps and farms, to help look out for our friends and make sure the generators kept running for the incubators. Anyway, I was making my rounds on Monday night and I thought I heard a boat leaving my farm. When I got there, I didn't see nothing, but I stopped to check on things just in case. There wasn't supposed to be nobody out there."

"Everyone else evacuated?" I asked.

"Yeah, they were worried about the flooding," he said. "I don't know what made me look in the incubator, but I did, and that's when I saw that two of my eggs were gone. I had just gathered them up, so I knew what I was supposed to have, and the first bin had two missing. That's when I knew what was going on. It's happened before."

He paused to snarl and adjust the sling that held his broken arm before continuing.

"I thought I heard the boat heading toward Sid's place, so I left on foot. There's a trail that leads from my place to Sid's, and I figured I could sneak up on the criminal that way. I was just getting to Sid's place when I heard the door to his incubator creak open." He smiled wickedly. "That's when I knew I had that bastard. I came around the corner and shoved my light in his face and aimed my rifle at him. He screamed like a little girl when he saw me. I told him to move to the alligator pit. I only meant to scare him, you know? If I would've wanted him dead, I would've just shot him."

I nodded, but didn't say anything. I knew why he didn't shoot him, and so did he. He wanted it to look like an accident.

"Go on," I encouraged.

"Well, he didn't move, so I dragged him by the hair until we got to the alligator pit. I kinda held him on the edge a little and asked him what he was doing there. He wouldn't talk, so I shook him a little, just to scare him, but…well, I accidentally lost my grip and he fell. There was nothing I could do. Sid's gators were on him in a flash."

"Did he say anything to you as you held him there?"

"Nope."

"Did you say anything to him?"

"Nah, I just asked him who put him up to stealing my eggs, is all." Brennan nodded. "Yeah, I just asked him why he was doing it and then he slipped."

"What happened next?"

"Um, well, you know, that was about it."

"How'd the body get to the other side of the lake?" I pressed. "I mean, you say it was an accident, but why would you bring the body to the other side of the lake?"

"That wasn't me," he said. "That was Sid."

"Really?" I asked. "What would you say if I told you we have evidence that you left there with the kid and the boat? That it wasn't Sid, but you who drove it out of there?"

Brennan's eyes narrowed and he hesitated for a long moment. "Well, I did manage to get the alligators off of the kid and pull him out of the pit, but it was too late for him. I did bring him to the boat, but only because I wanted to turn his body in and tell y'all what had happened. I drove the boat to my farm and then towed it in with my aluminum hull. When I got back to the camp, that's when Sid said we should bring the boat and the boy to the other side of the lake."

"Why would he suggest that?"

"I guess to keep it safe until after the storm." Brennan shrugged. "I mean, it all happened on his property, so it was his call. He drove the boat to the other side of the lake and I followed and picked him up."

"And who threw the body out of the boat?" I asked. "Because when Red and Paulie found Ruben, he was nowhere near the boat."

"That, I don't know."

"You know what I think?" I asked. "I think y'all went to Red's cabin hunting the other two boys."

"You're wrong. We didn't even know about the other two boys."

"Then why'd you and Sid show up at his camp?" I pressed. "You already said your camp has withstood Betsy and Katrina, so why leave it?"

He hesitated, but clamped his mouth shut.

"And if it was an accident, why would Sid murder Allen in cold blood and then attempt to murder Melvin?"

"You got me there." Brennan raised both hands in a surrender gesture. "That was crazy! I can't believe he thought he could do that and get away with it. I don't know what he was thinking."

"He was thinking of covering your ass," I offered. "He would've killed Cory, too, if given the chance. With both witnesses dead, you would've been in the clear. Thank God Paulie put a bullet in the back of Sid's worthless head before he shot Melvin."

Brennan's face hardened, but he pursed his lips and took a breath. Finally, he spoke again, and his voice was surprisingly calm.

"Look, I've got a lot of respect for y'all." He indicated Melvin with a nod of his head. "He's like family to me. I grew up with his grandpa. I would've killed Sid myself if he would've hurt Melvin."

"But you're okay with him killing Allen Foret, right?" I shot back. "Because Allen could've identified you as a murdering piece of shit."

"I didn't murder nobody!"

"You know, Brennan," I said, ignoring his outburst and leaning back in my chair, "I always figured you for an honorable man and a man of courage—a man who wasn't scared of shit."

"I ain't scared of shit," he said flatly.

"You're scared of the truth." I shook my head. "If you were a man of courage, you would just come out and admit what you did without trying to sugarcoat it. You're like a child who's too afraid of his father to admit what he did wrong. You're just a scared little boy."

"How dare you talk to me like that!" His eyes flashed. "You aren't even from the bayou. You don't know nothing about this place or our people. You're just some outsider who couldn't last a day in my world—"

"I'm from this place," Melvin interrupted coolly, "and I've saved your ass out on that water more than once. And you know what else?"

Brennan blinked, but didn't say anything.

"You're a coward." Melvin leaned close to make sure the older man knew to whom he was referring. "You murdered a helpless kid in cold blood over your precious alligator eggs, and you're too much of a coward to admit it. Like Clint said, you're a scared little boy."

Brennan wilted under Melvin's hard gaze, but he didn't say another word. He just sat there brooding as he cradled his broken arm.

I scowled. I needed him to admit that he had intentionally pushed Ruben into the alligator pit. If he didn't confess, the case against him would be weak. Sure, he had tried to hide the body, but that and everything else that happened since the murder didn't matter as much as the murder itself. Everything he and Sid had done afterward could be attributed to a fear of being liable for a horrific accident on Sid's property and in Brennan's presence. Brennan had no involvement in the shooting of Allen, so that information couldn't be brought up at his trial.

As it stood now, we had no direct evidence that Brennan had intentionally pushed Ruben into the pit. Cory had witnessed the act, but he was too far away to refute Brennan's claim that it was an accident, and it was quite possible that a jury might believe Brennan.

I was about to ask Brennan another question when there was a knock at the door. I turned to see a corrections officer standing in the square window. He waved to me, so I got up and stepped into the hall.

"There's a call for you at the desk," he said. "It's Detective Cooke."

CHAPTER 53

I quickly left the meeting room and followed the officer down the long corridor. Amy and Shade had recovered the bodies of Elton White, Ray Foret, Ruben Foret, and Allen Foret, and had taken them to be autopsied. I hadn't heard from her in hours, and hadn't expected to hear from her this soon. I was hoping she had something I could use to twist Brennan into confessing.

"What's up?" I asked when I answered the phone.

"Hey, they're doing the autopsy on Ruben right now," she said, speaking quickly. "They already did Elton, Ray, and Allen—those were easy because of the gunshot wounds—but we found something interesting in Allen's pocket."

"Oh, yeah?"

"Yeah, it's an SD card from a trail camera," she said. "I shoved it into my laptop to open the file, and guess what?"

"What?"

"It's got thirty-four one-minute videos on it, and one of them shows the moment when Brennan pushed Ruben into the pit. It's got audio, too, and you can hear Ruben begging for his life while Brennan's telling him that it's the last time anyone ever tries to steal eggs on Lake Berg. He told Ruben that his death would serve as a lesson for any future would-be thieves."

"What?" My jaw went slack. "How in the hell did Allen end up with a video of the murder?"

"That's what I wanted to know," she said. "I got Susan on the phone and asked her to talk to Cory about it. He told her he'd forgotten all about the game camera. He said that after they ran away from Sid's farm to hide, he mentioned to Allen that he'd noticed a red light go off in the area where Ruben had been pushed in the pit, and he asked him what he thought it could be. At first, he thought it might've been an alarm that let the alligator farmer know they were there."

"But it wasn't an alarm," I mused aloud. "It was the infrared glow from a game camera."

"Yep!" she said. "Allen knew what it was, and he told Cory it was a game camera. He said his dad had used them before, so he knew how they worked. They figured no one would believe them about the murder, so they went back to get the SD card. Since Allen knew how the cameras worked, he retrieved the card while Cory kept an eye out for Brennan. Cory said Allen came back with two of them. They didn't know if there was anything on the cards, but they planned on giving them to the cops once they got to town."

"Is there anything on the second card?" I asked.

"Nah, you only see some legs moving around and then you hear a scream, which is probably from Ruben."

"That might help, but the first video is pure gold," I said. "It's just what I needed!"

When I entered the meeting room, Brennan looked up. There was a curious expression on his face, as though he had been waiting for the second shoe to drop. I casually took my seat and stared at him for a long moment. Finally, I glanced at Melvin.

"Hey, Mel, did you know that Sid Punch had game cameras set up on his farm?"

The corners of Melvin's mouth turned up slightly. "Is that a fact?"

"Indeed." I turned my attention back to Brennan and watched the color drain from his face. "But you already knew that, didn't you?"

The old alligator farmer hung his head. "It was an accident," he repeated. "I caught the kid stealing and he slipped into the alligator pit. That's what happened."

"You know, Brennan," I said, pushing each word forward like a slow dagger to the heart, "Dexter would've been ashamed of you. If he wouldn't already be dead, this would've killed him. He would've denounced you and disowned you from the family. He was a true man of courage. You, you're just a common criminal who doesn't have the courage to stand up for what's right or admit when he's made a mistake. I thought you were the fabric of this community, but you're not."

Brennan raised his eyes and glared at me under bushy eyebrows. "After what you did to the Parker Brothers, how dare you talk to me that way," he said with a snarl. "You're nothing but a common murderer."

He was referring to the time when the Parker Brothers had broken into my house to murder me for killing one of their brothers, whom I had killed during a robbery incident that had left my first wife and daughter brutally murdered on the floor at my feet. I almost didn't make it through that period in my life, but I felt like I had come out the other end stronger—scarred, for sure, but stronger.

"The difference between you and me," I said with a nod, "is that I owned what I did. I didn't try to lie like a little bitch. I threw myself on the mercy of the justice system and I left law enforcement in shame. I was cleared in the eyes of the law, as you know, and eventually made my way back here, but I never once denied what I did. I owned it. Besides, the men I killed were murdering thugs who killed your brother and sister-in-law. The boy you killed only tried to swipe an alligator egg."

Brennan was brooding now, but he didn't say anything.

"Do you remember hiring me during my lapse in law enforcement to do some swamp tours?" I asked. "You didn't think less of me then. In fact, I remember you telling me once that you would've done the same thing I did. Remember that? You said you respected me for having the courage to do the right thing and for owning it even though I could spend the rest of my life in prison."

I paused for a second to let my words get through that thick skull of his, and then continued.

"Why don't you be the man that Dexter knew you to be?" I coaxed. "You were defending your livelihood out there in all of that chaos. There was a storm approaching, which threatened to destroy your very way of life, and here were these kids trying to add to the damage by stealing eggs that you had risked your life to gather. In defense of your property, and those of your neighbors, you fed this one kid to the alligators and then you went after the other two. While it isn't right, one can understand the stress you were under—"

"That's not the way it happened," Brennan interrupted.

"Oh, no?" I asked. "What'd I get wrong?"

"I wasn't going after the other two boys," he said. "I didn't know there were more. I thought it was just the one kid."

I cocked my head to the side. "Then why'd you track their boat to Red's house?"

He took a deep breath and let out a long sigh. "We were looking for the SD card from the game camera."

Had I been one of my dogs, my ears would've perked up. "Go

on," I said. "I'm listening."

"Look, I'm a man, and I own what I do," he said, clearly trying to regain some level of stature. "I'm not afraid to face the consequences. Sure, I killed that kid, but he deserved what he got, and so did the others. Don't you understand they were taking food from my family? If they do that, then my own family dies, and I would kill anyone who threatened my family."

I didn't agree with his sentiment at all, but I nodded to keep him talking.

"Anyway, after the gators had done their job, I pushed them back and pulled that boy out of the pit," he continued. "I dragged him to his boat and then drove the boat to Sid's farm. From there, I towed it to my camp and told Sid what had happened. He followed me across the lake and we tied the boat up in an area where we knew there would be some wild nests with eggs, and that's where we left the boat. We, um, we tossed the kid in some low-lying branches not far from the nearest gator nest. We wanted him to be found while the wounds were fresh, so everyone could see that he had been eaten by gators. We left the two eggs they had stolen in the cargo hatch, so whoever found him would know he was stealing eggs and that's how he died."

I nodded encouragingly when he stopped to catch a breath. The digital recorder was running, and we were capturing everything he was saying. This confession, along with the video evidence Amy had recovered, might be enough to compel his attorneys to strike a deal with the prosecutors at a later date, and that would save Cory and Mrs. Foret from taking the witness stand to relive the horrors of the last two nights.

"Well, after we placed his body there, we headed back to Sid's place to lock up the incubator, and then we went back to my camp." Brennan used his good arm to shift his broken one inside the sling. "It was the next day when we were making our rounds again—we decided to go together from then on, in case we ran into any more trouble—that I saw Sid's trail cameras and remembered that he had them. I asked him if they were live, and he said he had put fresh batteries in them for the storm. That's when we went around pulling the cards from the cameras, and we realized the card from the ones near the incubator and the alligator pit were missing. The best we could figure, the boy had pulled the cards before he went for the eggs, so he wouldn't be caught on tape."

"Did the other cameras have cards?" I asked.

"Yeah, all of them except for those two," he said. "When we

realized the cards were gone, we headed across the lake to check the kid's pockets, and that's when we saw the tornado coming. We had to take shelter for a while, and when we finally made it across the lake, we saw that the boat and the body were gone. We didn't know if the law found them or if they had been blown away with the tornado, but we knew we had to find them, so we started searching."

"That's what y'all were doing when y'all ended up at Red's place," Melvin said.

Brennan nodded. "When we saw the boat at Red's camp, we checked to see if the boy was onboard, but he wasn't. That's when we went inside and saw that you and the other officer were involved. When y'all told us there were two more boys out there, we figured they took the cards. We knew we were screwed at that point."

"What was the plan going forward?" I asked.

"I'll be honest, the plan was for us to find the boys before they did"—Brennan indicated Melvin—"and feed them to the gators, but when Melvin split us up, I knew we were screwed. My only hope was that the boys had been killed during the storm."

I grunted as I looked across the table at this evil man. I had worked more murder cases than I could count, but I had never worked one where the murder weapon was an alligator. Of all the horrible ways one could die, being eaten alive by a giant prehistoric lizard had to rank somewhere near the top of that list.

"Brennan, you're under arrest for second degree murder in relation to the killing of Ruben Foret," I said with a shake of my head. "My only regret is that you can't be charged with first degree murder, because you definitely deserve to die for feeding that kid to a pack of alligators."

CHAPTER 54

Clint and Susan's house

The chainsaw screamed in my hands as I cut through the thick tree limb that rested against the fence in our back yard. Other than a few broken branches, one downed tree, a busted window in the gym, and some missing shingles on the old woman's shelter, Hurricane Ursula had spared us much of her wrath. Some folks in town had fared better than we had, while others had done worse, but luckily, we hadn't lost anyone to the storm.

When the blade sliced through the large oak limb and it fell to the ground, I stepped down off the ladder and surveyed my handiwork. All that was left to do now was repair the damaged fence, and it would be safe for Grace and our dogs to enter the back yard once again.

Before I could even ground my chainsaw, I heard a delightful screech and turned to see Grace running for all she was worth, trying desperately to keep up with Achilles and Coco. Susan, who was standing at the back door wearing loose shorts, a tank-top, and a smile, had been watching me. Her swollen breasts pushed up through the top of her shirt and her beautiful belly protruded from the bottom. Although she often complained about being pregnant, her face was always beaming.

The dogs reached me first and began sniffing the downed branch aggressively, trying to figure out what had changed and who was responsible. I stepped in front of Grace and scooped her up in my arms.

"Stay away from the chainsaw," I warned. "The exhaust on it is hot and could burn you. Understand?"

"It's tired like Mommy?" she asked, a deep frown forming on her face.

"Not that kind of exhausted, Pumpkin Seed," I said with a laugh. I was about to explain the difference when Susan called out to tell me that my cell phone was ringing.

It was a Friday, and Susan and I had both taken off from work to clean up around the house. Over the past two months we had been going around town helping those who needed it, and it was past time we took care of our own property. I put Grace down and glanced back at the fence, thinking it might be the last time I'd see it for a while.

I kissed Susan on the cheek as I walked by and found my phone where I'd left it on the table. A quick glance told me it wasn't the office, and I was a bit relieved. That might mean I wouldn't have to leave.

"This is Clint," I said, wiping a bead of sweat from my face.

"Clint, it's Britt," said the district attorney for Chateau Parish. "How are you?"

I stood a little straighter when I heard Britt Lucas' voice. "Hey, what's up, Britt?"

"I need to talk to you about Brennan Boudreaux," she said. "I just got out of a long meeting with his attorneys."

I sighed, wondering where this was going. I was pretty sure Brennan's lawyers were looking to make a deal, and whatever deal they wanted would be in their client's favor.

"What do they want?" I asked. "Probation?"

"Almost," she said with a chuckle. "They said he's willing to plead to manslaughter and take the max, and he'll do it at our next hearing which is in two weeks."

"And what did you say?" I asked hesitantly. Britt had been tough on crime while she was an assistant district attorney, but she wouldn't be the first DA to lose her backbone after getting the top job. I had been disappointed by more than a few of them in my time.

"I told them I would take nothing less than a full guilty plea and life imprisonment without the benefit of parole, probation, or suspension of sentence," she said, "but I also told them it wasn't entirely up to me. While it is my decision to make, I want to hear from the family. You're close to Cory, his mother, and Mrs. Foret, so I was wondering if you could ask them how they felt. If they want to go forward—and I hope to God that they do—then we'll fix it for trial."

I assured her that I would speak with them right away, and I ended the call. I didn't waste time getting dressed. I stepped out back to shake the sawdust off of my clothes and to let Susan know where I was headed. Grace wanted to come with me, but I explained that I had to have an important conversation for work, and she understood.

"Finish cutting up that tree while I'm gone," I said to my four-year-old daughter.

"Really?" she asked, her eyes lighting up. "I can use the saw chain?"

I laughed and patted the red hair on her head. "No, Pumpkin, I'm kidding."

She folded her arms in front of her chest and her face dropped into a deep pout.

"Meanie!" she called after me as I turned to walk through the house.

I stopped and turned to face her. "Will I still be a meanie if I take you for ice cream when I get back?"

"Ice cream!" she cheered.

Susan was standing behind her smiling, and she said, "I'll need two of them—one for me and one for our son."

I started to laugh, but then stopped short. "Wait...*what?* We're having a boy? How do you know?"

She frowned. "I was scanning the ultrasound pictures to send one to my mom, and I accidentally saw one that showed his gender."

I studied her face carefully, wondering if it had been an intentional accident. The technician who performed the ultrasounds was always careful to seal the pictures that revealed the gender in a separate envelope and she was careful to never mention *him* or *her*, considering we didn't want to know until our baby was born. The only way Susan could've accidentally found out was if she opened the *sealed* envelope that read, *Do Not Open!*

"Accident, eh?"

A broad smile spread across her face. "It was killing me."

"Me, too!" I rushed forward and wrapped Susan in my arms. I was beaming on the inside. We were having a boy!

"I don't want a brother," Grace said. "Brothers are mean!"

I laughed, but it was brief. I sobered up as soon as I got in my truck and backed out of the carport. I didn't relish having the upcoming conversation with Cory and Wendy. It was bad enough that just seeing me would remind them of that awful time in their lives, and now we had to talk about it.

CHAPTER 55

As I drove through town, watching the progress of the rebuilding, and admiring the resiliency of our people in the aftermaths of the latest storm, I wondered how our victims would react to the news of Brennan wanting to plead to a lesser deal. While I also hoped that he would spend the rest of his life in prison, I knew it wasn't my call.

Cory was standing on a ladder and his mom was handing him screws to reattach a broken shutter when I pulled into their driveway. Wendy Foret was sitting in a rocker on their porch watching. I had heard a rumor that Wendy had allowed Valerie and Cory to move in with her when their house had been repossessed by the bank, and then she had turned around and purchased it from the bank with her husband's life insurance money. From what I understood, she had signed the house over to Valerie free and clear, with her only stipulation being that the Verdins never sell it or move away.

"Detective Wolf!" Cory said from his perch atop the ladder. "What's up?"

I waved and stepped out of my truck. "You're doing such a good job that I might hire you to do my shutters."

He laughed and descended the ladder to shake my hand.

Valerie offered me some lemonade, and I gratefully accepted. I had gone straight from my chainsaw to my truck, and I could use something to drink. Once she'd brought the glass of cold refreshment, I sat in one of the rockers and explained to them my reason for being there. They all listened intently, nodding their heads every now and then, and scowling at other times.

"DA Lucas would like to know how y'all feel about the offer," I said in closing. "She wants y'all to know she would like to see him spend the rest of his life in prison, but she wants some input from y'all before making her decision."

"I want him to die in jail," Wendy said flatly. "That bastard has robbed me of everything that was sacred. I want him to pay with his life, but if I can't get that, then I'd at least like to know that he'll live a miserable life in prison until he dies alone in a dirty jail cell." She paused and sighed heavily. "Of course, I'm not the one who has to testify. Cory's the one who has the difficult job going forward, so I'll leave it up to him and respect whatever he decides. I know it can't be easy to come face-to-face with the man who killed your best friends and then wanted to kill you."

Valerie turned toward Cory, who would be the only eyewitness in the case. I could see in her eyes that she was concerned for her son, but I saw something else in that expression—it was admiration. Cory had grown a lot in the months following his harrowing experiences, and in my few meetings with him since that first encounter, I could tell he had matured beyond his age.

Cory nodded reassuringly in Wendy's direction, a somber expression on his face. "You're gonna get your wish, Miss Wendy."

Wendy's eyes clouded over and she rushed forward to hug Cory. I remained for a few minutes—answering questions about the case and talking about the clean-up efforts in town—and then I excused myself. As I drove back home to pick up Grace for ice cream, I called Amy.

"Oh, no," she said in a fluster, "please don't tell me Susan's in labor!"

"No," I said, "she's still holding on."

"Thank God!" She let out a breath of relief. "While I'd love for your new baby to be at my wedding, I don't want to postpone it again. I'm ready to get tied down so I can start making babies myself. Oh, and you'd better wear a tux tomorrow! Susan said you mentioned wearing cargo shorts and water shoes. If you do, I'll have you thrown out."

"I'll wear a tux," I said with a laugh. "I won't like it one bit, but I'll wear it."

I went on to explain about the phone call from Britt and my conversation with Cory, Valerie, and Wendy.

"I'm glad Cory's willing to testify," she said when I was done. "I'd hate the thought of Brennan going free someday. If he's willing to kill over an alligator egg, there's no telling what else he might do."

I nodded thoughtfully. "I would've never thought him capable of such things."

"Me neither." She took a breath. "Oh, Shade's bringing Alice to the wedding. They seem to be getting along nicely. I talked to her the other day and she really likes him. Do you think he feels the same about her?"

"It's early still, but he seems to like her a lot." I slowed as I reached the street to my house. "What about Takecia? Does she have a date?"

I had been worried about her ever since her last relationship went up in flames.

"She does have a date," Amy said. "I don't know who he is, but she said she's definitely not going stag."

"That's good."

"Well, they're giving me mean looks. I've got to get back to practicing how to get married. You'd think that kind of thing came naturally." She laughed, and it sounded giddy. "You'd better be here tomorrow, and you'd better be dressed up."

I laughed along with her, glad to hear her so happy. I promised we'd make it to the wedding come hell or high water.

"We're going even if Susan's in labor," I said, to which she laughed again before ending the call. I smiled as I turned into my driveway and saw Grace waiting in her Barbie Jeep.

"What's up, Pumpkin?" I asked when I stepped out of my truck and approached her Jeep. There was a pink purse over her left shoulder and she wore heart-shaped sunglasses. Susan was standing in the doorway watching, a wide grin on her face.

"I'm moving away," Grace said. "I don't want a baby brother. They stink."

I laughed as I snatched her from the Jeep and kissed her cheek. "Let's go get some ice cream and talk about it," I said. "I think two scoops of chocolate fudge might make you feel better."

"No," she said with a pout. "I'm gonna need *three!*".

BJ Bourg

BJ Bourg is a former professional boxer and a lifelong martial artist who retired as the chief investigator for a district attorney's office. A thirty-year veteran of law enforcement, he has worked as a patrol cop, detective, detective sergeant and police academy instructor. He has investigated thousands of felony cases and trained hundreds of law enforcement officers in self-defense, firearms, and criminal operations.

Throughout his career, Bourg has served on many specialized units such as SWAT, Explosives Search Team, and Homicide Response Team. He founded his agency's sniper program and served as its leader and trainer for nearly a decade. A graduate of seven basic and advanced sniper schools, he deployed as the primary sniper on dozens of call-outs, including barricaded subjects, hostage rescue operations, and fugitive apprehensions. He also served as the sniper instructor for the 2001 Louisiana Tactical Police Officers Association's Conference.

Bourg has been the recipient of numerous awards, including Top Shooter at an FBI Sniper School, the Distinguished Service Medal, and Certificates of Commendation for his work as a homicide detective. In addition to speaking at numerous law enforcement and writer's conferences, he has written dozens of articles for leading law enforcement and tactical magazines covering a wide range of topics such as defensive tactics, sniper deployment, suspect interrogation, report writing, no-knock search warrants, and more.

Above all else, Bourg is a father and a husband. The highlight of his life is spending time with his beautiful wife and wonderful children. Originally from Louisiana, he now proudly calls Tellico Plains, Tennessee home.

www.bjbourg.com

Made in the USA
Columbia, SC
29 March 2024

33811415R00143